THE MILLENNIAL MANIFESTO

By Michael R. Fletcher

ALSO BY MICHAEL R. FLETCHER

GHOSTS OF TOMORROW
BEYOND REDEMPTION
THE MIRROR'S TRUTH
SWARM AND STEEL
A COLLECTION OF OBSESSIONS
SMOKE AND STONE (CITY OF SACRIFICE #1)

UPCOMING RELEASES

ASH AND BONE (CITY OF SACRIFICE #2)
BLACK STONE HEART (THE OBSIDIAN PATH #1)

The Millennial Manifesto

This is mostly a work of fiction. Names, characters, business, events and incidents are mostly the products of the author's imagination. Any resemblance to actual persons, living or dead, or actual events is mostly coincidental.

The Millennial Manifesto Copyright © 2019 by Michael R. Fletcher

All rights reserved. No part of this publication may be reproduced, distributed, or transmitted in any form or by any means, including photocopying, recording, or other electronic or mechanical methods, without the prior written permission of the publisher, except in the case of brief quotations embodied in critical reviews and certain other non-commercial uses permitted by copyright law.

Cover: Michael R. Fletcher
Editor: Sarah Chorn

SOME

    BRIDGES

        NEED

            TO BE

                BURNED

CHAPTER – INANNA

"This is killing me."

That's what Julia had said as she watched Gartner's Audi enter the gate at Tessier Waste Disposal Systems. "We have to *do* something." She'd looked at Inanna then, eyes desperate. "We have to do something or admit there's nothing we can do."

That moment, seeing defeat and surrender in the eyes of someone so indomitable, set everything in motion. For years Inanna's mom's words, *Make the world a better place,* had haunted her, ever teasing despite their simplicity. Yet how did one improve the world?

What they'd been doing wasn't working. That was obvious.

Picketing. Angry signs.

No one gave a fuck.

It was time to change tactics.

Now, a month later, Inanna sat with her three friends, Aarush, Chen, and Julia, in the kitchen of the house Chen and Julia rented on the outskirts of Bay City. Not far from the sugarbeet factories, they lived in the smelly end of town a famous singer once called the toilet of north Michigan. The previous tenant decorated the faded lime-green walls with nick-knacks from the 1970s. Cats and dogs with over-sized eyes, Amish figurines made of iron sitting on dusty wood shelves, and dozens of hand-carved wooden fish. The kitchen was at odds with the couple's disciplined military neatness.

Julia, a tight-wound bundle of adrenaline-junkie energy, stood at the kitchen counter making tea. She claimed to be only one of the group capable of making a decent pot, and wouldn't let anyone else try. She once threatened to break all of Aarush's limbs if he ever poured the milk in before removing the tea bag again. Inanna was damned sure she knew who would win a fight between Julia, a semi-pro MMA fighter carved from stone, and Aarush, a scrawny film student who lived off fast food and energy drinks.

So normal, thought Inanna. How many times had they sat around this very table talking about what they could do to force Tessier to stop dumping toxic shit in the poor end of town?

Julia turned from the counter and deposited a huge hand-made pottery mug in front of her husband, Chen. "Three heaping sugars."

Hair military immaculate, tall, broad shouldered, and well-muscled, the Chinese American seemed oblivious to the aesthetic of his surroundings. He might not appreciate the kitsch, but Inanna knew that if she shifted one of the many military strategy books lining his bookcases by even an inch, the ex-Marine sniper would give her that 'I'm deciding whether I should kill you' look. The look, he admitted, back when they first met, had been intentionally cultivated over the years. Its most regular recipient, Julia, was a master at both causing and ignoring it.

"Just milk," as she delivered Aarush's. He nodded thanks, dark, expressive eyes watching everything from behind thick-rimmed glasses and an unruly mop of black hair. He once told Inanna he liked the way his glasses framed the world, made every moment feel like he was watching a movie.

"Milk and sugar," as Julia slid one to Inanna. "Black, as god intended," as she took her own.

"Can we start now?" asked Aarush, impatient as ever.

"Only barbarians plot terrorism before tea," said Julia.

Inanna winced. "I think terrorism is the wrong word."

Humor gone, Julia turned pale blue eyes on Inanna. "Jenny died over a year ago. Since then we've picketed Tessier Waste Disposal every weekend. We've attended marches. We launched a civil-suit against them which went nowhere. Last week our neighbor's son, Kevin, died in the hospital from pneumonia-related complications. He was three." She blinked down into her tea, jaw clenched. "Everyone knows it's the water." Her lip twitched. "That fucking prick, Gartner, smiled and waved at me as he drove past us today."

"But terrorism—"

"Call it what you want. You know what the press are going to call us."

She was right, of course.

"You don't see it in your neighborhood," said Julia. "But at this end of town, people are dying. Half the folks have weird rashes from their bathwater. Almost everyone I know has had pneumonia in the last few years. Two people died of Legionnaires Disease!" She looked from person to person. "So yeah. Terrorism."

The Millennial Manifesto

My end of town. Unlike her friends, she came from money. They never rubbed it in, never let it get in the way of their friendship, but they also never forgot.

"Is that what we're doing?" asked Chen. "Is that our goal, to be terrorists? To terrorize?"

Julia grunted a laugh. "He's the only one in the group who has actually killed anyone, and he's the most squeamish about violence."

Chen had done a four-year tour in the Middle East and never talked about it. "You might want to think about that," he said.

I bet he talks to Julia about the war. The girl had a knack for getting people to spill their deepest secrets. Of course, she cheated by plying them with liberal amounts of alcohol first. *I can't believe I told her I had a crush on Aarush.*

The film student sat to her right, tinkering with his latest toy, a high-def GoPro. How he got the gear, she had no idea. Sometimes he signed it out of the university's equipment, but as often as not, he owned it.

"It's not about terror," said Inanna, trying to frame the discussion in a way she felt comfortable with. "It's about change. We've exhausted every legal means. We've been over every option and come to the conclusion that these tactics—"

"Terror tactics," said Julia.

"—will be most effective in forcing corporations to change."

"You know they'll catch us," said Chen. "Eventually we'll make a mistake and they'll get us. If we're lucky, it will be the FBI or the law. If not, it'll be some private corporate security firm."

"We know," said Julia. "But what we start will spread. When people see our success, they'll join our cause."

Everyone nodded. This was well-tread territory. Chen, ever detail-focused, needed to be sure everyone was aware of how it would end.

A month of planning for something none of them really believed they'd do. It had been catharsis until talk was no longer enough.

He's only guessing. He doesn't know. Not really. Inanna examined her friends as they sipped tea. *If we win over the people—if we're careful and never hurt the public—we'll be heroes.* And in America, heroes had a way of avoiding justice.

Chen nodded, face serious. He rubbed at his square jaw as if checking for stubble, found none, and said, "We're really going to do this?"

Julia needs this.

Maybe if they stopped TWDS from dumping toxic shit into the local ground water, Inanna's friend could find some kind of closure.

"We're going after Anthony Gartner, CEO of Tessier," Inanna said.

"You know I'm in," said Aarush, glancing up from the GoPro, attention darting to Inanna and away.

Tessier was one of those corporations no one ever heard of because they had virtually no interaction with the public and no public presence. The company specialized in hazardous waste disposal and had been burying toxic material in Michigan for over two decades. Their research, shoddy and driven by self-interest, claimed that the hazardous waste they buried deep underground wouldn't surface or reach local water tables for thousands of years. They said that by then it would have been filtered by miles of earth and would be safe. They were either lying or wrong. Seeing that smug grin on Gartner's face, Inanna suspected she knew which was more likely.

In several Michigan towns, children were being born with birth defects, and the water was undrinkable in a dozen more. Furthermore, half the county's population had developed strange rashes. The press had been all over Tessier for a week before the next political stumble distracted them and they were once again off chasing the President for tweeting something stupid about China. Chen and Julia's lawsuit were one of hundreds, but no progress had been made, and no charges filed.

So many times, they'd talked about this. Kidnap Gartner and force him to drink water from one of the rivers his company polluted. Capture video of the event. Post the whole thing online for the world to see.

Everything could still fall apart. Were they going to change the world, or go back to their shallow lives and admit it had all been talk? She half hoped everyone would decide this was insane.

It's only your *life that's shallow*, Inanna chastised herself.

Chen and Julia had each other, if not much else. She darted a quick glance at Aarush, which went unnoticed. He had his art, his photography, and a burgeoning career as an underground film-maker with a rabid cult-like following. Inanna… she had nothing, no one. She hadn't completed her degree, though often talked about returning to do so. She didn't have a job. What was the point when she didn't need one? And the only guy she liked couldn't pull his face away from a camera long enough to talk to her.

He looks up to watch SpongeBob SquarePants.

This was it. This would be her contribution. She would fund their activities.

"If we force Gartner to drink the water," said Chen, "we might kill him. He might die."

"Probably not," said Julia. She bared teeth in a sick grin. "At least not according to Tessier's research."

"He'll be in a hospital soon after," added Inanna. "They'll pump his stomach and flush it from his system."

"And if he later develops some cancer as a result," said Aarush, "that sounds like justice to me."

Everyone except Chen nodded agreement.

"Julia?" said Inanna. "How did your recon go?"

"I've driven past his house. He lives about forty-five minutes north. All multi-million-dollar homes. Luckily, it's an older community and not gated. Suburbia for the quietly wealthy."

Money. The great American divide. Inanna tried not to let it bother her.

"Chen?" she said, glancing at the man.

"We know where he works, where he lives, and have a rough idea of his schedule. I tailed him a couple of times. He always takes the same route home, and it always takes about the same amount of time. Barring accidents and traffic."

"Traffic in Bay City?" joked Aarush. He flashed a quick grin at Inanna and returned his attention to the camera.

Chen continued. "Easiest will be if we grab him the moment he gets home. Lots of tree cover. Trying to get him mid-commute would be difficult and dangerous. Too many opportunities for things to go wrong."

How many times did he do something like this in Afghanistan? Had he followed his victims, learning their habits, before killing them? Knowing what he was—having some idea of the things he'd done—made it difficult to equate the Chen she knew, the tender and loving, if overly serious man, to the Marine sniper. What had he felt when studying his targets through the sniper's scope? Did he have regrets?

"Aarush?" Inanna asked.

He looked up from the camera, blinking. "A little smashing would look good. We have to sell the drama."

His job was to record everything and post the videos to YouTube and anywhere else he could. Too many years of John Woo movies, however, had no doubt shaped his expectations.

"We aren't being violent for ratings," said Chen.

"We kind of are," argued Aarush.

"No. We don't hurt his family no matter what."

"Could we trash his car?" Aarush asked.

"No time for drama," said Inanna. "In and out fast. You have what you need?"

Aarush nodded and a lock of curly black hair fell forward to curtain his milk-chocolate features. He exuded boyish charm and energy and his easy grin got him into as much trouble as it got him out of. Sometimes Inanna wanted to smack him and tell him to grow up, that this was serious, dangerous. Sometimes she wanted to kiss him and drown in those dark eyes.

"I've signed a bunch of gear out from Northwood University," said Aarush. "Lights, audio recording equipment. I've got my two serious cameras, this GoPro—"

"Those always make me puke," said Julia.

"Folks love 'em," he said. "Puts the viewer at the scene. Anyway, I also have a microcam hidden in a pair of glasses. Real spy-level stuff. For audio I've got lavalier microphones. One for our friend, Mister Gartner, and one for each of us. I'm recording multi-track audio so I can later disguise our voices but leave his untouched."

"Great," said Inanna. "I've found the perfect place. Gartner's house is half an hour from the countryside. Farms and dirt roads. No people around. There's a motel we can stay at. I was thinking maybe we do two nights, make a weekend out of this."

Everyone nodded agreement.

"It's be nice to get out of town for a couple of days," said Chen.

"And," said Inanna, "I collected the water sample he'll be enjoying."

"Two rooms?" Aarush waggled eyebrows at her. "Finally making a play for me?"

"Me and Julia in one," said Inanna, "you and Chen in the other."

"Hot lesbo sex?" No matter how serious things got, Aarush couldn't help but joke to relieve tension.

"You wish."

"Indeed I do."

The Millennial Manifesto

"Let's not get distracted here. I've also found a dozen free Wi-Fi hotspots we can hit for the upload. We won't even have to enter the business, we can access the Wi-Fi from the parking lot. You can do the editing in a single night?" she asked Aarush.

"As long as there's lots of coffee."

"Good."

"And," added Aarush, "I set up a dozen YouTube accounts using false info and collected email contacts for all the major news companies across the country including several underground sources like Tinfoil Hat News, BlackListed News, Truth Out, and a dozen others."

"The authorities will take the video down," pointed out Chen.

"But not before a few hundred thousand people have seen and shared it. You can't stop the web," said Aarush. "I also have a few dozen folks ready to share anything that appears on any of the accounts I set up, just to get things moving."

"Ok," said Inanna, "are we missing anything?"

"Yeah," grumbled Julia. "I don't get to blow shit up." She said it like she was joking, but her eyes held an edge. Like Chen, she'd done a tour in the Middle-East, though she'd been in bomb disposals and was an explosives expert. The two met there while deployed.

"A crucial part of terrorism is the escalation," said Inanna. "Blowing up factories won't win hearts and minds. It'll paint us as violent and dangerous." They'd talked about this before, but Julia always seemed to come back to the demolitions. "And it would change the nature of how law-enforcement pursues us. Our path to success is through the people. We need the populace to be on our side, and that means no violence."

"I think a little violence would win some people."

Inanna ignored the interruption. "We need to attack the corporations on a human level. We *must* hit the people who make the choices, make it personal. Make them see change as their best bet for personal safety and security."

"Gotta build a backbone of trust among the public," agreed Chen.

Julia said nothing, but nodded with grudging acceptance.

Killing Gartner won't bring Jenny back. Inanna knew better than to voice the thought aloud.

"The car," said Chen, business as always. "I bought us a beater, an old Dodge van for five hundred bucks. The engine is in good shape though the body is badly rusted."

"That'll stand out in Gartner's upscale neighborhood." said Aarush.

Chen shrugged. "We don't have the budget for an Audi, and the dealer asked no questions and was disinterested in seeing ID. It's as invisible as we can get."

We're doing this. We're really doing this.

"Good." Inanna raised her tea mug and took a calming breath. "Tomorrow we pay Anthony Gartner a visit. Tomorrow we change the world!"

Everyone lifted their mugs.

"Cheers!"

"Let's get a real drink," said Aarush.

No one disagreed.

CHAPTER – HIRAN

"Hiran," said Chuck over the earbud, "I have eyes on the target."

Chuck called everyone a 'target' like they were going to kick in doors and shoot someone instead of remaining hidden to take a few pictures. In this case the target was a Michigan politician of some repute and power.

"Great," said Hiran, sipping his Thai coffee in the Hilton Inn restaurant. "Stay well back."

"Duh, Boss. Looks like he's coming your way."

No surprise there.

Hiran and his team had been working for Anthony Gartner, CEO of Tessier Waste Disposal Systems and all-around sociopathic douche-bag, for years. They did the dirty things he couldn't get done legally through the company. Mostly that meant strong-arming noisy members of the public, bribing politicians, and interacting with various aspects of the criminal underworld.

This last week they'd been following this gentleman—the target—gathering intel and trying to take naughty pictures of the man with his mistress. Their target's routine never changed. He met the woman at the same Hilton restaurant and they always sat for three drinks before disappearing to their room. Today, Hiran and his team were finally going to hit gold. Fana, their resident hacker and IT specialist, the only one of the three who could use a computer with any modicum of skill, managed to arrange for the target to be given a specific room. She'd wired the target's room with hidden cameras and microphones.

Tomorrow, if all things went well, they'd play show and tell, sharing their dirty pictures with the target. They'd explain that when their employer called and asked him to do a small favor, regarding the zoning of a certain plot of land Gartner wanted to bury some toxic waste in, he'd best play ball or face a costly divorce.

The Millennial Manifesto

It really is easier to think of him as 'the target.'

Better not to think of the man as a person, as someone with a family, whose life Hiran and his team were likely going to ruin. Once you were under Gartner's thumb, there was no way out. One little favor was never just one little favor, as Hiran knew all too well, having seen it from both sides of the relationship.

Chuck, however, possessed neither the wit nor the empathy for such a reason. He just liked to pretend they were still in the military, still kicking in doors and taking out persons of interest. The man was a goon, a killer for hire. Had he not found the military and been embraced by Special Forces, no doubt he'd either be dead or in jail by now. Working for Hiran kept Chuck out of too much trouble by giving him paid work *causing* trouble. Hiran kept a sharp eye on the man, distracting him and redirecting his violent tendencies when needed. Having grown accustomed to following Hiran's orders when in Special Forces, Chuck never thought to stop following them after.

The target entered the Hilton restaurant with a gorgeous woman on his arm who couldn't have been more than half his age. Hiran, who'd been married for twenty years and had two daughters, understood the attraction, but not the willingness of some men to be led by their pricks. He'd seen pictures of the target's wife. In her mid-forties, she was still stunning and in great shape. She clearly worked hard at maintaining herself. Yet here was the target fucking his future away. Except he'd no doubt worm his way out of this, do as Gartner wanted, and be back to fucking girls young enough to be his daughter inside a week.

If that long.

Glancing left, Hiran saw Chuck, two hundred and thirty pounds of muscle with a blond crew-cut, ice gray eyes and a cheap suit stretched near snapping, loitering outside. He stayed far enough away he wouldn't be noticed by anyone not looking for him. The big guy chain-smoked filterless Luckies, flicking the butts out into the street.

The target and his girlfriend took the same booth they always did and ordered the same drinks they always did.

"Target just ordered the first round," he muttered into the mic hidden in the lapel of his jacket.

"Hey Tick Tock," said Fana over the earbud.

"Don't fucking call me—"

"Chuck," interrupted Hiran.

"Sorry."

"Tick Tock, you sound just like Chuck Tingle."

"Who the fuck is Chuck Tingle?" Chuck demanded, immediately suspicious.

"Award winning science-fiction writer. You'd like him."

"Why would I like some fucking nerd?"

"*Fucking* nerd," said Fana and Hiran heard the grin in her voice. "Tingle works out a lot. Abs like you wouldn't believe."

Chuck, who spent hours a day working on his own abs, couldn't figure out her angle. "Stay off the channel unless you have something important to report," he said.

"Chuck Tingle would *really* like you."

"Fana," said Hiran. "Not now, please."

"Just cranking the cracker."

"Well don't." *Because that cracker will crumble and make a fucking mess of you.*

"Sorry, Boss." Fana had a way of talking that let you know when she wasn't sincere. Come to think of it, if she was talking, she was probably lying or making fun of you. She had a ninth-dan black belt in sarcasm.

Finishing his coffee, Hiran ordered a double Jameson, neat.

Watching two people drink, a middle-aged man with more money than class or intelligence, and a girl who could only be gold-digging his dumb ass, was boring as hell. Spying on people stopped being exciting years ago. Nothing lasting would come of this. They'd take their pictures, pass them on to Gartner and have their chat with the target. They'd get paid. Chuck would drink his share or spend it on girls or whatever stupid things he did in his spare time. Fana would buy science fiction and fantasy novels and watch movies. Hiran would put his in the bank, saving towards his girls' education when they finished high school. They'd all wait around until Gartner needed them again. It was never long.

The target and the girl finished their third drink as Hiran finished his first. He waved at the bartender for another. Whiskey warmth undid the knots life tied in him. The two were so lost in each other, already fumbling at clothing on their way to the elevator, he didn't bother disguising his attention.

Could that be real?

Could they just be madly in love?

Hiran remembered being like that with his wife, the need to touch, to taste. It was like her very saliva was addictive, the taste of her tongue, his cocaine. He still loved her. More than ever. You don't share a life, raise two girls together, without forming a deep bond far beyond mere physical attraction. Hell, Miriam was a damned fine looking woman. The curve of her ass still lit warmth in Hiran's groin.

But this—what these two shared—was gone. Or maybe just faded, a fire burnt down to embers but all the warmer for it. Still, part of him missed that desperate need for contact, the thrill of the new.

Yeah, the young and stupid part.

The two disappeared into an elevator.

Three minutes later, Fana, in the room beside the target's, said, "They're in," over the earbud.

"Come on in, Chuck," said Hiran.

Chuck entered the restaurant and sat across from Hiran, collapsing into the seat like a petulant child. "Who the fuck is Chuck Tingle?"

"No idea. SF writer, apparently."

"I think he'd make Chuck tingle," said Fana over the earbud.

"I don't tingle," growled Chuck.

"I bet I could make you tingle," she purred.

Hiran watched the big idiot be confused by conflicting desires, his racism battling the fact Fana was gorgeous.

"I'm going up to the room," said Hiran, tossing back the last of his Jameson. "You wait here. Let us know when they're gone."

"Right, Boss."

"Don't get drunk."

"I don't get drunk. I once downed an entire—"

"Don't. Get. Drunk."

"Right, Boss. No more than eight then."

"Don't—"

"Kidding. Relax. Sure you don't wanna join me for a beer?"

"Work before pleasure," said Hiran to deflect that he had no desire to drink with a confused racist. *Or am I being a racist now?* He wasn't sure. Didn't care.

"Sure thing, Boss," said Chuck, eyeing the empty whiskey glass.

The elevator played a jazz version of Iron Maiden's Run to the Hills with a swank sax soaked in reverb taking the vocal line.

Hiran sang along: "White man came across the sea. He brought us pain, and misery."

The Millennial Manifesto

The elevator dinged and spat him into a hallway of pastel and gray so air-conditioned he wanted a parka. Entering the room, he found Fana at the desk. She'd cleared it of hotel detritus and arrayed six large monitors to give her every angle on the target's dalliance. A pair of Yamaha NS10 speakers played the sound collected by the condenser microphones she'd hidden about the target's room.

"Boss," she said, not looking up from the screens.

Hiran coughed quietly and drew a line across his throat when she glanced at him.

Fana understood. "Coms are muted. Chuck can't hear anything you want to say about him."

"Thanks. Please don't play with him like that. He doesn't understand, won't get your weird nerd references, and will likely someday kill us both for not being white."

"Chuck doesn't scare me."

"Then you're not as smart as I thought." Hiran hired her straight out of school, offered her a job breaking the law instead of following the corporate route of her classmates, and she'd jumped at it without a moment's hesitation. Everything about her screamed good girl, from the way she dressed to the way she was unfailingly polite to people she didn't know, and it was all a lie.

"Yes, Boss."

"You're going to keep doing it."

"Yes, Boss."

Hiran sighed and collapsed onto the bed.

"Were you born in a barn?" asked Fana. "Take your fucking shoes off."

He kicked his loafers away. "What are they up to?"

"I call this act *Prelude to a Blowjob*. John Williams has been contacted to score the movie."

He had no idea what she was talking about. *She never gives up.* "All channels recording?"

She gave him her patented 'don't be an asshole, I know my job' look.

He ignored it. "After they're finished, put together a dozen stills we can show the target. We'll catch him on the street tomorrow as he returns to the office."

"Want me to catch the Big O moment?" She shrugged when he glanced at her. "That seems to be important. In every dude-oriented porn I've ever seen, they're all about capturing the instant when he—"

"We're not filming porn."

"We kind of are."

"We're going to blackmail him, not make him famous." *Unless he doesn't take well to blackmail.*

"No reason we can't take pride in a job well done." She held up a hand to stall him. "Wait. Boss, we have achieved blowjob." She darted him a look of teasing naughtiness, dark eyes and an inviting tilt to full lips, that totally would have worked had he not known she was messing with him.

"Pass," he said, lying back and closing his eyes.

Two hours later Fana woke him by poking him in the ribs with a pen.

"They're gone," she said. "And they made a hella mess of those sheets. For an old guy the target has rather impressive stamina. Is that an old man thing?"

Hiran ignored the question. "Pick your stills. Make them good. Make sure there's no doubt who's there and what they're doing"

"I know my job, Darth."

"I'm going to get Chuck and order room-service. You want anything?"

"Burger and fries and the biggest piece of chocolate cake they have."

Shaking his head, Hiran left the room. He was pretty sure he gained a pound just listening to her order. Tomorrow they'd have a chat with the target about some zoning issues standing between Anthony Gartner and a plot of inexpensive land perfect for dumping toxic materials.

"Good times," muttered Hiran, entering the elevator.

On the way down, he listened to Rod Stewart muzaked to the point he couldn't tell which song it was. He had no doubt the target would fold under pressure. They always did. Sure, he'd bluster and threaten, but when it came down to it, if the pictures were leaked, his wife would leave him. No matter how unhappy the target was with his wife—if he was at all—he could never handle losing half of everything.

Chuck still sat where Hiran left him, half a beer in front of him. Hiran pulled out a chair and sat across from the big man.

"Is that the same beer you ordered when I left?"

"Yeah, Boss."

Hiran waved down the waitress, ordered another double Jameson, and a Coors for Chuck.

"Chuck, does it bother you having a brown guy for a boss?"

"Nope." He was too dumb to lie, guileless by way of stupidity. "You aren't like the others."

The *others*.

Chuck shrugged. "You're different. Smart. Driven. We were together during the shit in Afghanistan. I've seen you shoot."

I get a pass because I can shoot?

"And I saw that match with Hideo," continued Chuck.

"He beat me."

"He beats everybody. But after, he bowed to you. When he kicked my ass, he just wandered away as I lay there wondering what the hell happened."

Hiran sipped his whiskey, felt molten caramel and smoke chase the tension from his shoulders.

"Most of you are meek, lazy little bastards," added Chuck.

"Most of *us*?"

"You know what I mean."

"You know a lot of *us*?"

"Sure, they're in every gas station, minimart, and cab. Thing is, you're different. You're a man. I mean, I know you. You're the exception."

And you're a lazy racist, confused when you meet someone who doesn't conform to your expectations. Instead of reevaluating your beliefs, you assume I'm different, the one brown guy in the world who is okay.

"Who the fuck is Chuck Tingle?" asked Chuck.

Hiran shrugged.

"Fana's smart for a black," mused Chuck. "Too smart for her own good."

Unable to listen to more, Hiran downed his whiskey. "I'm going to grab a burger and fries for Fana and bring it up to her. You want anything?"

"Nah. I only eat paleo. No processed foods. My body is a fucking temple." Chuck finished his beer and ordered another. Fishing out a crumpled pack of filterless Lucky Strikes, he said, "I'm going for a smoke."

CHAPTER – INANNA

Sunday morning, Inanna stood waiting just beyond the gate at the end of her driveway. The plan was to scout Gartner's neighborhood while he was at work, and then grab the CEO when he returned home.

Her friends had all seen her house, they knew she inherited everything when her parents died, but she still felt uncomfortable about it. She'd never worry about money. She couldn't spend extravagantly, but her parents arranged for a monthly stipend that more than covered her costs. Employment was something she would only have to think about if she was looking for something to fill her days. Her friends' lives were so different. Chen worked as a mechanic at small garage. Julia taught MMA and women's self-defense classes at a local gym. Aarush waited tables and picked up odd work editing films or doing sound for live bands. Her wealth was an uncomfortable topic for all of them; it was rare anyone brought it up. And it always ended in an awkward and apologetic silence. So far, no one mentioned the disparity between them, or how she could fund their efforts to save the world far more easily than they. Everyone paid an equal share of the costs, and no one grumbled.

Should she pay more? Would it upset them if she offered?

The guilt wouldn't leave her alone.

Chen pulled up in a white Dodge van. There were no windows in the side panels and those on the back door were covered in peeling decals advertising a variety of tools and local hunting and sporting goods products. Julia sat in the passenger seat.

Swinging open the side door and adjusting his glasses, Aarush said, "My Lady, your chariot awaits."

Inanna climbed in. The seats were stained, the fabric torn and faded. There was room for two rows of bench seating, but the middle row had been removed. Aarush had already wired the van for sound, and four small microphones hung from the ceiling. Battery-powered LED lights had been taped to the inner panels, though they were currently all off. Tucked against one wall lay a solid-looking camera tripod and camera case. Aarush fiddled with a smaller camera, delving into various settings to get it ready to shoot in the van's interior. It smelled like Inanna's grandmother the week before she died.

"It's real?" she asked. "We're doing this?"

"We can still back out," said Chen. "We haven't kidnapped anyone yet, haven't forced them to drink contaminated water."

Part of her wanted that, to go back to her easy life, to putter about pointless hobbies. *No. I'm going to make the world a better place.* "Do any of you want out?" she asked.

"No way," said Julia.

"Are you kidding?" answered Aarush. "Miss the opportunity to film the rebellion of our generation? Never!"

Or the catastrophic flop of our generation. Inanna kept her fears to herself.

Chen shook his head. "I have to keep you lot out of trouble."

The half-hour drive to the motel was a war of musical tastes. Chen wanted to listen to death metal fronted by someone who sounded like Cookie Monster. Julia wanted what she called Post-Metal, which to Inanna sounded suspiciously like grunge, and Aarush wanted to hear whatever was top of the pop charts. Inanna, trying to play the peace-keeper, kept her own preferences—straight up rock, never heavier than Tool—to herself.

Chen, shut the radio off. "In sniper training," he said, voice deep and mellow, "there are games we play to test and increase perception."

"Sounds fun," said Aarush, brushing dark hair from his eyes that immediately fell back into place.

"Fine," said Chen. "I spy with my little eye…"

Everyone groaned and Julia, in the passenger seat, punched him in the arm.

Two minutes later, Aarush, looking through his camera bag, said, "Fuck."

"What?" asked Inanna, sitting beside him.

"Forgot to pack my toothbrush."

After checking into the cheap roadside motel—the bored-looking old man behind the desk accepted cash with no questions—they sat in a cramped room drinking warm white wine from plastic cups. Julia and Inanna sat on the bed while Aarush took the single armchair, feet up on a collapsible TV tray table he found in the closet. Chen sat at the small desk in an unforgiving wood chair. As always, he seemed immune to discomfort.

The Millennial Manifesto

Inanna glanced about the room. "Why are all the pictures of boats and docks? The nearest decent-sized lake is half an hour away."

Chen turned to peer at the art hanging behind him. "They look like paint-by-numbers done badly." He leaned closer. "And the frames are all screwed straight into the wall."

"Who'd want to steal that?" asked Julia.

Aarush raised a hand. "I'd totally steal one. I'm an avid collector of motel kitsch."

"Of course you are," said Julia, sipping wine and grimacing. "Christ, this is sweet. What the hell is it?"

"Chardonnay," answered Chen, checking the wine box sitting on the desk.

"Get a dry pinot grigio next time."

"This box already blew the budget."

"First," said Julia, "wine in a box is a sin. Second, what was the budget?"

"Six bucks."

They drank and they talked about inconsequential nothings, everyone avoiding the topic of why they were there, what they planned on doing the next day. Finally, sharing out the last of the wine, making sure everyone had a splash in their glass, Chen stood. He was the only one who seemed unaffected by the booze.

Raising his plastic cup, he said, "To tomorrow. To making the world a better place."

"To not getting caught," added Aarush. "And to not going to jail. I am way too cute to do well in prison."

"True," deadpanned Chen. "You are." He looked them all over. "Chances are none of you will sleep tonight. It's just nerves. Don't worry about it. Totally normal."

"Of course *he'll* sleep like a damned log," said Julia.

Chen nodded. "You'll all feel like shit in the morning. You'll be groggy, easily distracted. You'll worry that we aren't ready. Don't. We are ready. When the time comes, you'll be pumping so much adrenaline you'll be as sharp as you need to be. Remember, if shit goes sideways—and it probably will—you listen to me. Do as I say. I'll get us all out."

"He's so dramatic," said Julia.

Inanna lifted her own plastic cup. "To shit not going sideways."

Everyone muttered "Cheers" and drank.

"You suck at toasts," Julia told Chen. "Next time keep it short and positive."

With the wine gone and the sun long set, the motel grew quiet as their neighbors beyond the thin walls turned in for the evening. The stuttering whistle of crickets and the hum of cars on the highway made for a hypnotizing background noise.

Chen and Aarush retired to a second room and Julia sprawled out on the queen-size bed and immediately began to snore.

Inanna paced the room for a while before giving up and shoving Julia to one side to make space. The woman didn't so much as stir.

Morning came after a thousand years of tossing and turning.

"You look like shit," said Julia, stretching. Even when relaxed she was hard and ropy in a way Inanna couldn't imagine achieving. Staying slim was difficult enough.

"You snore like a truck driver," said Inanna.

"Liar."

"It's true," said Chen, exiting the bathroom.

Inanna hadn't seen him enter their room. *He must have come in while I was asleep.* An extremely light sleeper, she wouldn't have thought it possible. Him in there, seeing her while she slept, left her feeling oddly uncomfortable, vulnerable. *No one should be that quiet.*

Seeing her look, he shrugged apology. "Aarush takes forever to do his hair. I couldn't wait."

Julia threw a pillow at Chen on his way out.

"Let's go, you lazy slack-asses," he called over his shoulder. "The van is already packed."

****

Inanna claimed the front seat, and Julia and Aarush sat in the back.

"How we going to do this?" asked Julia. "You could drop me off downtown near Gartner's work. I can let you know when he leaves."

"I don't like splitting up the team," said Chen. "Learn from Napoleon."

"Don't invade Russia in winter?" quipped Aarush.

"A man like Gartner," said Chen, "will always take the fastest route, and will always take the same route. Once he nears his home, there's really only one road he'll be on. We'll wait there, follow him home the last half mile and grab him in the driveway."

"Grab him," said Aarush. "I volunteer Chen for that job."

Inanna laughed, imagining the slim cameraman trying to force anyone to do anything. *Not that I'd do any better.* She suddenly regretted all those years her father tried to enroll her in martial arts lessons and she always refused, disinterested in sports and rough things in general.

Arriving ahead of schedule, as Chen always did, he took them on a leisurely drive through Gartner's neighborhood. The others ogled the huge houses, four-car garages, and driveways filled with BMWs, Audis, Mercedes, and Lexuses. Inanna tried to ignore that these mansions looked a lot like her own home. If the others noticed, they made no mention of it. Gartner's house looked like the others, if slightly bigger.

"Why do rich people love black, white, and gray cars so much?" asked Aarush. "I haven't seen a single red one."

"They're afraid that if they pick a color," said Julia, "everyone will know they lack taste and class."

Inanna thought about her Mom's white Porsche SUV and her Father's black BMW 750. Both still sat in the driveway, unused since their deaths. "Or maybe they just like gray," she suggested.

"I like white cars," said Chen.

"Yeah," said Aarush, "but you're the most boring person on the entire planet."

The Marine sniper shrugged.

Finding a playground with a picnic area down the street from the Gartner residence, they pulled over for lunch. Chen made sandwiches on thick slabs of soft white bread, slathering on mayo and laying enough ham in there to clog an artery.

Taking a monstrous bite, Aarush grinned. "These are even better than my mom's," he mumbled around a mouthful of beef and cheese.

Chen ate like a drill sergeant ordered him to. He did his duty, mechanically shoving sandwich in his face whenever he swallowed the previous bite. If he tasted anything he showed no sign. Aarush finished with a pile crusts on his lap which he then fed to the birds.

"You want one?" Inanna asked Julia.

"She's on this 'Eat Like a Predator' kick," said Chen. "She gorges and fasts, never eating before six in the evening. No processed foods. She's basically carnivorous."

"Eat like a carnivore," said Julia, "think like a carnivore, live like a carnivore." She flexed wiry muscles and showed bright teeth in a feral grin.

Whatever she was doing, it worked for her. Where Inanna was all softness and curves, Julia was lean muscle and whiplash speed.

"Personally," said Aarush, "I find I thrive on a vegetarian diet."

"You just ate beef," said Inanna.

"And that cow probably ate vegetable matter. The animal eats the veggies, digests them for me, and I eat the animal."

"Christ," said Chen. "You sound like Julia."

Aarush and Inanna sat on the picnic table, feeding the birds, while Chen walked a grid pattern, picking up any garbage or recyclable material he found, and depositing it in the correct bin. Julia stretched and worked through increasingly difficult yoga poses.

Inanna watched Chen. "I think I have to step up my 'make the world a better place' game," she said, nudging Aarush. "I've been so focused on the bigger picture I've been ignoring the small things. They make a difference too."

"They do," agreed Aarush, brushing hair from his eyes. "But anyone can do those things. And everyone should. What you're doing... what *we're* doing, it's bigger. Not everyone can. Not everyone will." He shrugged. "You can't do everything."

"Chen can."

"Yeah, well Chen is Chen. You and me, we're not Chen."

But maybe I should be. Could she ever do enough? It was, she realized, a slippery slope. The world would never be perfect, there would always be something that could be done to make it better. *That sounds like a reason not to try.*

They watched as Chen stopped to check his phone. After tucking it back into a pocket, he returned to the picnic area.

"Gartner should have left work by now. Assuming he comes straight home, his commute should be about forty-five minutes."

"Waiting around here for another hour might be pushing it," said Aarush.

"Agreed. We'll drive around a bit, hit a convenience store for any last-minute supplies. Then, in say thirty-five minutes, we'll park near an intersection he drives through on his way home and wait."

The four friends returned to the van. Chen took the driver's seat while Inanna claimed the passenger seat and Aarush and Julia sat in the back.

After stopping at the local gas-station for corn chips and energy drinks for Aarush, and leathery beef jerky for Julia, Chen parked a few car-lengths back from an intersection he said Gartner drove through on his daily commute home.

"When Gartner drives past," Chen said, "I'll follow him home, and pull the van into the driveway behind him. I'll grab him. Inanna, once I'm out, you take the driver's seat. Aarush, be ready to open the side door when I bring him over. As soon as we're in and the door is closed, Inanna, you get us moving."

Inanna nodded. *Bring him over.* She wasn't exactly clear on how that would happen, but Chen seemed confident. They'd talked about this for days, gone over details dozens of times, Chen drilling every aspect into them until he was sure they remembered. But now, sitting in the van, it suddenly felt too rushed. She remembered nothing. *Jesus, what the hell are we doing?* Kidnapping was a serious offense! Yeah? And how about poisoning the water people needed to drink? Wasn't that serious too? And yet here was Gartner, years later, still free. Not only had he gone unpunished, but no one even really talked about the possibility of punishment. Tessier paid a few fines and those towns still didn't have drinking water.

"You got it, Boss," said Aarush, interrupting Inanna's thoughts.

Aarush. He was supposed to bring something. Part of the plan. Critical.

"Did you get the masks?" Inanna asked.

Grinning, Aarush fetched a bag from the back of the van. Pulling the masks out one at a time, he held them up for inspection. "I have Spider-Man, Wonder Woman, Captain America, and Green Lantern." They were the expensive rubber ones that pulled down over the head. No chance of one slipping off and exposing the wearer.

"Only one female super hero?" asked Inanna.

"Best I could do."

"I want Captain America," said Chen.

"Of course you do," said Julia.

Aarush passed him the mask.

"I'll take Wonder Woman," said Inanna. "If that's okay with you?" she asked Julia.

Julia waved off the question. "Go ahead, I don't have the tits to be Wonder Woman."

Aarush, looking like he desperately wanted to say something about tits, passed her the mask and examined the last two. "God, that Green Lantern movie was a turd. Sorry Julia, but I'm taking Spider-Man."

"No worries. Ryan Reynolds is hot as fuck."

"Even in Dead Pool?" asked Aarush.

"*Especially* in dead Pool."

While they waited, Aarush used the time to check the cameras he'd mounted in the rear of the van. Three GoPros were clipped around the interior giving a selection of angles. He planned on combining the three with his hand-held camera in editing. Next the film student clipped wireless lavalier mics to everyone, testing the feeds.

"Each lav mic is recording to its own track," he explained. "This way I can distinctly process our voices to disguise them. I'll attach one to Gartner once he's in the van."

Forty minutes later, Gartner roared through the intersection without so much as slowing for the stop sign.

"There are kids in this neighborhood," muttered Chen. "This asshole deserves everything he's going to get."

"Fucking right," said Julia, eyes hard behind her mask.

Last chance, thought Inanna. *We can stop now. Everyone can go home. No one will get hurt, my friends will be safe.* But Gartner would be free to continue making the world a shittier place, and Julia would have to go on knowing she'd done nothing to the man responsible for her daughter's death. "Let's do this."

"Masks on," said Chen, sliding Captain America into place. Throwing the van into gear, he followed the Audi.

"Cameras all rolling," said Aarush pulling Spiderman into place. "Damn this rubber smells funky."

Inanna suddenly wished she'd thought to put more effort into disguising herself beyond the mask. It was still obvious she was a black woman. Too late, nothing she could do now. *Live and learn.* Next time she'd do better. If there was a next time.

"There should be university classes on terrorism," she joked to Aarush.

"There are," said Chen, pulling on a pair of close-fitting rubber gloves. "At least in military college."

He pulled the van into Gartner's driveway, neatly blocking in the Audi.

Seeing Anthony Gartner climb from his car, Chen stepped from the van and Inanna slid over to take her place behind the wheel. The CEO looked immaculate, black suit and tie over a dark blue shirt. This was no fat old man, but someone who clearly went to great efforts to take care of himself. Wiry and fit, his face was all angles and hard planes.

"Mister Gartner," said Chen, approaching.

The CEO looked up, eyes widening as he noted the van and masks. He managed a step away before Chen closed and caught him with a fast punch to the chin, dropping him. Chen caught him as he crumpled. Dragging the unconscious man back to the van, he pulled him through the open side door.

"Go," said Chen, sliding the door closed. "Don't speed. Don't rush. Drive slow and easy."

Putting the van in gear, Inanna backed out of the driveway and into the street.

"Shit," said Aarush. "We left his car door open. That'll look weird."

"Doesn't matter," said Chen. "People will notice he's missing soon enough."

Inanna, driving, could only hear what went on behind her and catch brief glimpses over her shoulder. She heard Gartner mumble something confused and unintelligible as Chen zip-tied the man's wrists.

"Mister Gartner," said Chen, "if you cooperate you will walk away from this unharmed. Resist, or cause problems, and I *will* hurt you."

"But you'll probably want to get your stomach pumped," chipped in Aarush.

"Probably," agreed Julia.

"The fuck?" said Gartner, clearly still dazed.

"Tessier Waste Disposal Systems buried toxic waste in shoddy underground silos that you said wouldn't leak. That waste is now poisoning the water supply in half a dozen towns in Michigan."

"What?"

"Cancer rates among children have spiked. People can't drink the water. Bathing in it leaves open sores. People are dying."

"What?" Gartner demanded, incredulous. "No." He rubbed his chin. "You hit me!"

"Yes," said Chen. "Tessier seems to be on the brink of quite literally getting away with murder."

"The charges were dropped due to lack of evidence," said Gartner. "There are four other companies burying waste out there. There's no hard proof that it's our silos that are leaking. We build quality storage facilities. It's one of the other companies' silos!"

"Yours are closest to the rivers," said Inanna, over her shoulder as she turned onto another side street. "Anyway. It doesn't matter."

"Doesn't matter?" She heard the confusion in the CEO's voice.

"You're going to be an example." She flashed a grin at him in the rear-view mirror. "The first of many."

"First of... You're eco-terrorists!"

Inanna shrugged. "Today. Tomorrow we'll be some other kind of terrorist. We're going to make the world a better place."

Gartner laughed, a cruel bark of derision. "Fucking hippies. Look. Try to understand. We didn't murder anyone. There's no evidence—"

"The shit your company leaked into the water killed my daughter," growled Julia. "You're lucky we aren't doing this my way."

"We are not here for a discussion," said Chen. "That is not what this is about."

"You're not on trial," agreed Julia. "We've already found you guilty."

Aarush, remaining silent, leaned forward to capture a close-up of Gartner's expression.

Gartner eyed Chen. "So what is this *really* about?" Now that he was getting over the shock, he looked a lot less afraid. He looked angry. Coldly angry. "Making the world a better place like this curvy black bitch says?" He laughed. "Yeah, I can see the color of your skin and I can see your eyes." He nodded at Chen. "Asian." Glancing at Aarush he said, "Your camera man is brown, and the skinny bitch is white. Blue eyes. Probably blond." He shook his head as if disappointed. "It won't be hard to find you."

Somehow Inanna got the feeling he wasn't talking about the police.

Chen hit him, hard. And again.

Gartner curled up, making a noise like a stomped kitten and a rush of guilt surged through her.

Chen frisked him with sharp efficiency, found his phone and keys. "Window," he said. When Julia lowered the van window, he tossed them out.

Aarush handed Chen a lavalier mic and Chen clipped it to Gartner' suit lapel.

What are we doing? Inanna hated violence; it was the final refuge of the stupid. This wasn't her, and it wasn't her friends. *He poisons children,* she reminded herself. *We're doing this for Julia. We're doing this for Jenny, so that no one else has to lose a child.*

Another turn, and they were on a long and winding road. A few ranch-style houses, massive sprawling bungalows, and then empty road.

"We're almost at the field," she said. "Maybe twenty minutes. Julia—" *Fuck!* The name just slipped out. "The water is in my duffel-bag." She felt

Chen's eyes on the back of her neck and hated herself for the stupid mistake. This wasn't going at all like she'd thought.

"Mister Gartner," said Chen, "we'll be stopping soon." Inanna heard him draw his gun and rack the slide. "If you try and run, I will put a bullet in your skull and we will move on to our next target." He sounded so calm, so matter of fact, like blowing this man's brains all over the van interior would be nothing.

He's killed before. It was easy to forget that Chen did four years in the Middle East as a sniper. She imagined him peering into people's lives through the scope of a rifle, dropping them with the same efficiency he did everything.

"Do you understand?" Chen asked.

Gartner said nothing.

She heard the hammer *click* into place.

"Tell me you understand," said Chen.

"I understand," said the CEO.

"Good. Here," she heard Chen say behind her, "use this to wipe the blood from your face."

They drove in silence, Inanna careful not to speed and to stop completely at each stop sign.

"Where are you taking me?" Gartner asked

"You'll see," said Aarush.

Ten minutes later Inanna found the dirt road she'd picked on Google Maps. It led to nowhere, ending in a field run rampant with clover and weeds. It looked like it hadn't been farmed in decades.

Dropping the old van into park, she killed the engine and turned in her seat. "Ok, folks. Let's get this done. Spiderman," she said, "you ready?"

Aarush nodded and flicked a switch, and harsh white LED light filled the van's interior. "Right," he said, setting a small digital camera on a stand and checking to see his hand-held was also running. "Good to go. Cue Wonder Woman."

Chen, gun in hand, finger clear of the trigger, watched Gartner, attention never straying.

Inanna cleared her throat. "Anthony Gartner, CEO of Tessier Waste Disposal Systems, your company is one of many dumping toxic waste into American soil. You're poisoning the land and the people."

"There's no evidence—"

The Millennial Manifesto

"Silence," said Chen. "This is not a trial. There is no defense. We know you are guilty. The American people know you are guilty. *You* know you are guilty."

"We have decided," continued Inanna, "that simply paying a few fines—which you'll likely write-off as a business expense anyway—is insufficient. We want you to stop poisoning us. We want all the companies around the world to stop poisoning our planet. You are merely the first." She paused, gathering her thoughts. *Maybe next time you do a better job of scripting and memorizing this.* "We are going to terrorize every corporation guilty of such crimes. You will fold to our demands because we will not attack your wallets. This is personal. You, the CEOs, are going to pay the price."

Julia dug the jar of murky water out from within Inanna's backpack and held it out to Gartner. "Take it."

"No."

"Take it," said Chen. "Plan B is much worse."

It was a lie, a bluff. They'd all agreed they wouldn't kill anyone. They weren't murderers. Now, looking at Chen, seeing the flat death in his eyes, Inanna wasn't so sure. *He's just pretending.* Though Jenny's death always seemed to have hit Julia harder, she was Chen's daughter too. What if he wanted vengeance, no matter the cost?

Gartner took the jar.

"Open it," commanded Inanna with a wave of relief.

The CEO shook his head.

Chen raised the gun, pointed it at Gartner's face.

Gartner opened the jar and a foul stench filled the confines of the van.

"I'm gonna puke in my Spidey mask," said Aarush, gagging.

"Do you know what that is?" Inanna asked the CEO.

He shook his head, lips pulled back in a grimace of disgust.

"Water from the river half a dozen towns use as their main source. Water *your* company poisons."

Gartner looked from the jar to Inanna, face pale. "I'm just the CEO."

"Lift it to your face, asshole," snapped Julia. "Take a deep breath and describe the smell to the camera."

Gartner's attention darted to Chen and the gun and back to the jar. He lifted it, took a tentative sniff, and retched.

"Deeper," said Julia. "Suck it right into your lungs."

Shooting her a glare of venomous hate, he did as instructed and promptly puked all over his expensive suit.

"Describe it," said Inanna.

"It's fucking disgusting. It smells like… eggs and rust and rotting meat."

"With just a hint of wild berries," said Aarush, "a soft nose, and a long finish."

"Spiderman," scolded Julia.

Aarush grinned behind his mask. "Sorry."

Inanna watched Gartner hold the drink away from his pale face. *Am I really going to do this?* The man was directly responsible for poisoning people. Folks had died. Cancer rates were way up in the area. There were children covered in strange sores from bathing in tap water.

Jenny. She wasn't the only death.

Just the beginning. Make the world a better place. "Drink."

Gartner's attention snapped to her. There was something there, something reptile cold and calculating. He was scared, but more than anything he was angry. "You're the leader of this little circus, aren't you." It wasn't a question.

"There's no—"

"I'm going to get you, you know." He showed teeth in a rabid snarl and Inanna remembered Julia's talk of predators. This man was the real thing, an apex predator. No hint of compassion. Cold death. "I will."

"You're not getting anyone," said Chen. "Now drink."

Inanna hid the sigh of relief when Gartner's shark-like attention returned to Chen and the gun.

"I can't," the CEO said.

"Drink," said Julia. "What's to be afraid of, if you haven't poisoned the water?"

"It's dirty," he said, holding the jar well away from his face. "I can't."

"You can," said Chen. "You will."

"It's disgusting!"

"Yes," said Inanna, "it is. And your company helped make it that way. Drink."

"It's poisonous!"

"Thank you very much," said Aarush. "That'll look great on YouTube."

Gartner blinked at Aarush, torn between relief and anger. "That's it? That's all you fucking wanted?"

They'd talked about this. How much was enough? Would a confession suffice?

"No," said Inanna. "Drink it. Drink it all or Captain America puts a bullet in your brain-pan and we leave your corpse at the side of the dirt road. Someone will find it, some day."

"Look," said Aarush reasonably. "You'll get to a hospital and get your stomach pumped. You'll be fine."

"Hell," said Julia, "you can puke it all out the moment you're out of the van. But if you don't drink it…" She leered behind the Green Lantern mask. "Bang!"

Gartner twitched, glancing around the superhero masks surrounding him. His shoulders sagged. "I drink this and you'll let me go?"

"Unlike corporations," said Inanna, "We're not liars."

Gartner's eyes locked on Inanna. "This is your last chance. You can stop this, save your friends. Drive me back to my fucking house right now and I'll pretend this never happened."

"Five," said Chen. "Four…"

"Fuck," said Anthony Gartner, seeing the cold stone of Chen's eyes. He drank the jar in one long go.

Sliding the van door open, Chen shoved him out onto the gravel before the CEO began retching and puking. Exiting the vehicle, he stood waiting, gun pointed at Gartner, until the man stopped. Aarush filmed the whole thing, leaning out the door with his hand-held.

"Strip," said Chen.

"Oh c'mon," said Gartner. "Really?"

"Five…"

"Fucking hell." He stripped down to his socks and underwear.

"Good enough," said Aarush. "This is a family-friendly show, after all."

Julia climbed out of the van, collected the puke-stained suit, and tossed it inside. "Shall we leave him his shoes?"

Aarush leaned forward, focusing the camera on Gartner. "Tell us you knew you were poisoning the water but didn't give a fuck because of your profit margins, and you can keep your shoes."

Gartner eyed him, jaw set.

Julia shrugged and tossed the expensive alligator shoes into the van. Pointing back up the dirt road she said, "A couple miles up that way you'll find a house where you can make a call. Have a nice day, asshole," she added, climbing back into the van.

"I'll email you a link to the video once it's up," called Aarush as Chen slammed the sliding door closed.

Inanna pulled away, giving the van some gas and spraying the CEO with dust and pebbles.

"That went well," said Aarush, pulling his mask off.

Everyone removed their masks, all grinning except Chen.

"We should celebrate," said Julia. "I'm starving."

"I could seriously go for a beer," said Aarush.

Chen mulled this over for a moment and then nodded agreement. "A beer wouldn't be terrible. First, we hit a car wash. Clean the dust off the outside, vacuum and clean the puke from the interior. We ditch the clothes in the garbage and the van somewhere else once it's cleaned."

Aarush let out a whoop as he peered into the small screen on the camera. "Guys, this looks amazing. With some editing, it's gonna be gold. Everyone, hand in your lav mics. I gotta return them to the college."

All three unclipped their wireless lavalier mics and handed them to the film student. Hunting through Gartner's crumpled clothes, Aarush retrieved the last mic.

"That went pretty much to plan." said Inanna.

"Nothing ever goes to plan," said Chen, ejecting the chambered round from the gun and putting the safety on. "We just don't know where things fucked up yet."

****

Hours later, back at the hotel, Inanna went through her mental checklist, making sure they hadn't forgot anything.

After downing a round of celebratory Coors, the group had gone about their various tasks. Aarush spent the evening editing the video down to a tight two minutes, a fast montage of the kidnapping, followed by the beautiful scene of Gartner refusing to drink and then finally drinking it and immediately puking it back up.

The video ended with a shot of the CEO in his boxers as they drove away. Aarush had shotgunned energy drinks and eaten an entire family-sized bag of peanut M&Ms before finishing.

Chen and Julia took the van into a nearby industrial site, doused the interior with gasoline, and set it ablaze. They caught a bus back to the motel.

The Millennial Manifesto

Since they both stunk of gas, Inanna washed their clothes at the motel's coin-op laundry facility while the two showered together.

Once Aarush finished the video, Julia downloaded it onto her phone and went for a walk, looking for free Wi-Fi. She found it outside a coffee shop called the Galaxy Diner. After creating a quick Explodemail account and using it to create a YouTube account, she uploaded the file. She then used the Explodemail to send copies to every TV, radio, and internet news source they'd found contact info for. Half an hour later the Explodemail account self-destructed, leaving no trace it ever existed.

Now, back at the motel, the four sat in a loose circle, Julia grinning, her blond hair still damp, as she leaned against Chen. A cooler sat at the foot of the bed filled with ice and tall cans of Coors.

Aarush, sitting on the bed, back against the headboard, legs stretched out before him, claimed the remote for the TV.

Almost every news channel was playing their video, and the ones that weren't were decrying those that were, saying it only furthered the terrorist agenda. They were, however, still talking about it, still describing it in loving detail. Some of the trashier stations hosted call-ins where the average Joe America could voice their ill-thought opinions. The four got called everything from superheroes to terrorists and they either ought to be shot, or they hadn't gone nearly far enough.

The news stations speculated wildly based on what little information was available. The terrorists were a small, poorly organized group. They were international and well-funded. They had corporate backing and the eco-terrorism thing was a flimsy cover. There were independent cells operating across America. This was the work of a rogue YouTube comedy troupe. It was part of a larger art exhibit.

They decided, at the beginning, not to name the group. This was about saving the world, not getting credit. And being unnamed made it easier for copycats to take up their cause. Eventually, everyone would understand. This wasn't just about the environment.

They were going to do everything in their power to make the world a better place.

CHAPTER – HIRAN

Hiran sat reading in his hotel bed, pillows piled up behind him. The book, borrowed from Fana, was a strange fantasy novel about a world where reality was mutable to the beliefs of the masses and the insane were capable of terrible magic. He couldn't decide if it was horribly derivative, or completely unlike anything he'd ever read. The writer was obsessed with semicolons; he used them far too often.

His cell phone rang. Glancing at the display, he saw it was Chuck.

"Great." Picking up the cell, he accepted the call. "Yeah?"

"Boss, you in your room?"

"Yeah."

"Turn on the TV."

Hiran sighed. "If this is because you want me to see some woman's tits—"

"No, Boss. Not this time. Though the reporter chick—"

"Chuck."

"Sorry. Gartner is on TV. Local station, channel 42."

"He's CEO of a corporation. He's—"

"Someone kidnapped him. Eco-terrorists or something."

Hiran's guts fell. Gartner had employed him—and through him Chuck and Fana—for years. For the most part it was an easy gig. Sometimes they were bodyguards, there to look impressive, but stay quiet and out of the way. Sometimes they ran errands for him, putting pressure on competitors and politicians, like they did with the man they photographed with his mistress.

No way this would end well. At best Gartner would be pissed they weren't there to protect him, and at worst Hiran would have to go in search of a new employer. *So close to retirement.* Could he and his wife and daughters live off what he'd squirreled away over the years? *College. Two girls.* What if they wanted more than just a bachelor's degree? Nope. Not a fucking chance.

The Millennial Manifesto

With a sinking feeling, Hiran found the remote and turned on the TV.

Sure enough, there was Gartner, harried and wearing what looked like a police coat thrown over his shoulders. He also didn't appear to be wearing pants or a shirt. Paramedics were assisting him into the back of an ambulance, and Hiran saw he wasn't wearing shoes either. His feet were filthy and bloody.

Fuck.

"I'll call you back," he said to Chuck, disconnecting.

Gartner is going to be murderously angry. And that meant someone would have to get hurt. The man was a cold fish with a mean streak, a pure sociopath with power and money. If he didn't pay so damned well, Hiran would have left him years ago.

Hiran watched as the reporter—an attractive woman in a business-like blue skirt-suit—explained Anthony Gartner's ordeal. The CEO of Tessier Waste Disposal Systems, a company recently acquitted of accidentally releasing toxins into several Michigan water sources, had apparently been kidnapped by eco-terrorists. He was, she said, forced to drink the water from one of the very rivers his company was accused of polluting for the last two decades.

Bloody feet aside, Gartner seemed unhurt, more angry and embarrassed than scared. Which, Hiran mused, was bad. Gartner wasn't a bundle of hugs and warm words at the best of times.

And then the news channel played a YouTube video.

It was slick, well shot, and nicely edited. Totally professional. The sound was top quality.

"The video has already been removed from YouTube," the reporter said, "though not before it got three hundred thousand hits. Thousands of copies have already sprung up on similar sites. We estimate it has been seen and shared over four and a half *million* times since it was released."

The irony of the station playing the video it was already calling banned was apparently lost on the news anchor.

Hiran watched his boss cower in fear, groaned as they tossed Gartner from the van and forced him to strip.

"Shit," he said to the empty room.

Gartner was going to be so far beyond pissed. Would he let it slide? Would he let the authorities deal with it? This was bad on so many levels. He'd been forced at gun point to drink the water, and called it poisonous. That wouldn't sit well with the board. Then there was his seemingly infinite ego and pride. They made a fool out of him on TV, got him to admit, albeit not legally admissibly, that Tessier poisoned the water.

They embarrassed him. Gartner would never let this go.

With the damning pictures already in Hiran's possession, this op was finished. They were due to report back to Gartner the next day. The CEO liked doing these kinds of dealings face to face, just as it would be Gartner who met with the target and showed him the photos. Gartner said he liked to see defeat in the eyes of his victims. He said he loved that beaten look people got when they knew he'd fucked them good.

Hiran's phone rang that special piercing ring that meant it was Gartner and he'd better fucking answer or the asshole would scream abuse at him later. *Not worth it.* Except it was. *College*, he reminded himself. *You're putting the girls through college.*

Hiran answered. "Sir."

"You watching TV?" demanded Gartner.

"Yes, sir." God he hated calling this sociopathic ass 'sir'.

"Tell me you know why the fuck I'm calling."

"You want us to find these eco-terrorists."

"Fucking right I do."

"You want us to hurt them?" *Please don't tell me to kill them.* Hiran had killed before. You don't spend that much time in Middle East without wracking up a few scalps. Unlike Chuck, however, he never developed a taste for it.

Silence.

Finally, "No. Bring them to me."

"Is that a good idea?"

"It's a brilliant idea. Now tell me you've got some good news."

"We have the pictures."

"At least something has gone right today. I want to see you here, stat. Bring the pictures. I'll give you everything I remember about these fucking hippies."

Gartner hung up without another word.

"Shit."

Hiran hit the speed dial for Fana.

"S'up, Boss?"

"We're reporting back to Gartner now rather than tomorrow."

"Nice. Time to wind up Tick Tock."

"Please don't. We're going to be in the car together for an hour."

Hiran killed the call.

Half an hour later, they met at the stolen black Chrysler 300 in the hotel parking. For all Chuck's many faults, he was an accomplished car thief. Though, for reasons Hiran would never understand, the man insisted on stealing Chrysler 300s.

"Shotgun!" called Fana. "Tick Tock is riding bitch in the back."

"That doesn't make sense," groused Chuck. "She's tiny. She doesn't need leg room. Sitting back there hurts my knees."

"Sorry," said Hiran, climbing into the driver's seat. "She called shotgun."

Once everyone was strapped in, Hiran accelerated hard out of the parking lot.

"Boss," said Chuck from the back, "where we going?"

"Gartner."

"I can hear the gears grinding in Tick Tock's brain," said Fana, curling her legs up on the seat and using none of the excessive leg-room supplied.

Hiran ignored the legs, thought about his wife.

"Is it because of the kidnapping?" Chuck asked.

"You know how everyone says there's no such thing as stupid questions?" said Fana. "Well, Tick Tock just proved them all wrong."

"Don't fucking call me Tick Tock," growled Chuck.

"Tick," said Fana.

"Seriously, woman. Don't."

Fana flashed an innocent smile, batting eyelashes. "Tock."

Chuck glared at her, fists clenched, jaw working like he was trying to figure out what to say.

"Yes," said Hiran, ignoring them both. "Because of the kidnapping."

Turning from Fana, Chuck scratched at his chin with cigarette-stained fingers. "So we're gonna hurt someone?"

"Probably."

"They really made a fool of Gartner, eh? He's gotta be pretty angry about that."

"Aren't you the goddamned Grand Master of Understatement," said Fana.

Christ, imagine if he says something like that to Gartner. "Chuck, when we get there, I don't want you to say anything. Keep your mouth shut, okay?"

"Me? What about the ape with the huge hands in the front seat?"

"My hands aren't that big," said Fana.

"You could crush a child's skull with those mitts!"

"I could crush yours."

"Enough," said Hiran. "Let's pretend to be professionals, just for a little while."

Chuck giggled in the back seat while Fana ground her teeth and tried to hide her hands—which really weren't that big—between her lovely legs.

Don't look at her legs. Think about your wife.

Hiran focused on the road.

****

Gartner's neighborhood consisted of turn of the century bungalows, quaint and well-maintained with little flower gardens, manicured shrubberies, and huge eight thousand square-foot modern homes with solar panel roofs.

There were no visible police cars, but Hiran noted the blue Dodge Charger with two men sitting in it across the street. Both men wore identical mustaches and crew cuts.

"They should just put the donuts on the dash," said Fana.

Chuck grunted agreement. He hated cops almost as much as he hated immigrants, brown people—with Hiran, maybe, being the one exception and Fana occasionally getting a pass because she was beautiful and female—and hippies.

At least they aren't bickering.

A Channel 7 news van also sat parked across the street, but the film crew were nowhere to be seen. Probably inside, viewing the day's footage.

Wheeling the 300 into the driveway, Hiran dropped it into Park and climbed from the car with a grunt as his knees twinged and his lower back sent a friendly little reminder-stab of pain.

"Chuck," he said, as the big man clambered from the back seat. "Not one word."

"What if he asks me a question?"

"Does anyone ever ask you questions?" demanded Fana.

"You just did."

"Chuck!" Hiran took a calming breath. "If he asks you a question, answer. Otherwise, silence."

"I bet I can trick him into talking," said Fana

Chuck shook his head. "No way."

"Both of you behave, or you're staying in the car." Christ, it was like dealing with the girls when they were little. Fana opened her mouth to speak.

"And you'll be riding in the back for the rest of time." She closed it, dark eyes glinting daggers.

The two pouted but said nothing.

"Let's go."

Chuck waved to the cops and gave them the finger. "What?" he said, sounding wounded, when Hiran shook his head in exasperation. "I didn't say anything. And anyway, we're not even inside yet."

Anthony Gartner was waiting at the front door to let them in. He wore neatly ironed khakis and a red polo shirt tucked in tight to show off his trim frame.

"Sir," said Hiran as he passed.

Fana and Chuck followed him in, both remaining silent.

Passing Hiran with quick and impatient strides, Gartner led them into a colossal kitchen of black granite counters, white marble floors, and over-sized stainless-steel appliances. Collapsing onto a chair, the CEO rocked back onto the two rear legs. Hiran sat across from him, with Fana taking the seat to his left. Chuck remained standing at the door, muscled arms crossed, scanning the surroundings like he expected to be attacked at any moment.

"Coffee?" said Gartner. "Beer?"

Chuck glanced at Hiran, one eyebrow creeping up.

"Thank you, no," said Hiran.

"They made me drink fucking river water," said Gartner. "I had to get my stomach pumped. You ever had your stomach pumped? Not fun. I've been dosed to the tits with antibiotics and god knows what else because of all the ecoli and shit in there. Probably die of cancer next week."

He looked more annoyed than angry or scared. "The doctors—"

Gartner waved him to silence. "Fuck 'em. I want the four assholes who did this. I've been fucking humiliated. Tessier could drop me for this if I didn't hold dirt on just about every asshole on the board."

Having helped Gartner get most of that dirt, Hiran was pretty damned sure the man's job was safe.

"I've transferred funds into your account already. No expense spared. A sweet bonus if you find them within the week." He paused in thought. "I want to know who these people are and what they *really* want. I want to embarrass them. I want to pull their lives apart. People are calling them heroes! They're terrorists, plain and simple. I want every detail of their lives. Homes. Family. Employment. I'm going to break them, leave them nothing."

Hiran sat through the tirade, nodding as if all this were perfectly reasonable. "Of course, sir."

Gartner glanced at Fana. "You're information systems, right?"

She nodded, darting a look at Hiran.

"Facebook. Twitter. Fucking Instagram, and snapchat. I want to know who they're fucking. I want to know where their goddamned mothers live. Find them." Gartner turned to Chuck. "And you're Special Forces, right? Covert Ops? Black bag and all that shit?"

Chuck nodded.

"Then fucking find them." He returned his attention to Hiran. "The second you know who they are, call me." He scratched at his chin. "Maybe it'll be better if they just disappear. No need to let them spout their shit on TV or whine and cry to the authorities."

"Legally," began Hiran, but Gartner stopped him with a look.

"The law only applies to poor people and you fucking know it."

Having done all manner of illegal things for Gartner, Hiran did indeed.

"If I decide they disappear, you'll disappear them. Tessier… We're talking billions of dollars every year, thousands of employees, all of them American citizens. Tessier shutting down would cripple this county."

Hiran stifled a laugh. *Sure, this isn't personal at all*. That, however, wasn't Hiran's problem. Gartner was, as Chuck liked to say, the wallet. He kept his face blank. He'd hurt too many people, committed too many crimes, while working for Gartner to let guilt get in the way now.

"If you could tell us everything you remember, sir, that would be a huge help. Every detail, no matter how small."

Gartner grinned professionally straight teeth, crisp and white. "There are four of them. One big Asian male, Japanese descent, no accent. I'd say he has military training. He reminds me of Chucky-boy here." He waved a dismissive hand at Chuck. Thankfully Tick Tock remained quiet. "The camera man was a skinny brown kid. There's a white girl, blue eyes. Probably blond. One of them let her name slip: Julia. She looks like a workout freak, all lean muscle. The leader is a black girl, short and curvy as hell. Fantastic tits. I think she's the driving force here, the brains of the operation." Finally remembering his beer, Gartner took a long drink. "They were all in their early to mid-twenties. Fucking millennials."

He hadn't shared any of this with the police.

"Anything else?" asked Hiran.

"Yeah. I got the license plate of the van they were driving."

CHAPTER – INANNA

After several rounds of drinks, Aarush snapped off the TV. "I'm going to call that a qualified success," he said. "Next time I'd like more time with editing. It felt a little rushed."

"Next time," said Chen.

"What *is* next?" asked Julia. For the first time since Jenny's death, she seemed relaxed, like a weight had been lifted from her.

All eyes turned on Inanna. "I'm open to suggestions," she said. She had ideas, but wasn't quite ready to share.

"Tessier Waste Disposal Systems is refusing to comment," said Chen.

"We should hit them again," said Julia. "*Make* them react. Is there some way we can force them to admit they knew they were poisoning the water?" She chewed gently on her bottom lip. "I want every single board member to drink a pint of that river."

"Yeah," agreed Aarush, pushing the thick-rimmed glasses back up from where they'd slid down his nose. "The entire corporate office. What if we replaced all the water coolers with contaminated water?"

"We'd have to filter it enough to at least looked clear," Inanna pointed out.

"Doable," said Chen. "The problem would be delivering the bottles. No doubt they have a contract with someone for that." He scratched at his chin. "It'd be easier to inject the bottles with contaminants after they'd been delivered. Couriers come and go all the time. Faking uniforms would be easy. Baseball caps to keep our faces off camera."

"I like it," said Inanna, "but it sounds a little dangerous."

"And I'd rather not poison the guy who mops the floors," said Aarush. "It's the people who make the decisions that we want."

"We should kill Gartner," said Julia.

Aarush's eyes widened. "Kill him? Just… murder him?"

She studied the group, eyes again hard. Her moment of peace had been brief indeed.

"We aren't murderers," said Inanna. "Remember, the punishment fits the crime. We decided that day one."

Everyone nodded, except Julia, who shrugged. "How about we kidnap the fucker again and this time we inject him with the same level of toxins someone would have if they'd been drinking the water for the last three years?"

"That's good," said Chen. "Tessier has been polluting a lot longer than that. He'd be getting off easy."

"How dangerous would that be to Gartner?" Inanna asked.

"Who cares?" demanded Julia. "He deserves to die."

"Let's sleep on it," suggested Aarush, ever the peace-keeper. "I want to see that clip again." He turned the TV back on to forestall further disagreement. "Who wants a beer?" Without waiting for answers, he handed out another round of icy Coors.

"Hey," said Julia, pointing at the TV. "That's Gartner's house."

Everyone focused on the screen. The scene looked to be hastily shot through a vehicle window.

"Maybe he's going to make a statement," said Inanna. "It'll be interesting to see how he backpedals after begging not to drink the water."

Instead, a Chrysler 300 pulled into the driveway and three people exited the vehicle. The image froze while the reporter blathered on. There were two men with military crew-cuts. The brown one, clearly in charge, wore tan khakis and a blue button-down shirt. He was well into his fifties, but still looked lean and muscled. The other one, a white guy in a short-sleeved shirt with even more muscle and no neck, made a rude gesture to someone off camera, his hand fuzzed out to hide the offense. The third, a young black woman with curly shoulder-length hair, was at odds with the ramrod straight bearing of the others.

"Turn up the volume," said Chen

"…what looks to be private security contractors enter the Gartner's household," said the reporter. "Our camera man caught this through the van window after we'd finished filming and had been told to vacate the property. We've done some digging, and the two gentlemen pictured are both ex-Navy Seals with several tours of combat-heavy duty under their belts. At this time, the woman remains a mystery." The reporter went on but no one was listening.

Chen shook his head. "Shit."

"Why shit?" asked Inanna.

The Millennial Manifesto

Chen took a deep breath and let it out in a slow hiss. "It means Gartner is angry and maybe scared. It might mean he's hoping to deal with this—with us—outside the confines of the law." He nodded at the TV. "She'll be an information specialist, a high-end hacker for hire."

"We were careful," said Aarush. "They won't find us."

The set of Chen's jaw said he was less certain.

"Maybe they're just bodyguards," suggested Inanna. *Which means there's no way we're going after him a second time.* That was a relief. She didn't want to see the man again.

Chen slowly nodded, but looked unconvinced. "I recognized the tattoos on the white guy. He's a killer. Up close, with a knife. Two clicks away with a rifle. Everything in between. He's a one-man strike-team."

"You and I," said Julia. "We aren't exactly kittens. If they're so bad-ass, let's hit them before they're ready. You're a Marine sniper. I'm a demolitions expert. They won't even see us."

"No," said Chen. "We stay clear. We were careful. We'll be fine."

Julia studied the TV with narrowed eyes. "This would be a perfect time to grab Gartner again. Snatch him right from under their Special Forces noses. Embarrass them and Tessier."

"Too dangerous." Chen's voice left no room for argument.

"Let's sleep on it," repeated Aarush. "I'm exhausted."

Everyone nodded agreement.

Julia gave Chen a kiss on the cheek, and then shoved the two men—who were staying in an adjacent room—out the door.

"What about me?" asked Aarush on the way out.

Julia blew him a kiss and then punched him in the shoulder hard enough to make him wince. She closed the door and turned to lean her back against it. She stood, examining Inanna. "You know, we won't change the world by backing down."

"And we won't change it by getting caught."

"Then we have to be smart."

"Smart is choosing our targets wisely, not throwing ourselves at a giant we've already kicked into a state of high alertness."

Julia cocked an eyebrow. A scar, a thin white line, ran through it. A memento from some MMA cage match. Her career as a pro-fighter hadn't been much more than four years, but she'd retired unbeaten, claiming that fighting by the rules was for pussies and cowards. She told Inanna she wanted *real* tests, where the fight meant something beyond a few thousand dollars. She wanted battles where wit and skill were everything and no one could hide behind a technicality, where nothing *ever* got left to the judges. She told Inanna all this one drunken night after a fight where she broke her opponent's arm. She'd been suspended for six months afterward.

"Fine," Julia finally said. "We all agreed you were in charge. We did that for a reason."

"You did?" Inanna asked, startled.

Julia nodded. "We trust your judgment. *I* trust your judgment."

Inanna drew a deep breath. "I think we should hit a radically different target. Everyone is labeling us 'eco-terrorists'. That's not what we are. That's not *all* we are."

Julia perked up, eyes bright with excitement. "You have a target."

"I saw a news report last week about a company called The Children's Dream Foundation. They raise money for children dying of cancer or whatever."

"I heard of them."

"In the last decade they raised over one hundred and ten million dollars. Less than a million of that actually went to the kids. The rest goes into their pockets and to pay the companies promoting them."

"So they've already been busted?"

"Nope. They do actually donate some money, and there's no law saying how much they have to give. Technically, they *are* a charity. Just one that's really expensive to run and pays the founding members really well."

"Dirt bags."

"Indeed. So how do we make the punishment fit the crime?"

"They need to lose everything. Their wealth. Their homes. Everything."

"But if we just blow it all up they'll make insurance claims and have it all back a year later."

"Damn," said Julia. "What if we can make it look like they did it, like it was arson, an insurance scam?"

"People need to know *why* this is happening. We can't terrify corporations if they don't know it's us."

"Wait. You said founding members. Plural."

"Husband and wife team."

Julia's eyes lit up, her fingers twitching and fidgeting with nervous energy. "We take the wife, kidnap her. Hold her for ransom. We post videos on

The Millennial Manifesto

YouTube—showing her—with our demands. If the husband doesn't sell off all their properties and donate every last penny to the charities of our choosing, we'll make her wear Walmart brand clothes or something." Julia always made fun of Chen for doing all his shopping at Walmart.

"Julia, you're a genius."

Julia made a show of looking smug and checking her fingernails, which were cut short and in need of a good manicure. "I know."

"Everyone will understand why we're doing it. The news stations will replay the original reports and put it back in the news."

"And those assholes will be left with nothing." Julia grabbed two more beers from the cooler, cracked them open, and handed one to Inanna. "Details," she said. "We need to scope their security."

"They operate out of a warehouse behind a gas station. Probably because it's cheap."

Julia's smile grew, spreading from her eyes to her lips and lighting her face. She never wore makeup, never seemed to put much thought into her appearance at all, yet Inanna saw a simple beauty in her. And so much strength.

"You've already been researching them, you little sneak. This is perfect. Where do we hold the woman once we have her?"

Inanna considered the options. "We could rent a cottage? We need somewhere remote with Wi-Fi access."

"Better to stay on the move," said Julia. "We can rent a little camper or motorhome and upload from a different town each day."

"I like it."

"If they have a really nice car," said Julia, "I'm going to blow it up."

Inanna laughed. "Yeah, I'm fine with that. As long as no one gets hurt."

"We need a list of their properties, vehicles and investments," Julia pointed out.

"The woman will give us all that once we have her."

"Why are we both assuming we grab the wife?" asked Julia. "Kinda sad."

She's right. "Men… They're more prone to violence. The husband is more likely to put up a fight. Women…" Inanna sighed. "When cornered or threatened we tend to shut down, to retreat and try and protect ourselves."

"You've seen me fight," Julia said.

"I doubt the wife is an MMA fighter."

The two sat in silence for several minutes.

Finally, Julia said, "We grab the wife. You're right. It's likely to be easier."

"We'll have the wife tell the world how much they stole," said Inanna.

"And since we're not taking a penny, there's no dangerous drop-off or trade. When the money is donated, we release her with a quarter for a phone call."

"What if the husband refuses?" asked Inanna.

"We tell his wife he refuses to buy her freedom and we show the world the video and then we let her go. She'll divorce him and take half of everything. And the whole world will know what kind of shitheads they are."

"I like it," said Inanna. "We'll tell the others in the morning."

They drank several more beers, fantasizing about how it would all go down, building the perfect heist in their minds, arguing about which charity the money should go to.

Eventually, Julia sprawled out on the bed, long limbs thrown wide, and snored like a fat truck driver.

In the morning, Inanna woke as Julia let herself back into the room.

Inanna groaned at the hangover. "Where were you?"

"Went for a walk." Julia lifted a cardboard tray with two steaming coffees. "Got these on the way back."

"Praise the lord."

An hour later, they trooped to the bus station and returned home.

CHAPTER – HIRAN

"Well that's a fucking dead end," said Chuck, looking over the burnt husk of a van.

Fana had intercepted police communications regarding a van which matched Gartner's description, and they'd trooped down to check it out. Luckily there were enough onlookers around they didn't stand out.

The police had taped up the scene and were keeping the rubberneckers and kids filming with their phones at a safe distance. Hiran saw them make note of Chuck and himself and decide they weren't likely suspects.

Only because we're clean and well-dressed.

Smoke still rose from the wreck, spiraling into the sky and filling the air with the stink of melted rubber, gasoline, roast upholstery, and burnt metal. Absent, happily was the barbecue aroma of cooked flesh. Hiran had seen and smelled enough charred bodies in gas-drenched cars to last a lifetime.

Though that really would have made my job a lot easier. Would he still get the bonus if he reported back that the eco-terrorists had committed suicide instead of facing justice? Probably not.

Something was wrong here. He couldn't quite put his finger on it. Something didn't jive with this being the work of eco-terrorists.

"Eco-terrorists," he said aloud. "*Eco.*"

"Boss?" said Chuck.

"Burning tires is bad for the environment," said Hiran.

Chuck glanced at the smoldering wreck. "Only four tires. Not too bad."

"Eco-terrorists, Tick Tock," said Fana. "Ecological. As in they care about the environment."

"They lit this thing with half a tank of gas inside," noted Hiran. "Left it to burn on the street."

"Maybe they just didn't think it through," said Chuck. "Maybe this wasn't planned or they panicked."

"No." Hiran shook his head. "They were meticulously destroying evidence." Turning, he took in their surroundings. All the street lights in the neighborhood had been smashed, though not recently. The few buildings fronting onto the intersection were boarded up. There were no street cameras anywhere. "They put some thought into this."

"You think they're pros?" Fana asked. "Maybe a corporate team?"

"But to what end?" asked Hiran. "What was their objective?"

This felt all kinds of wrong. Nothing fit where it should. Kidnap a man and force him to drink poisoned water. That was hardcore. But Gartner's report on the perpetrators suggested only one had any military training. The others, he'd said, seemed like a bunch of post-college hipsters.

"Maybe it's one man using the others. Maybe he's corporate and the others are being played." It sounded wrong even as Hiran said it. Gartner told them the group acted like friends, like they knew each other well. One even slipped up and named another Julia. That wasn't pro at all.

Chuck lit a cigarette, drawing smoke deep into his lungs and letting it curl out through his nose like a dragon. "What's next, Boss?"

Hiran glanced at Chuck. Only when he had a cigarette in his face did he stop fidgeting with nervous energy. "Let's play the odds. If they're eco-terrorists—"

"Fucking hippies."

"If they're hippies," continued Hiran, darting Chuck an annoyed look which was ignored, "how are they getting home?" He waved his hands at the abandoned buildings. "Assuming they don't live here?"

"Hippies love public transit," said Chuck.

"And bicycles," piped in Fana.

"Right. If they're on bikes, we're screwed. Chuck, that's your job. We're looking for four people in their early to mid-twenties traveling together. Asian male. Indian male—"

"As in tomahawk and scalping kinda Indian, or like a brownie? Like, the dot, or the feather?"

"Indian," sighed Hiran, "as in brown, like me."

"Right. Gotcha."

"May I continue?"

"Yeah. Sorry, Boss. But it needed clarifying."

"Can I shoot him?" Fana asked.

"Later. So. One big Asian male. One slender Indian male. One tall and wiry white female with blue eyes—"

"What color were the brownie's eyes?" asked Chuck, drawing hard on his cigarette.

"I'm going to go out on a limb here," said Hiran, "and say brown. And there was one black female, short and curvy."

"Gartner said she had fantastic tits," added Chuck.

"Great. That's who you're looking for. They may have split up, so also keep an eye out for pairs. Hit all the coaches that run buses anywhere even close to this neighborhood and report back." Hiran tossed him the keys to yet another stolen Chrysler 300. "And don't smoke in the car."

Chuck nodded, barely refrained from saluting, and left.

"Christ he is dumb," said Fana.

"Yeah, but he was right about the bus thing."

"How bad is that newscast for us?" she asked. "Everyone knows we're working for Gartner now. Well, at least they know about you two goons."

"We're going to have to be a little more careful. If anything happens to these folks, all eyes will be on us. If we end up having to disappear them, we have to make sure we do it right."

"Good luck with Captain Subtle on the team. I put a hundred bucks on this ending with a gunfight downtown and Tick Tock getting killed by a hippie."

Hiran grunted a half laugh. "He'll do his job. He might not be subtle, but he obeys orders." He glanced at Fana, "The news folks identified Tick Tock—" He grimaced. "Chuck and I, pretty quick. How come they weren't able to identify you?"

Fana shrugged, batted long lashes at Hiran, and said, "A girl's gotta have her secrets."

Surprised there were this many people in such a rundown neighborhood, Hiran scanned the gathered crowd. Maybe twenty pedestrians stood around watching the cops do nothing. It was a cliché, but criminals really did return to the scene of the crime with surprising regularity. Maybe it was a secret desire to get caught, or maybe they just wanted to feel smugly superior, be the only people to know the *why*. There were several people in this crowd who matched the near-useless descriptions Gartner was so proud of. There were at least two Asian men and several white girls in the assumed age range. There were even three skinny brown kids and a couple of black women. None looked pleased or smug or any of the other emotions common to criminals who think they've gotten away with something.

He noticed one of the white women, a tall blond girl in her early twenties with her hair tied back in a pony tail, staring at him. A thin scar bisected one eyebrow. She glanced away, like it was nothing. To get a reaction, Hiran raised a hand and nodded to her. She blinked, and waved back. Then she checked her phone and wandered off. Hiran watched her leave. Attractive and athletic, there was a hardness to her. That scar in her eyebrow was similar to those commonly found on MMA fighters and boxers who've been busted open in the same place a few times.

She doesn't look anything like a hippy eco-terrorist.

"What's next?" asked Fana, interrupting his thoughts.

What *was* next? The odds of Chuck finding anything useful—or even the bus station—were slim.

Hiran turned on Fana. "You are going to back-trace the original YouTube video. Figure out where it was uploaded."

The chances of the terrorists being so sloppy as to upload it from home were minimal, but it might at least give them a rough location.

"Already did that. Unlike Tick Tock, I actually know my job."

"Why haven't I heard your report?"

"I want you to feel useful, like you come up with this stuff all on your own and we'd be lost without you." She patted him on the arm. "Tick Tock probably really is lost. Expect a phone call asking how to use Google Maps."

"The report, please?"

"The video was uploaded in a coffee shop with open Wi-Fi, no password required."

"That should be illegal," grumbled Hiran.

"Yeah, okay, old man. You can't stop the flow of information. Cyber security—"

"Damn. We have a cyber-hippie right here in our midst. The *report*."

Fana rolled her eyes. "I went down there and asked around. No one remembers anyone suspicious. No group of four fitting the description. The diner is in a shitty part of town. No street cameras to hack. The owner said the camera inside the diner didn't actually work."

"Dead end, then."

"Not quite." Fana grinned. "There are a lot of divey motels near the diner. I asked around, some of Gartner's money helped people remember, and I found something." She crossed her arms and stood waiting and smirking, one eyebrow cocked.

"And?"

"At one motel there was an Asian man and an Indian man sharing a room. Next door was a black woman and a white woman. All were in their early twenties. Unfortunately, no one saw them leave."

"I don't suppose—"

"They made no use of the motel's Wi-Fi."

"Shit."

"And they paid cash."

"The room?" Hiran asked.

"Already cleaned before I got there. I bribed a maid fifty bucks to let me look around, but the place was spotless. There was a pile of anti-bacterial wipes in the garbage."

Anti-bacterial wipes tossed in the garbage. This sounded less and less like eco-terrorist hippies.

"They cleaned up after themselves," continued Fana. "Like pros. Real methodical. The place stunk of disinfectant and it didn't seem the kind of motel to care that much about cleanliness."

Hiran contemplated the burned wreck of a van. Could they be professionals? Unfortunately, at the moment it looked like the work of eco-terrorists with military training who didn't mind burning tires and using anti-bacterial wipes.

"What's next?" Fana asked again.

"Breakfast."

****

They found a greasy spoon around the corner called Mel's Diner and claimed a booth. Hiran ordered coffee and three sides of bacon while Fana devoured a mountain of syrup-drenched pancakes and a chocolate milkshake.

Where the hell does she put it all? He missed being able to eat like that. Between his slowing metabolism and the fact he no longer ran ten miles every day with full combat gear and some asshole drill sergeant shouting at him, he had to be careful what he ate. His wife, Joan, introduced him to the low-carb thing—she'd always eaten like that and always been thin—and after some adjustment, he decided it really did make controlling his weight a little easier. He figured he looked pretty good for a man on the wrong side of fifty and still snuck in weight workouts at least twice a week. But he felt his belt tighten just looking at that milkshake.

The diner, red pleather faded almost yellow with green Formica tables, smelled of decades of deep-frying and spilled coffee. The waitress, a big woman well into her fifties, feigned bored friendliness and didn't screw up their orders.

Half an hour after calling to find out where they were, Chuck arrived. He glanced at the small space on the bench beside Hiran and the much larger space beside Fana, muttered "Fuck" and sat beside her.

Drumming blunt fingers on the tabletop, Chuck ground his teeth and stared at the waitress until she came to the table.

"Striploin, medium rare. Four eggs over easy," he said the moment she arrived. "Coffee, black. No toast. No potatoes."

She nodded and left, not bothering with the feigned friendliness.

She knows it's wasted.

Chuck drummed on the table again, attention darting about the room like he was checking escape routes.

"Forgot to have a cigarette before coming in, didn't you," said Fana.

The drumming stopped. "I'm fine."

"Tick Tock is gonna blow," she said.

"Pancakes will make you fat," said Chuck.

She blinked. "Do I *look* fat to you?"

He eyed her as if measuring. "You carry some extra meat around your hips. It's fine now, but in a couple of years—"

"Chuck," said Hiran. "What did you find?"

"I got lost. Couldn't find the bus station."

"Told you," said Fana, pinching her hip and frowning,

"You guys have any luck?" asked Chuck.

Hiran filled him in on what little they'd found and shared his suspicions regarding the inconsistencies with the hippie eco-terrorist theory.

"So either they're smart hippies," said Chuck, "or the hippie thing is a cover."

"Or they're not hippies and not eco-terrorists and we've got it all wrong," added Fana.

When Chuck's food arrived, he ate with monomaniacal focus, barely pausing to breathe.

I wonder if he tasted any of that.

The Millennial Manifesto

No one bothered talking until he was done; they knew better. Chuck couldn't eat and communicate at the same time. Or think and chew. Fana, Hiran noticed, had slid the rest of her pancakes away untouched. *She never does that.* He'd never seen her not polish the plate. She stared longingly at the milkshake.

One point for Chuck. It was rare, but the big man did occasionally land a blow in this on-going and senseless war.

Chuck finished, belched loud and deep, and then wafted it toward Fana with a hand. She rolled her eyes. "What's next?" he asked.

I'm going to call home and talk to the girls and glory in something that is beautiful and pure and I'm going to tell them that I love them and I miss them.

"I think at this point we're waiting to see what these eco-terrorists do next," he said.

"Wave bye bye to that bonus," said Fana.

Chuck resumed fidgeting and eyeing the sidewalk beyond the grimy diner window.

"Go smoke," said Hiran.

Chuck nodded thanks like he needed permission—though maybe in some strange way he did—and left.

"How many people do you think Tick Tock has killed?" asked Fana, watching the man pace outside, drawing on the cigarette like he was mad at it.

They bicker, but on some level there's a fucked-up fascination there. And it went both ways.

Chuck had served under Hiran in the Middle East, so Hiran knew exactly how many confirmed kills the man had. What he didn't know was how many Chuck had killed or crippled in bar fights.

"Enough," he answered.

"What's enough? Six? Twelve?"

"We'll leave when he finishes his cigarette."

"He's gonna stink the car up."

Can't wait to call home. His wife would be pissed he wouldn't be back when he'd promised, but she knew the job. God, he missed her. Couldn't wait to hold her, to smell her hair.

"You're smiling," said Fana.

"Thinking of home."

She grunted. "Empty condo, Ikea furniture, a room full of old computer parts." She scratched at the table. Someone had carved MF+EC into the Formica. "I do miss my bed."

Chuck rapped on the window with a meaty knuckle. "Let's go!" he barked like he'd been waiting for them.

While Hiran paid, Fana wandered out the front door.

"Hey Chuck, guess what?" he heard her say.

"What?"

"Shotgun!" she crowed. "You ride bitch again."

"Fuck."

The three climbed into the Chrysler 300, Hiran driving as always, and went in search of the bus station. Fana only let them wander lost for half an hour before pulling out her phone and finding the station in ten seconds. She mocked them the rest of the drive.

CHAPTER – INANNA

At Inanna's suggestion, they used the bus trip to plan their next action. They claimed four seats, Chen and Julia sitting in the front two, and turning to speak through the gap between the chairs. The bus being mostly empty, they weren't worried about being overheard.

Inanna went over the details she'd already shared with Julia, bringing Chen and Aarush up to speed.

"Why this one?" asked Chen. "You said there were dozens of charities guilty of similar practices."

"They were recently in the news," she explained. "Their name will still be fresh in folks' memories. Everyone will understand why we did this. Also, not only do I know where they're doing business from, but it's only two hours from home."

Chen looked thoughtful. "I know where we can get a motorhome for a few thousand. It's old, but the engine is in good condition. It's got a chemical toilet—"

"Yay," deadpanned Inanna.

"—and two small beds with privacy curtains," finished Chen.

"We keep the wife on one of the beds so we can conceal her with the curtain if needed," said Julia. "We'll have to take turns sleeping. One pair on watch at all times. I'd suggest me and Aarush—"

"You just want to get me alone."

"—and Chen and Inanna."

As the only two with military experience, it made sense to divide Chen and Julia.

"How fast can you have it ready?" Inanna asked.

"How fast can we scrape together the cash to buy it?"

An uncomfortable silence.

Inanna knew they didn't have the luxury of her economic situation. "I'll buy it," she said. "Just need an hour to go to the bank and get the cash."

There was another uncomfortable moment as everyone wanted to demure but knew they had few other options.

"We can't let Inanna pay for everything," said Julia. She looked them over, gaze lingering on each of her friends. "How much would you spend to save the world? How deep in debt would you go to make the world a better place?" She held up a hand to forestall reactions. "I'm not judging. We all have different levels of risk we're comfortable with."

The corner of Chen's mouth twitched like it wanted to smile but wasn't allowed. "I was Marine sniper. I spent weeks behind enemy lines with only my spotter. Julia, here, is an adrenaline junkie. Who the hell else goes into Bomb Disposal? Who else becomes an MMA fighter on a whim?"

Julia sketched a mock bow. "I've also been dabbling in parkour." She poked Aarush. "How do you feel about risk?"

"Dudes," he said, adjusting his glasses, "I'm a film maker. I have one of two paths: Either I'll die broke and unknown, or I'll be stupidly rich and famous." He shrugged. "To be honest, I don't really have a preference. But at the end, when all this is done, I'm going to edit everything together—keeping our identities hidden, of course—and release it as a movie." He laughed. "Though since I can't claim responsibility for it I'm not sure how I'm going to make money off it."

When all this is done. When would that be? By some unspoken agreement, they never talked about it. *When we get caught?* Was making the world a better place something you could retire from? When were you finished? Would her friends at some point want to settle down, have normal lives? Would she?

I can't imagine it. How could she ever rest when the world was in such a shit state, when people like Chen and Julia lost children because of people like Gartner? The government whittled away at the freedoms of the American people and were cheered on by the very folk it stole the most from: the poor. *Somewhere, somehow, we started thinking actors, reality TV stars, wrestlers, and sociopathic failed business tycoons were good leaders.*

It was insane.

Then there were the corporations polluting the lakes and rivers and selling bottled tap water to those they poisoned. When had American cheese become an edible oil product? Everyone was so focused on themselves, so focused on making or saving a buck, they'd lost sight of the bigger picture. What was the point of any of this if they lost their humanity?

When the robots have taken every job, from flipping burgers to building cars, what do they think we'll do? How will they sell all this shit to people with no money?

Humanity was tragically short-sighted, a trait shown over and over through the centuries.

We talk about 'those who forget the past' while we ourselves make the same mistakes.

It was too much. There could be no end.

Inanna wanted to give up, to go home and live her life of quiet obscurity. But she had so much more than most, and she knew it. She had it easy. She could do nothing, and that was why she had to do something.

Work forty or more hours a week in a job you tolerate, at best. Eat. Sleep. Slave. Live for the weekend and your few hours of freedom.

Land of the brave. Home of the free.

We sold it. We bought lies and badly made Chinese junk. Our own government lied to us about terrorists and, in spite of overwhelming statistics to the contrary, we believed the world was out to get us.

The brave? People cowered in their homes, clutching their guns, living in fear of their neighbors and the very government they voted into power.

Land of the scared, home of the wage slaves.

It was too much, too big. What could four friends do against centuries of corruption?

Go home. Give up. You can't win.

But this wasn't about winning, it never had been. This was about trying, about showing people they didn't have to be victims, that the government served at the whim of the people, and that corporations could be brought low.

Inanna didn't have to win. If others saw her efforts and followed, that would be enough.

When people see the corporations bend before us, cave to our demands, they too will rise.

Governments might say lofty things like, 'we will never cave to the demands of terrorists,' but corporations were different. Profits margins were god. Move the money, and the corporations would follow.

Scare the people in charge, make it personal, go after their families, and they will do as we demand.

She wanted to believe that, on some level, these people, these CEOs and CFOs, these leaders of industry, were decent humans. She wanted to believe they'd see the benefits to everyone, make the right choices if pushed. She wanted to believe they secretly *wanted* to do the right thing, but couldn't due to pressure from investors.

But she couldn't take that chance. Years of watching corporations make choices that were clearly harmful to the American people left no doubt in her mind. The soulless drive for profit, making money, the bottom line in every decision, was anathema to humanity.

Others will follow.

Inanna reined in her thoughts and fears. Doubt was death. What was that line from *Dune*?

Fear is the mind-killer.

"I'll front the cash for the motorhome," she said.

Chen accepted this with a curt nod. "I'll pick the vehicle and make the purchase."

"We're really going to do this?" asked Aarush. "We're going to kidnap this woman and ransom her back to her husband, demand he gives everything to charity?"

Inanna nodded. "You okay with that?"

"Fuck yeah! Fuck those people who collect donations for dying children and then pocket it."

Everyone else grinned agreement and flashed a thumbs up.

The bus dropped them off a short walk from Inanna's house. Chen and Julia climbed into his pickup truck and disappeared into traffic. Aarush hung around talking about cameras and lenses and SpongeBob until he spotted his city bus approaching and jogged off to catch it. Inanna watched him go, waved at his boyish face as he grinned through the bus window, and walked home.

The house, six decades old, was located in a wealthy neighborhood of doctors and lawyers. Old growth trees lined the streets, oak and maple. Every lawn was lush and green, bordered by neatly trimmed hedges. Her parents left her this house when they died. Now, she lived alone. Five bedrooms, four bathrooms, two kitchens, and over six thousand square feet of comfort. With her monthly stipend she could cruise through life, never work a day. She could have been an eternal student, learning something new all the time, collecting degrees and knowledge like she did books. The idea appealed.

But such a life achieved nothing. Such a life took from the world and gave nothing back.

The Millennial Manifesto

Passing into the front hall, she wandered past the portraits of her parents. They were as she remembered from childhood, not the gaunt skeletons cancer would later turn them into. Her mom died first, her father less than a year later. They'd been doctors, saving lives every day of their adulthood. They'd made the world a better place. She couldn't live with herself if she did nothing to honor their memory.

What am I doing with my life? She remembered the first time she thought that, sitting alone in the palatial living room. She had everything and nothing. She'd been empty, gutted by loss. Now…

Now I have purpose. And purpose was worth more than anything. It was worth more than a comfortable life, more than a good job or collecting university degrees. *It's worth more than this huge house.*

The thought stopped her. How much *was* the house worth?

Putting on a pot of coffee, she paced the kitchen, walking circles around the massive granite breakfast bar. Last year, the Johnstons across the street sold their place for two and a half million dollars, and it was a third of the size with a much smaller lot.

I could sell the house and fund our efforts for years.

She'd still have to live somewhere, but Aarush had a second bedroom in the apartment he rented that was littered with old camera crap. Maybe he'd be willing to sublet.

Should I tell them?

Interesting question. They knew she came from money, but also knew she didn't actually have much herself. Or at least that the wealth she had was tied up in equity.

"Shit! The beach house!" She hadn't been there since her parents died. That had to be worth a couple million too. "Why the hell do I have a beach house?"

But suddenly having money, being able to fund their efforts, would that bother the others? She didn't want to change their relationship, didn't want to put unfair pressure on her friends.

They'll understand.

Their goals were her goals. They'd see this as proof of her commitment, that she wasn't just a spoiled rich girl.

This was my parents' home.

Pouring a mug of coffee, she meandered from room to room, touching each piece of tasteful furniture as she passed. So many memories here. Her whole life, really. She remembered balancing on the back of the sofa when she was six, the way her mom watched, worried she'd fall, while her dad urged her on. She remembered the meals they ate together in the kitchen, breakfasts of conversation and laughter. Those rare occasions when they had company and ate in the dining room at the colossal oak table.

The furniture and art alone must be worth a fortune.

Would she sell her life to fund a revolution?

Yes.

These things—these luxuries—meant nothing. She hadn't *earned* this. She would not live out her days in this cage of wealth. She would not take the easy path.

"I will change the world, or I will die trying."

Inanna returned to the kitchen and poured herself another coffee. She glanced at the huge espresso machine taking up most of one counter.

How much did Dad pay for that? Four thousand dollars?

Grabbing the iPad off the breakfast bar, she opened a browser window and set about researching real-estate agents and how to go about selling the entire estate. The house. Her parent's cars, both of which gathered dust in the driveway. The beach house and boats. All the furniture. The art. Everything.

Her stipend would still come in each month, and that was easily enough to live off.

Two hours later, research finished, she began making phone calls.

CHAPTER – HIRAN

Fana was right. The car stunk of Chuck's cigarettes.

Hiran spun the 300 into the bus station parking lot and stomped into the terminal, Fana and Tick Tock hot on his heels.

"Bus route 314 goes past the hotel where the four stayed who match Gartner's description," said Fana, catching up with Hiran.

He grunted his thanks.

When asked for the bus driver of route 314 the Dispatcher tossed a thumb over his shoulder without so much as glancing up from his phone. They found the man, tattooed from his hairline to his knees in an incomprehensible swirl of red, green, and blue art, smoking behind the station. No more than five and a half feet tall, he gave them the stink-eye from under twin rows of eyebrow rings as they approached. He also wore a large bull's ring in his nose and had over-sized plugs stretching his earlobes.

Chuck, immediately noting the hard and wiry physique of a fighter, made a show of sizing the man up with a dismissive grunt.

The driver inhaled smoke with casual insouciance, leaning against the wall, and blew it at them.

"You drive route 314?" asked Hiran.

The driver squinted at Chuck. "Cops?"

"No," said Hiran. "There were four—"

"You look like cops."

"Fuck you," said Fana.

The driver glanced at her, eyes lingering, raised an appreciative brow, and said, "Fine, not you." He jabbed his cigarette at Chuck. "But he screams pig."

"I'm not a fucking cop," said Chuck, moving closer, threatening with his bulk.

The driver looked unimpressed and certainly in no way intimidated. He sniffed at Chuck. "Cop."

"He's right," said Fana. "You guys really do look like cops. Maybe if Tick Tock kept a slightly smaller pickle up his ass he might be able to relax."

"Fana," said Hiran. "You're not helping."

"Sorry, Boss." She grinned in that way that said she wasn't at all sorry.

"Well," said the driver filling his lungs with smoke and blowing it at Chuck. "If you're not cops, I don't see as we have anything to discuss. So fuck off."

"Boss?" asked Chuck.

"Not yet."

"Uh oh," muttered Fana. "Here comes Tick Tock."

Hiran fished out his wallet and slowly counted out two hundred dollars in twenties. He wafted through them for the driver to appreciate. "How much do you make a day? Would you like to double it for answering a few simple questions?"

"Take your dirty money, you stinking fucking curry-eater, and jam it up your ass."

"I fucking hate white supremacists," said Chuck, which caused both Hiran and Fana to gape at him for a moment.

"What?" he demanded when he noticed them staring at him. "They're always the most embarrassing inbred shitheads. Can I hurt him now?"

Glancing around, Hiran noted there were no cameras mounted in the alley. No street cameras in sight. He didn't see anyone with a phone either. They were alone in the alley with the driver. With a sigh, he stepped back. "Don't kill him. He needs to be able to answer questions and that means he has to be conscious and have a working mouth."

"I know what it means, Boss."

The driver came off the wall as Chuck moved in. He had no fear in him. Flicking the cigarette at Chuck's eyes, he followed it in with a spinning head kick. Chuck batted the butt away and swayed out of range of the kick.

"You telegraphed that," he said.

Chuck rocked his head from side to side, loosening his neck and shoulders.

Hiran and Fana backed away to give the two men more space. Chuck had an easy thirty pounds of muscle and four inches of height on the driver, but the man moved well, perfect balance, light on his feet. Hiran gave him the edge in speed, whereas Tick Tock clearly had the strength advantage.

The Millennial Manifesto

The two men circled each other, jabbing and feinting, watching for reactions and tells, judging the other's skill. Both looked relaxed, unworried. In fact, both seemed quite happy.

I will never understand these asshole macho types.

While Hiran had done his time with the Special Forces, could hold his own against any of them—at least back in the day—he'd rather read a book or play with his daughters than fight. The contest might be fun, pitting one's skill and strength against another, but getting hurt wasn't. You only had to wake up from a knockout once, dazed and confused, and spend the next week wondering why you could no longer spell simple words, praying it was temporary, to know you didn't want to do it again. After that, all Hiran's fighting was either sparring, with rules and gear, or for life and death.

The driver pushed in, chin tucked, and unleashed a flurry of punches, most of which Chuck took on his arms. When they once again parted, they both wore huge smiles.

"Assholes," said Fana.

"How's your ground-game?" asked Chuck.

"Come find out."

Again, the smaller man bulled in, lashing out with hooks and jabs, ending the combination with a tight uppercut up the middle. Again, Chuck leaned back just enough for it to *whish* past him. This time, however, he followed with his own series of punches. The driver ducked and weaved, blocking many with his arms. Chuck fired a series of fast hook punches at the man's face and, when the driver's arms lifted to protect himself, went low with a crushing punch to the kidney.

They parted, breathing hard, but still grinning.

"If they quit smoking," said Fana, "they wouldn't be wheezing like old ladies."

The driver lifted a hand, wincing. "Fuck. I think you cracked one of my lower ribs. Next route is gonna hurt like a bitch. Okay." He turned to Hiran. "Who were you looking for?"

Chuck relaxed like nothing happened. Fishing a crumpled pack of filterless Lucky Strikes from his front pocket, he fished out two cigarettes, lit them both, and handed one to the driver. The shorter man accepted it with a nod.

"Four people," said Hiran, ignoring Fana's rolled eyes. "Two young women, one tall, thin, and white, the other shorter, curvy, and black. Two men, also in their early twenties, a brown kid, and a bigger Asian."

"The brown kid is just a little guy," said the driver. "The Asian a big, strong looking dude."

"They were all together?" asked Hiran.

"Yeah, I mostly remember the girls. They were both hot, though really different from each other. The black chick was a lot softer, great tits."

"Soft can be nice," said Chuck, darting a glance at Fana.

The driver nodded agreement. "They all got off at the same stop. I saw the big Asian dude head off with the blond, and the black chick went with the brown kid."

"Which stop did they get off at?" asked Hiran.

"Corner of Wabash and Lake. That's an expensive part of town. Lots of lawyers and doctors. The black chick seemed like a spoiled rich bitch."

"Meaning she ignored the tattooed douche-nozzle bus driver?" asked Fana.

The driver shot her a dark look, but Chuck said, "Don't," before he could think of anything mean to say.

Will wonders never cease? It felt oddly like Chuck had been dangerously close to being protective of Fana.

They left the driver smoking and favoring the ribs on his left side, with two hundred in cash jammed into a pocket. He seemed pleased with himself. Chuck had even taken a moment to shake the man's hand and suggest that when he lifted his arms to block punches, he not take his eyes off his opponent.

Back in the car, Fana once again riding in the passenger seat, Chuck sat in the back bouncing like a little boy as unspent adrenaline hummed through him.

"I always feel like fucking after a fight," said Chuck.

"Forget it," said Fana. "Hiran doesn't like white boys."

Chuck ignored her. "What's next, Boss?"

"We're going to find somewhere to stay close to where they disembarked. We still don't know what they look like, but we'll keep an eye out for anyone matching what we have."

"We could do a door-to-door search in the rich bitch's neighborhood," suggested Chuck. "How many hot young black chicks can there be?"

The Millennial Manifesto

"Not yet. Fana, find all the open Wi-Fi networks in the area. I want a list. If there are street cameras, get access. If there are any local stores with cameras, I want to know."

Fana grunted. "I love how he says this shit like it's all gonna be super easy and like he has any clue what's going to be involved."

"Focus on the bars and coffee shops frequented by students," said Hiran. "Maybe we'll get lucky."

Once they reached the neighborhood, Hiran wheeled the 300 into the first hotel he saw. It was a clean family-run place called The Henry VIII and had a small pub attached to it.

After renting three rooms, Hiran met with the other two in the pub for dinner. Chuck ordered a steak without so much as looking at the menu, while Fana hummed and hawed and kept changing her mind between the lamb curry and the deep-fried calamari. While she waffled, Hiran ordered a steak and salad and a double Jameson. Finally, Fana settled on ordering the calamari as an appetizer and the curry as her main.

Chuck narrowed his eyes at Hirans' whiskey when it arrived. "That shit'll kill you, Boss," he said, guzzling a pint of Coors.

After everyone ate and Chuck had stepped out for a smoke and returned reeking of cigarettes, he and Fana turned their attention on Hiran.

"What are we doing while Fana is doing her computer-nerd thing?" asked Chuck.

"We're going to take our crappy descriptions and hit all the local university and college bars."

"Pub crawl!"

Hiran ignored him.

"Any chance of you two *not* looking like cops?" asked Fana. She laughed, punching Hiran in the arm. "Never mind."

****

The next morning, Fana looking like she'd spent the night cage-fighting a rabid raccoon, they set about their assigned duties. After grabbing several energy drinks, she mumbled something about not sleeping well and fired up her laptop in preparation of searching out any open Wi-Fi networks in the neighborhood. She said there was a site that listed most, but that she'd also do a walk around just in case she found anything not listed.

"She looks like shit," said Hiran as he and Chuck entered the Chrysler 300. Truth be told, Chuck looked pretty rough too.

The big man grunted, gave a confused half smile, and glared out the passenger-side window. His fingers drummed and twitched and several times he caught himself reaching for his cigarettes before remembering he wasn't allowed to smoke in the car.

Hiran glanced at Chuck, examining him from the corner of his eye. If anything, the crumpled state of his suit made him look even more like a cop. "I'll do the talking," he said.

Chuck grunted.

"If anyone assumes we're police officers, we will do nothing to disabuse them of the notion."

"Abuse?"

"Disabuse. You won't tell them we aren't cops."

"I knew that."

Five years to retirement.

"And you will not get angry. You will not punch or shoot anyone."

"Boss?" Chuck looked lost, oddly vulnerable.

"Yeah?"

"Nothing."

Five years.

****

They'd seen six cafes and three bars, all favorite hangouts for local students, when the universe finally smiled upon them. At each of the previous stops they'd been met with polite curiosity shaded with a not-so-subtle distrust. No one had particularly made note of groups similar to the four they were looking for, though there were usually several fitting the description in plain sight at that very moment, and promised to call the number on the card Hiran left if they saw anything. None of them waited until he and Chuck were out of sight before deep-sixing the card in the garbage.

Hiran turned away from another polite barrista with an ironic Iron Maiden t-shirt and an equally ironic beard, and spotted a young blond woman entering the cafe.

Their eyes locked.

I know her.

She was tall and lean, quite attractive. Blue eyes narrowed, and he knew she was thinking the same thing.

A thin scar bisected her right eyebrow.

Like the ones fighters get.

The burning van.

Casual as anything, the woman glanced at her watch and turned to head back out the door.

"Her," said Hiran. "Blond at the door. She was at the burnt van."

"The one just leaving?" asked Chuck.

"Yes. Get her."

Chuck moved and anyone in his way either moved or got moved.

The second the girl was on the sidewalk, she bolted like a startled dear, long legs carrying her away.

Not a chance I can keep up with her.

But maybe, if he guessed right, he could cut her off.

Hiran stopped, partway out the door.

What if she's coming here to meet with the others?

CHAPTER – INANNA

Julia answered on the first ring. "S'up, Inanna?"

"Are you with Chen?"

"Nope. He's at the garage." Chen worked as a mechanic at a Goodyear Service Center. Between getting to work with his hands, and not having to interact with too many humans, he claimed it was the perfect job. "He finishes in half an hour," she added.

"Okay. I have crazy news. Amazing news. But I want to share it with everyone."

"Christ, you're such a tease."

"Can you call Chen and ask him to meet at the Accretion Disk Cafe? I'll call Aarush."

"Yeah. C'mon. Give me a hint."

"Nope."

"You're finally going to fuck Aarush?"

"What? No!" Inanna killed the call.

Next, she called Aarush.

"Hey, sexy," he answered.

"I've got huge news," she said. "We're all meeting at the Accretion Disk to discuss it."

"When?"

"Chen gets off work in half an hour."

"Hold on, let me check my schedule."

"You're unemployed."

"I guess I'm available then."

"Good. And Aarush?"

"Yeah?"

"I may need somewhere to live soon."

"You getting evicted?"

"Something like that. When it happens, could I stay with you?"

"I knew you wanted me."

"In that second bedroom you keep filled with old camera junk."

"Those are collectors' items. Or will be. And of course you can. But no sneaking into my room and taking advantage of me."

"Aarush—"

"Unless you really have to, in which case I understand. Chicks love me."

"Thanks."

"No prob, Bob."

She hung up.

Inanna spent the next few minutes wandering around her house, wondering if she should keep any of the seemingly infinite number of knickknacks and mementos crowding the place. Maybe she could rent a storage locker.

No. No clinging to the past.

None of this stuff mattered if she failed. What use was a locker full of memories if she didn't save the world?

It's just stuff.

Figuring she could walk to the cafe in five minutes, Inanna went upstairs for a quick shower. After, she stood staring at her twenty-foot-deep walk-in closet loaded full of clothes and shoes and boots.

They say you don't know what you have until it's gone.

Taking a few minutes to peruse her wardrobe, she realized how little of it she would miss.

"Am I crazy?" she asked the closet. "Am I really going to sell my parents' house, my home, everything in it, all to fund a terrorist cell?"

The more she thought about it, the less she wanted to.

And the more she knew she had to.

In the end—and someday it *would* end—the law would catch up with her. They'd take everything, strip her of everything she owned. All this stuff was gone the moment she set all this in motion.

After getting dressed in some sturdy clothes, faded jeans, and a comfortable t-shirt with a second soft button-down flannel shirt thrown over top and left open, she went to her parents' room. While not quite avoiding it, she'd had little reason to visit the room since their deaths. Venturing into her father's closet, a deep room smelling of shaving soap, a scent that would forever remind her of him and bring her to the edge of tears, she shoved his shirts aside, exposing the wall safe behind. Entering the code—her birthday—she opened it. There, trigger lock in place, lay dad's Glock G30S. Beside it sat a dozen boxes of .45 ammunition and six empty ten round magazines. The mag in the gun was, she knew, loaded.

Home defense, he said. Dad even made her take a week-long gun safety course and get both her firearm permit, and her concealed carry permit. Reaching into the safe, she touched the gun. The key to the trigger lock lay right there beside it which always pissed Mom off. Somewhere, back in Inanna's closet, was her holster, a small leather contraption that held the gun neatly against the small of her back leaving it easily accessible, and yet almost invisible.

Should she take it? *Dad would want me to be safe.*

He also wouldn't want her to form a terrorist cell and attack corporations in an attempt to change the world.

"You said I could be whatever I wanted to when I grew up," she told his memory. "You said I could do anything." She blinked and a tear rolled free. "Were you lying? Was that just talk?"

Should she take the gun? Dad said he bought it at an outdoor and semi-legal gun show in Texas. He claimed it was untraceable, though she didn't know nearly enough to even guess at that.

"Not today."

Inanna closed the safe and locked it.

Lacing up her hiking boots, she left the house. Someday soon she'd leave it for the last time. She'd cry—she knew she would—but she'd get over it.

The sun shone, dappling the sidewalk through the canopy of ancient trees lining the street. A cool breeze rustled leaves, dancing the shadows in waves. Hints of fresh cut grass, the neighbor's small vineyard, and the scent of rosebushes feathered the air.

I'm going to miss this place.

The short walk to the Accretion Disk Cafe passed in a haze of scents and sounds. Sometimes she closed her eyes for a few paces, basking in the beauty and the memories of a lifetime spent growing up here.

Everything changes.

To cling to the past was to die, was to fail at the only important decision she ever made.

Half a block from the cafe, her phone rang. Pulling it from her pocket, she saw it was Julia.

Probably running late as always.

The Millennial Manifesto

"Yeah?" she answered.

"Where are you?" Julia sounded out of breath, panting heavily. Unusual, as she ran the New York Marathon the year before.

"Almost there. Not late, am I? I—"

"Stop! Stop walking!"

Inanna stopped. Up ahead she saw Aarush wander into the cafe. Staring at his phone, he missed her frantic wave.

"Julia, what's going on? You're scaring—"

"Shut up. Turn around. Go home. I'll tell you later."

"Aarush just went inside."

"Oh, fucking hell I hate you punctual people."

"I don't—"

"Shit! I thought I lost him!"

Then she was gone.

CHAPTER – HIRAN

Turning back, Hiran re-entered the cafe and reclaimed the table he previously sat at. The waitress raised an eyebrow and he grinned sheepishly and shrugged. Ordering another coffee, he sat back to wait. Chances were, Chuck would catch the blond girl and then she'd tell them all about her friends if they promised not to press charges. Hiran would promise all that and more and all of it would be lies. You could do that when you weren't a cop. Actually, come to think of it, cops did that all the time too.

Either way, sitting here sipping coffee was infinitely preferable to chasing people on foot. His knees ached and he hadn't popped any ibuprofen that morning. And who knows, maybe he'd get lucky and the other three would wander in for a coffee. If the universe really took a shine to him, and if Karma saw fit to ignore all his many sins and transgressions, they'd all be together, making it nice and easy to identify the group.

Skinny brown kid. Curvy black girl. Tall Asian.

A skinny brown youth with thick-rimmed glasses wandered into the cafe, poking at his phone. He bee-lined for the counter where he joined the lineup. The kid looked so normal, barest hint of a scruff of facial hair, boyish good looks and a ready grin, that Hiran discounted him as a hippie eco-terrorist.

When the boy's phone rang and he answered, "Hey future roomie," Hiran was already tuning him out and wondering if the black girl entering the shop qualified as curvy.

When he said, "Where are you guys?" Hiran perked up. "I'm already—" and then he was talking too quiet to overhear.

Hiran watched out of the corner of his eye as the young man ordered a coffee, collected it, and retreated to one of the tables near the back.

Hiran contemplated his options, He could try and spook the boy, maybe scare him into a confession, but then he ran the risk of going after the wrong person and scaring the others away. He checked the black girl who'd entered a moment ago, but she'd joined a table of other students and was discussing some philosophy lecture like it was the most important thing in the world.

Not curvy enough, Hiran decided.

The brown kid was his best shot.

I'll nurse my coffee and wait him out. If he left before the others arrived, Hiran would try and tail him. If he could discover where even one of these eco-terrorists lived, the whole thing would be over. Maybe he could even go home tomorrow, see the girls.

Don't get ahead of yourself.

Lifting his own phone, using its reflective surface as a mirror, he checked the youth behind him. Sure enough, he was staring at Hiran's back while tapping at his own cell.

When did I start thinking of twenty-somethings as kids?

Hiran watched the young man close his eyes for a moment, nod to himself, and stand.

Going to casually saunter past me, are you?

If he did, Hiran would wait until he was outside, drop a twenty on the table, and follow at a good distance. There was enough pedestrian traffic out there it shouldn't be too hard. Hopefully the kid wouldn't be too paranoid. Paranoid people were a bitch to follow.

Where the hell is Chuck?

About to text the big man, he paused when the kid turned and sauntered casually toward the back where the restrooms no doubt must be located.

Was there another exit back there?

Hiran sighed. *Of course there is.*

CHAPTER – INANNA

Inanna stood frozen, staring at her phone.

Turn around, go home.

That's what Julia said. She clearly didn't want Inanna going into the cafe. The cafe Aarush just entered. Was he in danger? Should she go home and wait, or try and reach him somehow?

Standing here in the middle of the sidewalk is probably a bad idea, dumbass.

Glancing around, Inanna spotted a side-street. Ducking into the alley, she pressed her back against the wall and called Chen. There was no answer. Either he was stuck working late, which happened fairly often, or he was already on his way to the cafe.

"Fuck!"

What should I do?

Why didn't Julia want her to go into the cafe? Had they somehow been found out already?

Her gut soured, twisted with nauseous fear. Were the police even now heading to her home? She glanced around. No sign of police cars.

Inanna called Aarush.

"Hey future roomie," he answered.

"Can you act?"

"Of coursh, shweet heart," he said, doing an awful Sean Connery.

"Then pretend to be calm and bored."

"I don't even have to pretend. Where are you guys?"

"Shut up. Julia just called. Told me to stay away from the cafe."

"I'm already—"

"I know! Don't talk. There must be someone there. Are there cops."

"Nope."

"Good. Well… Maybe good." There was a moment of silence and she heard him talk to the cashier, ordering a large coffee. True to his word, he sounded wholly unconcerned.

"Look," he said. "I'll text you later." He hung up.

A second later her phone pinged with an incoming text.

/There's a brown dude here who looks like a cop. I've never seen someone sit so ramrod straight except maybe Chen. Wait. No. False alarm. He isn't eating donuts./

Even at a time like this he's joking. She wanted to smack him.

/Does anyone seem dangerous or particularly interested in you?/ she texted back.

/Nope. He did check me out when I first entered, but I figured it was 'cuz I'm so fucking cute./

She was trying to figure out how to reply when her phone pinged again.

/Fuck. He just turned around and looked straight at me/

/Stay calm,/ she sent back.

/I am fucking calm./

An idea. /I'm checking the back door./

/Mine? It's super cute./

Inanna ignored the text. Clutching the phone tight, she did her best to saunter around to the rear of the coffee shop. The eyes of unseen watchers shivered up her spine like a cold breath, teased the hair on the back of her neck. As expected, there it was, garbage bins lined neatly against the wall, the smell of rotting food souring the air. The door was propped open with a milk crate like the ones Dad used to hold his vinyl collection. Glancing around, she saw a pile of broken skids, not much more than wood slats, stacked against one wall. If she wedged one under the doorknob…

Inanna hurried to the piled wood. Grabbing one end of a board about the right length, she pulled. Rusted nail groaned and squeaked and finally gave. She stood, in a dirty alley, surrounded by trash and the stench of sun-warmed food, clutching her slab of wood. She felt like an idiot. What the hell was she doing?

Fuck it.

Approaching the door, wood in hand, she peered in. Beyond, she saw the kitchen. Two sweaty bearded men bustled about preparing food. Neither noticed her. There, off to the right, she saw the hall to the restrooms.

Backing out of sight of the kitchen, she typed one-handed. /Go to bathroom. Leave out back door. I'm there./

/What if he follows?/

/Going to block door./

/You sure I shouldn't just drink my coffee and then go home?/

/What if he follows, wants to know where you live?/

/He looks familiar. Can't place it./

/Get. Out. Now./

/Fine./

A moment later Aarush appeared in the hall. Looking back through the door he just exited, his eyes widened.

Seeing Inanna, he ran toward her. "He's coming!"

CHAPTER – HIRAN

Hiran fished out a twenty, tossed it on the table, and rose to follow, knees groaning.

Glancing over his shoulder, the kid saw him. Eyes widening, he suddenly darted right and disappeared. The sign said the toilets were to the left.

"Shit!"

Hiran chased after him, knees grumbling a complaint. He'd feel this later in the evening. Pushing through the same door, he turned to see the exit on the far side of the kitchen slam closed. Charging the door, Hiran threw his weight against it, twisting the knob as he hit. Crashing into the door, he bounced back and landed in a crumpled heap. He was *definitely* going to feel that later. Somehow the kid must have managed to wedge the door shut in the few seconds head-start he had. How was that even possible? Hiran's ribs ached, his shoulder sending waves of pain through his spine.

"Too old."

"What the fuck?" said one of the cooks.

Rising, Hiran went after the door again, this time braced and ready for resistance. Whatever was outside splintered apart and Hiran staggered into the sunlight. The alley left in two directions, each with its own secondary alleyways.

Which way?

He listened. The city was too damned loud. Cars and pedestrians out on the main street. The squeal of bus brakes. Picking a direction, he sprinted as fast as his knees allowed.

CHAPTER – INANNA

The instant Aarush was out, she kicked the milk carton away and slammed the door closed. Within, she heard one of the cooks utter a startled "Hey!" as she jammed the plank under the doorknob, wedging it firmly. Grabbing Aarush's hand, she dragged him into a sprint toward the nearest corner. Behind them the door shook with a dull thud as someone ran into it from within. Seeing another alley, she pulled Aarush into it, thinking as she ran.

Running is dumb. We'll stand out. People will notice us.

What if the man in the cafe had partners outside? She heard the slab of wood crack and splinter as the door banged open.

"We have to get off the street." Turning another corner, she slowed to a walk. "Act casual. That clothing store." She nodded to the building ahead. "It'll have change rooms."

Aarush wheezed like he'd just sprinted a thousand-yard dash. He said something she couldn't understand and coughed.

"What?"

"You look fantastic when you run in that t-shirt."

She squeezed his hand, hard.

"Ow!"

Inside the clothing store, a boutique specializing in retro clothing from the 70s and 80s refurbished and sold for outlandish prices, she flashed a grin at the clerk.

"Christ, my lungs," said Aarush.

"Do you have anything in tie-dye?" Inanna asked the girl behind the counter, a teenager in bellbottoms.

The girl blinked and pointed at row after row of spiraling color.

"Thanks."

Inanna grabbed a couple of shirts and turned on Aarush. "Try to find some corduroy pants."

"I hate you."

"Make sure they're tight."

Snatching a pair of pants off the rack, she threw them at him. He caught them, grinning, and she felt a blush of heat work its way up from her neck to her forehead.

"Fuck off," she said, before ducking into a change room.

They spent two hours there, trying on clothes, before she decided it was safe to leave. Neither Chen nor Julia responded to any of Inanna's increasingly panicked texts.

Feeling guilty for wasting the clerk's time, she bought several shirts and a pair of bell-bottoms that made Aarush say "Holy fuck" when she turned in a circle to display them.

"Where now?" he asked as they left.

"My place. We find out what happened to Julia."

Inanna led the way, Aarush hurrying to catch up.

"Do you think she's okay?" he asked.

Inanna shrugged, angry at her own ignorance and unsure what to do. How could things fall apart so fast?

"She's tough," she said. "I'm sure she's fine."

CHAPTER – HIRAN

The sprint didn't last more than thirty seconds before becoming a quick jog, and then a pathetically slow shuffle.

Who the hell am I kidding?

Hiran stopped. No way he was going to catch a skinny twenty-something. Fishing out his phone, he called Chuck. "Tell me you got her," he said, when the big man answered.

"Sorry, Boss." Chuck sounded like he was in some pain and breathing hard.

"You hurt? What happened?"

"She uh… She got me. Sprinted around the corner and stopped. When I followed she was waiting. Tripped me and kicked me in the junk when I went down. I still chased her, but she was fucking fast. And my balls…" He coughed and spat. "I gotta quit smoking."

"Nothing too serious?"

"Scraped my elbow when I fell."

Poor baby.

"But I got some good news and some bad news," continued Chuck.

"If the bad news is that there's no good news, you're fired."

"What?"

"Never mind. The news?"

"She dropped her phone and I got it."

"But?"

"It's smashed pretty bad."

"Of course."

"I kinda stepped on it while chasing her."

"Of course."

"Sorry, Boss."

"Yep, well, bring it back and we'll get Fana to take a look. Maybe she can recover the data."

"I didn't—"

"Meet me back at the hotel." The big thug could walk.

Hiran killed the call, not wanting to hear the excuse, whatever it was. For a moment he considered going back to the coffee shop in case one of the others arrived late, but decided against it. Word would be out by now. Damned kids and their phones. Instead, he wandered back to the 300, wincing at the pain in his knees and shoulder and promising his joints all the ibuprofen they wanted, to discover he'd received a parking ticket.

"Great." Of course, since the car was stolen, as were the plates, it's not like it would cost him anything. Still, it seemed like adding insult to injury.

Back at the hotel he found Fana sitting in his room drinking a diet cola with her feet up on the desk. Seven empty cans sat lined up in a neat row and she'd moved her laptop in here.

"What's wrong with your room?" Hiran asked.

"Lonely."

"But there was no one here either."

She shrugged.

"Find anything?" he asked.

"What? I was supposed to do something other than lounge around your hotel room watching porn on your dime?"

He gave her the 'I'm not in the mood' look.

"I got fuck-all," she admitted.

"Tell me you at least have eyes on the intersection of Prospect and Kinnlos. The Accretion Disk Cafe."

"Which part of fuck-all did you not understand? No street cameras. Nothing."

"Fuck."

Chuck knocked once politely and waited. The man was an uncultured boar in virtually every possible way, and yet unfailingly polite in others. Hiran, who'd had etiquette and manners grilled into him as a child, had noticed that Chuck somehow always managed to use the correct cutlery and yet always failed to thank the wait staff.

"Pretend we're not here," whispered Fana.

Hiran opened the door and stepped aside.

Shuffling into the room, looking sheepish and embarrassed, Chuck collapsed onto the nearest chair with a groan. His already wrinkled suit was a mess of stains and he stank like a trash bin.

"What happened to Tick Tock?" Fana asked, sitting up.

"Got his ass kicked by a girl."

She laughed, and when Chuck failed to offer denials, stopped. "Really? A girl beat up the big tough Special Forces gorilla?"

"She surprised me. Kicked me in the balls." He winced in memory of the pain.

"Ha!" crowed Fana. "I bet tonight—" She cut herself off, glanced at Hiran, and then glared at Chuck.

The hell is that about?

Chuck missed it as he was too busy fishing bits of shattered plastic from his jacket pocket.

"What's that?" demanded Fana.

"Chick's phone. She dropped it."

"And?"

"I kinda stood on it?"

"Kinda?" Taking her feet off the desk, Fana downed the last of her diet cola and went to collect the shards. Searching through them she said, "You're an idiot."

Chuck looked hurt. "Why?"

"This is the battery. I need the damned memory card."

"I didn't see anything else. Anyway, I thought that *was* the damned memory card."

Fana tossed the phone battery in the trash. "Useless."

"Chuck," said Hiran. "Back you go. Search that alley. Find the memory card. Don't come back until you have it."

"C'mon, Boss. Let me have a shower first. I'm filthy and my balls are killing me."

"Now."

With a sigh Chuck pushed himself from the chair.

"Maybe I should go with him," said Fana, rising. "I actually know what to look for."

Groaning, Hiran lowered himself into the chair Fana vacated.

"Knees, Boss?" asked Chuck.

"Get the fuck out of my room. Both of you."

They left in a hurry.

Once the door closed Hiran ordered a bottle of Jameson Caskmates from the bar to be delivered to his room and used it to wash down a fistful of ibuprofen.

He was sprawled on his bed like a brown Jesus, dreaming of Joan and the girls, when his cell rang. It was Fana.

He answered. "Good news or your both fired."

"Found the Sim card. It's cracked, but I might be able to rescue some of the data."

"Good."

"Tick Tock and I are going to grab dinner on the way back. Want anything?"

"No. Get back here and crack that phone."

"But he's hungry."

Hiran blinked at the phone. "He's *hungry*? Well then, by all means, stop for a meal. Take your time. There's a lovely steakhouse across the street."

"We'll be back in three minutes," said Fana.

Hiran heard Chuck mutter, "I told you he was grumpy," in the background.

They were seven minutes.

An hour after that, Fana had a name—Julia Iliadis—and not much else.

"Didn't Gartner say one of his kidnappers accidentally called the other Julia?" asked Chuck.

Hiran, who'd totally forgotten, wanted to hug the big racist bastard.

"What else can you get?" Hiran asked Fana.

"Sorry," she said. "The Sim card is pretty badly damaged. But we know the phone's owner and the carrier they're with. Shouldn't be too hard to track her down."

"How?" asked Hiran.

"I can lift the number and some personal data off the memory. Then I call her cell provider, say it's Julia Iliadis and I just smashed my phone and I need a new one. They'll confirm my mailing address and off we go."

"It can't be that easy," said Chuck.

"It is when you're as sweet as me." She grinned saccharine. "Anyway, I have a backup plan.'

"Yeah?" asked Hiran.

"Make Chuck go through the local phone book looking for Iliadis. Then we drive out to each one."

Hiran nodded. "You did good." He regretted his earlier temper. Pain never brought out the best in him, and his knees still ached through the haze of whiskey and pain killers.

"Can we go get dinner now?" asked Chuck.

"Yeah. Sorry I was bitchy."

The two muttered about it being nothing and left.

Are they hiding something?

It definitely felt that way.

Pouring another whiskey, he returned to the bed. Whatever it was, he didn't care. More than likely Fana had pushed Chuck too far and Tick Tock got angry. He'd never hurt her, never lay a finger on her, but he was definitely dumb enough to say something he'd later regret. Fana would have reacted to his anger with another jab, ever pushing him, and probably now felt guilty.

It was like looking after children!

Except his kids were better behaved.

God, he missed them.

CHAPTER – INANNA

Inanna and Aarush were sitting in her kitchen trying to figure out what to do when Julia let herself in the front door.

"Thank god!" Julia said upon seeing them.

"Where's your atheism?" joked Aarush with a wink an Inanna.

"Fuck off. Chen—"

"We called him," said Inanna. "He got stuck at work. He should be here soon."

Julia held out a hand. "Give me your phones."

"Why?"

"Gotta take the batteries out."

"They're iPhones," said Aarush.

"Then turn them off. All the way off."

They did as requested, laying their phones on the table.

"What's going on?" asked Inanna.

"Yeah," said Aarush. "Who the hell was the guy in the cafe?"

Julia sat with a grimace. She bit her lip, staring at the tabletop. "I fucked up. Big." She rubbed hard at her face, angry at herself. "I went back to the van. I wanted to make sure we didn't miss anything. I thought maybe I might overhear something useful from the police. Anyway, there were a pile of cops. They didn't even notice me. And then I saw him."

"Who?" Inanna and Aarush asked together.

"The guys from the TV. The Special Forces goons that were at Gartner's house after the kidnapping."

"Oh fuck," breathed Aarush, removing his glasses to polish the lenses with the hem of his shirt. Examining the over-thick arms and rims, testing the hinge screws, he replaced them.

Anyway," said Julia, "one noticed me and so I left. No big deal, I thought. No real damage done. Then today, when I went to meet you guys at the cafe, there he was. He was sitting there, drinking coffee in the cafe where we were supposed to meet."

"You were early?" demanded Aarush, pretending incredulity.

"Now is not the time," she said. "I panicked and ran. The younger one, the big mean looking white guy with the Special Forces tattoos, came after me. I ducked around a corner and stopped. He came charging around the corner and I did a Judo throw. Tossed him into a pile of garbage and kicked his balls in."

Aarush winced. "That ain't cricket."

"Then I ran. He got up faster than I expected, but after two blocks he was wheezing and coughing. Smoker. I left him behind."

"So it's all good?" asked Inanna.

"No. I dropped my phone somewhere in there. It must have fallen out of my pocket." She swore, thumping the table with a fist. "Probably during the scuffle. I don't know."

"Oh hell," said Aarush. "They might have your phone."

"And all our contact info," added Inanna.

Chen arrived, still dirty from the garage. After he kissed Julia, a quick peck on the cheek, they caught him up. He sat in silence, looking grim.

Finally, he said, "We have to go to ground. At least for a while. Until we know for sure."

"Seriously?" said Aarush. "Just when Inanna was finally going to move in with me?"

Chen and Julia blinked at him.

"He's only kind of joking," Inanna told them. "I have…had…big news."

All eyes turned on her and she drew a deep, calming breath.

"I'm selling all this." She waved a hand. "The house. The beach house. The cars and boats. Everything."

"Why?" asked Julia. "This is your home!"

"We need money. This will fund our efforts for years. And this—Gartner's Special Forces goons looking for us—we always knew this would happen at some point. We always knew eventually the police would figure out who we were."

Everyone watched her, waiting.

"Whenever that happens," she continued, "I'm going to lose everything anyway." She went into detail, explaining her earlier thoughts, and they understood, if not agreed.

"I always wondered if you were crazy," said Aarush. "Of all of us, you kind of have the most to lose."

"It's just stuff. I didn't *earn* it."

"Yeah, but you're set for life. You don't even have to work unless you want to." He grinned that boyish grin. "Now I *know* you're crazy! Welcome aboard!"

"Are you sure about this?" asked Julia.

No, I'm really not. "I've already got things moving," she admitted. "The properties are on the market, and I have an estate seller coming to look at all this stuff. Best guess, we're going to have near five million dollars to fund our efforts."

They stared at her, shock painting their faces.

"If they're onto us, you're going to have to quit your jobs. Like Chen said, we need to disappear. Now we can."

"Julia," said Chen. "Your phone was password protected, right?"

"Of course."

"That'll only slow them down," said Aarush.

Chen nodded agreement. "We'll have to pray you manage to sell some of this before they figure out our identities."

"I already told the estate agent I was looking for a quick sell. I won't get top dollar, but now is not the time to be greedy."

"We can't go home," said Chen. "They may already be watching our house. In fact…" He looked around the table. "We should probably all leave now."

"Really?" asked Inanna.

"Really. If they crack the phone fast, they'll already have our cell numbers and email addresses. From there, I'm pretty sure they'll have some means of finding our home addresses."

Everyone stood.

"We'll take my truck," said Chen. He swore. "I'm going to have to change the plates."

"Sell it," said Inanna. "Or give it away. I'll buy you a new one."

She looked around her house, the only home she'd ever known. Was this really goodbye? She couldn't believe it. Surely not. Surely they were panicking over nothing and she'd be back tomorrow. "I'll meet you guys outside. Going to grab some clothes."

As the others filed out the front door, Inanna dashed upstairs. Grabbing a few changes of clothes, she tossed them into dad's old backpack. Halfway down the stairs, she stopped.

The gun.

Turning, she dashed back up to her parent's room. Ducking into the closet, she opened the wall safe and removed the gun case. Stuffing it into her pack, she ran back downstairs.

They were waiting for her, Chen's gray Silverado already running.

"Sorry," she said as she slipped into the back of the extended cab to sit beside Aarush. "I know you love this truck."

Chen shrugged. "We're all going to make sacrifices."

Yes. Yes, we are.

Staring out the window she waved goodbye to her home and the ghosts of her parents.

"It'll be okay," said Aarush, concern writ across his features.

Is this the first time he's ever been serious about anything? Ever?

"Going to take care of me, are you?" she joked, leaning against him.

"What? No! I was going to distract you by keeping you busy taking care of me."

He smelled good, warm and real, with a hint of man. It felt good when he put an arm around her. Slightly built, and not much over five-eight, he wasn't big. But he was solid, with not a hint of fat.

After making a stop at a local electronics store to buy disposable phones to be used as burners, they found a motel where the woman at the desk was willing to accept cash and not look at their IDs. She eyed the four of them as she handed over the keys to the two rooms. They'd discussed sharing a single room, but decided they weren't quite that desperate yet.

Convening in the room Julia and Inanna were to share, they ordered Chinese food. Aarush insisted they get chicken balls and that gooey neon red sauce that always comes with them. Shoving furniture out of the way, they ate sitting on the floor. Everyone used the little wood chopsticks supplied except Chen who used the plastic cutlery.

"Okay," said Inanna between mouthfuls. "We may or may not have some serious trouble on our hands. If these ex-military goons work for Gartner, and are onto us, what will they do?"

"Call the cops?" suggested Aarush.

The Millennial Manifesto

Julia gave him a withering look of pity. "For whatever reason, Gartner wants us for himself. Maybe he took it personally that we fed him poisoned river water."

"Speaking of Gartner" said Inanna, "how is our video doing?"

Aarush bounced with barely contained energy. "Better than our wildest dreams. The more Tessier demands sites remove the video, the more people are sharing it. It's all over every social media outlet. There are new copies popping up on YouTube all the time. Someone even did a techno-remix of Gartner begging not to drink it, saying it was poisoned."

"Someone?" asked Inanna.

He grinned purest innocence. She didn't believe it for a second.

"Anyway," he continued, "it's everywhere."

"Gartner probably wants us to make public retractions, tell everyone we were lying," mused Julia.

"Or he wants to disappear us," said Chen, licking Szeschwan sauce off his fingers. "If he's really angry…"

"I know we've had a scare," said Inanna, "but we can't rest on our laurels. We can't stop now." Groaning and stretching, she pushed herself off the floor and claimed a spot on the empty bed. Julia and Chen had already risen and claimed the room's two chairs.

"This is a perfect time to be off wandering the country in a motorhome," said Julia. "It'll get us out of Dodge and give us something to do."

"Agreed. I propose we continue with our plans with the children's charity. With our last action still fresh in everyone's minds, still receiving media attention."

"How will we know when it's safe to go home?" asked Aarush. Rising from where he sat cross-legged on the floor, he sat beside Inanna, leaning back against the headboard.

"We're not going home…" Three sets of eyes locked on Inanna. "You guys all rented. No reason to go back. We're done with that life. I'll give my estate agent the burner phone number. As soon as my place sells, we'll have all the funds we need."

"I know somewhere cheap we can rent for cash," said Chen. "No questions."

"Good," said Inanna. "We'll need that."

Chen suddenly flashed a rare grin and fished a credit card from his wallet. "I'm going to run this to the limit buying supplies."

Suddenly everyone was digging out their wallets and tallying their credit.

"At the least," said Julia, "we might as well hit the cards for cash. It's not like we'll ever be paying it back."

"And frankly," said Aarush, "fuck the banks and credit card companies. The interest rates they charge are criminal."

"They'll get their turn," promised Julia.

They spent the rest of the evening discussing their plans for the folks running the false charity. They knew where the husband and wife team worked. In the morning they'd swing by to pick up the motorhome Chen had arranged, and grab whoever they found at the warehouse the charity ran out of. Husband or wife, they decided they didn't care. They'd stay on the move, posting videos as they went and updating the world on how the kidnapping was going and whether the spouse had agreed to their demands.

"I still think we should blow something up," said Julia. "So they know we're serious."

"No," said Inanna. "That sends the wrong message."

"We're terrorists. Let's terrorize." Glancing around and seeing no one was going to back her, Julia snorted in disappointment. "Fine."

Inanna turned to Chen. "You already have handcuffs and anything we'll need to restrain whoever we take?"

"Of course he does," said Aarush. "Julia's totally into bondage. I bet they're pink and fluffy."

"Zip ties," said Chen. "Cheap, and easy to get."

"Actually," said Julia, "I kind of wanted to bring that up. Chen and I haven't had any alone time in a while. Would you mind if we shared a room tonight?"

Inanna glanced at Aarush, caught his suggestive leer, and rolled her eyes.

"Fine with me," said Aarush. "Inanna can sleep on the couch."

"As if!"

"It is a Queen-size bed," he mused. "I suppose…"

Inanna swatted his shoulder. "You guys go ahead."

After Julia and Chen retired to their own room, claiming a bottle of wine on the way out, Inanna found herself sitting on the bed with Aarush, staring at the now vacated chairs, and not wanting to move.

"Um…" said Aarush, glancing around the room, avoiding eye-contact. "I… Umm…"

"You've been trying to get me alone in a bedroom since we first met, and now here we are. What are you gonna do?" she teased, poking him with a finger.

"You know, all the things I said, I didn't…"

"You didn't mean them?" she asked, unsure how she felt about that.

"No. I mean yes. I mean, I totally meant them. But we're friends."

"Yeah," she said. "It'd be terrible to be with someone you actually liked."

A bit of that ever-present boyish grim returned, teasing the corners of his lips. "Well, it's never happened before."

"What the hell is wrong with guys?"

"I wouldn't discount stupidity."

"Aarush?"

"Yeah?"

"When I was leaning against you in the car, that felt nice."

"It did. I was totally sporting a monster—"

"Don't ruin it."

"Right." Charcoal eyes examined her, bright and playful. "You're just messing with my head, aren't you. This is payback for all the times—"

Inanna leaned in and kissed him. For an instant he froze, but then moved closer, leaning into the kiss. Soft, tentative, but not shy. More like he was making sure she was okay with this.

They parted and he stared at her, mouth open with a puppy-dog grin, irises so huge his pupils were nothing but black.

"Notice how I totally resisted the urge to grab a boob?"

"Always classy."

Removing his glasses, he folded them and dropped them into the drawer alongside the ever-present hotel bible. It was an oddly self-conscious action.

Sliding the drawer closed, he turned to face her. "Could I… Would it be okay if… Can I kiss you again?"

"Can you resist going for the boob grab?"

"No promises."

She studied him, narrowing her eyes as if making a really difficult decision. "Yeah, I'll chance it."

"You know I'm totally going for the boob."

"I know."

CHAPTER – HIRAN

The next morning Hiran met Chuck and Fana in the Henry VIII pub for breakfast. They claimed a bench finished in worn red velour, complete with a thick oak table shellacked black in thick paint. The room smelled of the ghost of French fries past, and the stale tang of ancient beer. Pictures of WWI fighter planes, German and English, adorned the walls. A hipster millennial, all neatly trimmed beard, tattoos, and man-bun, worked the bar.

Fana was already hopped up on energy drinks and Chuck had the most confused look on his face.

He looks like he's had his first thought and isn't sure if it's good or bad. Either he loves it and wants another, or he's afraid it'll send him to hell.

"What's up, Chuck?" Hiran asked.

"Upchuck," grunted Fana with a smirk.

Chuck smiled at her, an oddly lopsided thing wholly out of place on his cinderblock face. "What?" he finally managed.

"You thought of something to do with the case?" Hiran asked. "You remembered something about the girl who kicked your balls in?"

"What?" He looked dazed.

"Have you not had your coffee yet?"

Chuck's fingers fidgeted on the tabletop.

"Ah, you haven't had a cigarette yet."

Chuck shook his head and glanced at Fana. "I… I, uh… I think I might quit. That girl, yesterday. I couldn't catch her. I thought I was gonna die. It took ten minutes before I could breathe without sounding like a chainsaw."

Hiran glanced at Fana, but she busied herself with her phone. Was this her doing somehow?

"Fana?"

She looked up, eyes wide like she'd been caught with her hand in the cookie jar. "Yeah?"

"Make any progress last night?"

She darted a look at Chuck and the big man grinned and went back to drumming on the table. She stuttered, flustered. "Got a number off the SIM. The rest was toast. Couldn't get the phone's own number, too much damage. I made some calls, and turned that number into a name: Chen McClure. I did some checking, and I'm pretty sure I have an address for him."

"Is that all you did last night?"

Eyes wide she stared at him, mouth open.

"Did you track the name?"

"Right! Yeah! Ex-military."

"Special forces?" asked Chuck, suddenly interested.

"Marine sniper. Did four years in Afghanistan. Pretty much straight out of high school."

"How many confirmed kills?" asked Chuck.

"How did I know you were going to ask that?" asked Fana. "Seventy-two."

"Damn." He nodded in appreciation. "Kid's got some skills."

You don't kill seventy-two and remain a kid. "Four years," mused Hiran. "PTSD?"

"No record of him seeing a shrink."

"He's stone-cold," said Chuck, appreciatively. "A killer."

Hiran preferred not to leap to conclusions. Half the time 'confirmed kills' was something of a misnomer. Still, seventy-two put Chen on a very short list. Things just got a lot more interesting.

I hate interesting.

The tattooed hipster arrived at the table and everyone placed their orders. Steak and eggs for Chuck. A salad and coffee for Fana. An English Breakfast of sausage, bacon, fried eggs, brown beans, fried tomato slices, and toast, for Hiran.

"Does this sound like Gartner's description of a big Asian guy?" Hiran asked after the bartender disappeared into the kitchen with their order.

Chuck and Fana nodded.

"I think," said Hiran, "we may have misjudged the situation. These folks aren't hippy Greenpeace wannabes. They're a lot more dangerous."

He'd seen the blond girl at the burned-out van. She recognized him somehow, and hadn't twitched or blinked. He remembered that fighter's scar.

When she ran from Chuck, she didn't run blind. She stopped and took him out, threw him into a pile of garbage.

"What if the whole team has military training?" asked Chuck, drumming even faster in his excitement.

Tick Tock is too dumb to be scared.

"That scrawny brown kid wasn't military," said Hiran.

"I bet they have corporate backing," said Chuck. "It wasn't a random strike, and it wasn't about some shitty town's water being poisoned." He nodded to himself, warming to his theory. "Corporate for sure."

"Tessier's stock did a dive into the shitter," said Fana. "They still haven't recovered."

Chuck rubbed at his chin. "I bet it's another toxic disposal company."

While not impossible, companies didn't act like this in spite of what card-carrying conspiracy theorists thought. Collusion was easier and more profitable than competition.

"You said you got an address," said Hiran. "After breakfast, we're going to pay Mister Chen McClure a visit." He nodded at Fana. "Bring whatever hacking gear you need—"

"It's called a laptop, grandpa."

"Whatever. I expect he's gone, but maybe we'll get lucky and they'll leave behind a computer or a tablet and we'll get a lead on the others."

"We going in hard?" asked Chuck, eyes bright with excitement. "Should I bust out the tactical gear?"

He clearly found the thought of a gunfight more appealing than Hiran, who would quite happily go the rest of his life without being shot at again.

"No. We're civvies here. If some neighbor calls the cops because she sees us running around with assault rifles, we'll be in a world of shit." Hiran thought it over. "That said, throw your assault rifle and three vests in a duffel bag. We'll leave it in the trunk. Just in case."

"Sweet. I got a new Beretta ARX100. Modular. Totally ambidextrous controls. You can field strip in seconds without tools."

Chuck loved his guns.

"That's great," said Hiran, not listening as the big man continued to list off features. "Just put it in the fucking duffel bag."

"Hey, Chuck," said Fana.

"Yeah?"

"Did you bring a…"

"A what?"

"Shotgun!"

For the first time Chuck didn't grumble about sitting in the back.

****

They found Chen McClure's house at the far end of town from the coffee shop where Hiran spotted Julia. If that cafe was a central meeting ground, the whole crew might be located within a few miles of where he now stood.

The home was a small bungalow built back in the fifties. Yellowed steel siding, brown shutters finished in thick paint, and a front garden of roses and daisies gave the place a quaint, old lady feel. Wheeling the 300 into the driveway, Hiran dropped it into park. No point in hiding. There were too many neighbors around, too many windows that might hide spying eyes.

The three exited the car.

"Chuck, you got the lock-punch?"

This handy little device neatly gutted most doorknob locks.

"Yep. We going in hard and fast?"

"No. If there's a deadbolt, try and lean into it. Pop it as smooth as possible. Call out greetings like we've been invited in."

"Yeah, Boss."

Chuck loved kicking in doors. He was an artist at anything involving destruction.

They approached the front door, Chuck taking the lead. He knocked twice, tilted his head as if listening to someone within, and used the bulk of his body to block the view from any nosy neighbors as he popped the lock with the punch. He opened the door with one smooth motion.

"Hey, Gladice," he bellowed, "how are you!"

"Her name is Julia, you tit," muttered Fana, following him in.

The moment Hiran swung the door closed behind him, Chuck drew his SIG-Sauer P226. Chuck being Chuck, had of course opted for the .357 SIG, chambering a high velocity, high penetration cartridge.

Catching Hiran's eye, he shrugged, hefting the pistol. "I haven't had a chance to take the Beretta to the range yet. Gotta go with old faithful."

Hiran and Fana waited at the door as Chuck did a fast room-to-room search of the house.

He returned, two minutes later, gun once again in its shoulder holster. "All clear, Boss."

"Shame." It would have been nice to find one or more of them here and put all this to rest so he could go home. "Keep an eye on the street," instructed Hiran, "in case someone returns while we're here. Make note of what they're driving. Get the license plate. Write it down this time. If you tell me you can't remember what color it is, you're fired."

"It only happened once," said Chuck, defensive.

"Fana, take a look around." He didn't need to say more. Unlike Chuck, she knew her job.

Hiran did his own search, careful not to touch anything. He had rubber gloves in his back pocket, should the need arise, but hated the way they made his hands sweat.

There were two bedrooms, one with a Queen-size bed, two mismatched dressers—one filled with a man's clothes, the other with a woman's. There were curtains on the bedroom windows, but they were lacy, did nothing to keep out the light. Noting they were east facing, Hiran decided whoever slept here didn't mind rising with the sun. Nudging open the closet door with a foot, he examined the clothes within. Packed tight with both men's and women's clothes, there was nothing fancy, nothing girly. Even the woman's attire was sturdy and plain. Several pairs of USMC combat boots, some smaller, some larger, sat neatly arranged on the floor. It reminded him of the shared quarters back in the Army before he went Special Forces.

A man and a woman shared this room and shared a Marine's need for orderly neatness. Poking deeper into the closet he found Marine dress uniforms. The man's bore a selection of Marksman badges including the Distinguished International Shooter Badge, as well as the Marine Special Operator Insignia. The woman's included the Explosive Ordnance Disposal (EOD) Breast Insignia of a Master ECO.

Both ex-military. Both Marines.

Hiran wandered into the second bedroom and discovered it had been converted into a gym. Weights, a chin-up station, and a heavy bag filled the space. On the wall he saw newspaper clippings and MMA cage-match photos. 'Julia Iliadis Wins Debut Bout,' read one headline. He recognized the blond girl, bloodied, but grinning.

An MMA fighter. Chuck will be in love.

Back in the living room, he saw a wall of shooting trophies awarded to Chen McClure. There were also a couple of pictures of a tall, broad-shouldered Asian American, and a lanky blond with blue eyes.

The Millennial Manifesto

Chen and Julia. Hiran snapped a picture with his phone.

There were also pictures of the two of them with a little girl with mixed Caucasian and Asian features. She had Chen's eyes, and Julia's nose. All three grinned into the camera.

They didn't look like terrorists.

Hiran paused. One shared bedroom. The second bedroom converted into a gym. No child's room.

They made Gartner drink the water.

"Shit."

If this was personal, if Gartner had pissed off a couple of Marines, a decorated sniper and an explosives expert, things were going to get a lot uglier.

Should I call Gartner and warn him?

Hiran stared at the picture, the smiling little girl with her parents. He thought of his own girls, what he'd do to anyone who hurt them.

Fuck him.

Leaving the living room, he found the kitchen at the back of the house. Looking out the kitchen window, he saw the backyard was much lower than he expected, dropping down into a ravine. Spotting a door, he opened it to discover steps down into a dark basement.

Did Chuck check down here?

It'd be typical for him to miss a door and never think that there must be a basement with the backyard being that much lower than the front.

Basement must open into the yard.

Spotting a light switch, Hiran snapped it on. Rough wood steps led down to a bare concrete floor. Drawing his Glock 34S, Hiran took the steps slowly, stopping to listen. At the bottom, he found an unfinished basement, an ancient oil-burning furnace and water heater against one wall. A workbench took most of another, tools lined up neatly or hanging from nails driven into a sheet of plywood mounted to the wall. Each tool had its outline drawn on the board.

Every tool has its place.

At the end of the table stood a tall gun safe, large enough for a dozen rifles. The door hung open.

That's not right.

The rear wall had a door opening out into the yard. Confirming the basement was empty, Hiran approached the door, checking the backyard through the window, pushing aside the thin curtain just enough to see. The ravine, thick with leaves and unkempt bush, lay beyond the yard. Probably one of the city's 'wild space' initiatives. Through a part in the greenery Hiran saw a stream trickling past on its way to Lake Michigan. Glancing left and right, he noted that all the yards this side of the street opened on to that ravine. In most cases only a six-foot-tall picket fence separated the yards. None of this would even slow a Marine. Seeing no threats, he returned to the gun safe. Not knowing what was supposed to be in there, he couldn't guess what might be missing. Still present was a Marlin Model 39A lever action, a twelve-gauge shotgun, and an antique M1 Garand from World War Two. On a shelf within the safe sat several boxes of ammunition sorted by caliber. One box caught his attention, the lid left open.

7.62mm x 51mm NATO.

None of the guns present used that particular round. Lots of other weapons, however, did. Including the M40 sniper rifle, standard issue to all Marine snipers.

Fuck.

Using his sleeve to avoid leaving prints, Hiran checked the back door and found it unlocked. None of this, not the open gun safe and box of ammo, not the unlocked door, fit the rest of the orderly Marine life Hiran saw upstairs.

Double fuck.

Hiran retreated back up the steps.

"Bingo!" he heard Fana say from somewhere in the house. "I found an iPad!"

Returning to the front hall, he found Chuck thumbing through a well-read paperback instead of watching the street.

"Chuck—"

Chuck lifted the book, turning it to display the cover. "*Guns Up!* by Johnnie Clark," he said. "*This* is a book, not that escapist shit Fana reads."

"Chuck, did you check the basement?"

"Yeah, of course."

"You saw the gun safe down there?"

"Yeah."

"You noticed it was open?"

"Uh huh. So?"

"Did you notice the box of 7.62mm x 51mm NATO that was also open?"

"Oh. No." Chuck looked at his feet. "Fuck."

"Why fuck?" asked Fana, joining them in the foyer.

"M40," said Chuck. "Marine sniper rifle. It fires 7.62. There wasn't one in the case."

"And there wasn't anything in the case that does fire 7.62," added Hiran.

"My bad," admitted Chuck.

"You don't think…" Fana left it hanging.

"I really do wish you'd been watching the street," said Hiran.

"Sorry, Boss."

Stuffing the book into his pocket, Chuck went to the front door and peered out though the window. "Shit. There are a million places he could hide. Lots of trees. Buildings."

"You saw those trophies," said Hiran. "He could be a kilometer away and put one between your eyes."

Chuck stepped away from the window. "He probably grabbed the gun and ran. That'd be the smart thing to do."

True. Blowing someone's brains out in the middle of suburbia would draw a lot of attention. Attention, Hiran prayed, Chen wouldn't want.

The picture. The family. The little girl.

What does *Chen want?*

Vengeance?

"We going out hard and fast?" asked Chuck.

"Christ," said Hiran, "is everything hard and fast with you?"

Fana sputtered a cough and turned away.

The thing was, Hiran would love to go out hard and fast. He wanted something—anything—between his head and a Marine sniper with seventy-two confirmed kills and a room full of shooting trophies. Not that there was a lot out there that would stop a 7.62. Movies were shit on that point. Hiding behind a car door was fucking useless.

"We're going to play it cool," he said. "Wander out like we've had a nice visit and are going home."

"Your call, Boss." Chuck darted a glance at Fana who'd finally stopped coughing. "Stay behind me."

"The sniper," said Hiran, "could be anywhere. If there is one."

"Whatever." Chuck's eyes never left Fana. "First sign of trouble, get down. Move for cover. Follow me." He swallowed and turned back to the door. "Casual. Right."

Is he scared? That was impossible. Chuck wasn't afraid of anything! And then Hiran understood. Just like his wife said, when it came to people, he never saw what was right in front of his face. Chuck wasn't afraid for himself. He worried about Fana's safety.

Wonders will never cease.

"I'm out first," said Hiran. "Chuck is second, Fana last." Two big men ought to provide her with some decent cover. "Chuck, be a gentleman, and open the car door for her. We want this casual and smooth, but fast."

Fana, eyes wide, amazingly said nothing. iPad in one hand, she nodded her readiness.

"Let's go."

Hiran swung the front door open and strode purposefully toward the car like a man with somewhere to be. Not rushed, but under some time constraints. He felt like a walking target dummy, his neck itching with unseen eyes. He imagined how big his head was in the sniper's sights.

Wife always said I had a huge melon.

Chuck followed, swinging wide and picking up the pace so he could open the rear door for Fana. "Shotgun," he said, just loud enough for everyone to hear.

Fana shook her head, grinning. "You ass—"

The unmistakable *crack!* of a rifle interrupted her.

Hiran dropped and rolled, putting the Chrysler 300 between himself and where he thought the sniper might be. Chuck slid up beside him, SIG already drawn. There might not be much in the car that would stop a sniper round, but suddenly anything was better than nothing.

Fana lay in the driveway, bleeding from her side, just below the ribs. A grimace of agony stretched her face.

"Fana's been shot," Hiran said, stupidly. The iPad lay beside her, shattered. Had it saved her, somehow deflected the bullet? That made no sense.

"Cover fire," said Chuck, and he was moving.

Hiran popped up and snapped off two pointless rounds before ducking. Chuck scrambled to Fana's side, hurling himself flat when another *crack!* shattered the already brutalized suburban peace. The damaged iPad exploded into fragments of gray plastic.

"He's shooting the iPad!" Hiran shouted. "Get her away from it!"

Grabbing Fana's collar, Chuck dragged her back to the car. Two more shots smashed what remained of the tablet.

That was too slow. A Marine sniper could work the bolt and hit something the size of that tablet in a fraction of the time this shooter managed. That said, whoever the shooter was, they were skilled. They'd managed to shoot the iPad out from Fana's grasp without killing her or blowing her hand off.

Cowering behind the car, Hiran studied the ruined tablet. *There was something on there they didn't want us to have.*

There, in the shattered bit of plastic, he saw the memory card. Should he hope the sniper didn't see it and retrieve it later, or make a dash for it now? *Cops will be here soon. No time.* Gathering his legs under him, he prepared for a leap and roll. Already his knees hurt and promised tomorrow would be a world of pain.

Sniper already thinks it's fucked. I'll be—

The memory card exploded as the shooter scored a direct hit.

Hiran blinked at the space he'd been about to put his body in, the space through which that round just passed.

"Fuck."

Thank Christ I'm slow and old.

Maybe not a Marine sniper, but whoever it was, was a damned good shot. *Good enough to have killed us if they wanted.*

Hiran's heart slammed in his chest.

"She's bleeding," said Chuck.

Hopefully the wound was caused by bits of plastic and not fragmented 7.62.

"He isn't trying to kill us," said Hiran. "I'm going to get in the front seat and start the car. If my head explodes, you're on your own."

Chuck nodded once.

"Get her in the back seat as soon as the car starts."

Fana coughed a pained laugh. "He's been trying to get in my back seat since we met."

Hiran stood, opened the car door, climbed in, and started the 300.

Nothing. No crack of rifle fire. No exploding head.

Behind him, Chuck pulled Fana into the car. She cursed his clumsiness. Hiran dropped the car in gear and eased out into the street.

Still nothing.

Accelerating away, he left the bungalow and the shattered tablet behind.

"How bad?" he asked over his shoulder.

"Hospital," said Fana.

Chuck, meeting his eyes in the rearview mirror, nodded.

"Shit." He focused on driving, teasing the edge of what a cop would bother pulling them over for. "Chuck, bullet wound?"

Checking the rear-view he saw Chuck lift Fana's shirt just enough to see the wound but still maintain decorum. It was the gentlest thing Hiran ever saw him do. Fana kept her eyes locked on Chuck like she was afraid to see the wound herself, but okay with reading it in his reactions.

"No bullet," said Chuck. "But lots of plastic. If it was me, I'd say let's go home, pick the bits out with tweezers and pour some of that awful whiskey you drink on it." He winked at Fana.

"Not too bad?" she asked, face desperate for good news.

Hiran scanned the road for cops, the trees for snipers, and the rear-view mirror to watch his friends.

"Not too bad," agreed Chuck. "Classic flesh wound."

"Maybe we don't need the hospital," she said. "Maybe we can—"

"No," said Chuck, voice gentle. "That was if it was me. We don't risk you on some stupid macho stunt."

She reached up and touched his cheek and then Hiran was too busy driving to watch.

The Millennial Manifesto

CHAPTER – INANNA

Chen and Julia were in mid-argument when they returned to the hotel. He'd gone out to pick up the motorhome, and she'd left to do some shopping for supplies.

"This is bad," said Chen, when Inanna let them into the hotel room.

Aarush, glasses in place, sat cross-legged on the bed, cleaning camera lenses and checking the charge on battery packs. Though they hadn't talked about last night, his eyes followed her everywhere. Whenever she looked at him he flashed that boyish grin, pure unadulterated happiness.

Julia followed Chen into the room, turning to slam the door closed behind her. "It's not my fault!"

"What isn't?" asked Inanna. "What happened?"

"She went back to our place."

"With good reason," snapped Julia.

"I told you I could get another rifle."

"It wasn't just the rifle. My iPad was there. It's got everyone's addresses. All our emails. Everything."

"They already have your phone," said Chen.

"We don't know that."

"Then how did they find our place?"

"I don't know!"

"What happened?" repeated Inanna. They were both here, both fine. How bad could it be?

"They showed up while I was in the house," Julia admitted. "It was those ex-military guys we saw on TV. I was downstairs getting Chen's M40 when they came busting in the front door. I snuck out the back and then remembered I'd left the tablet on the dining room table."

"You didn't go back," said Inanna.

"Worse," said Chen.

The Millennial Manifesto

Oh god, she killed them.

"I stayed in the bushes, worked my way to the front of the house so I could watch." Julia closed her eyes, drew a deep breath. "I took the M40 and a pocketful of rounds."

"You—" Inanna stopped herself. "The sniper rifle?"

"I mostly wanted it for the scope, so I could see. Anyway, they weren't in there long. And then they come trooping out all causal-like, and the woman has my iPad."

Inanna's chest tightened. Her heart felt like it dropped into her belly to be devoured by her stomach. "No. Julia. No, you didn't."

"No! I didn't shoot her!"

"Thank Christ."

"I shot the iPad."

"She shot the fucking iPad," said Chen. "The woman had it in her hand, and Julia shot it."

"I was careful."

"You could have killed her. You're not a sniper."

"But I'm pretty fucking good."

"You didn't kill her?" Inanna asked.

"No. She probably got some shards of plastic in her side, but nothing serious. I blew the iPad to dust. Totally destroyed it."

"Having ex-military goons sniffing around was bad enough," said Chen. "But a whole pile of neighbors basically heard or saw a gunfight. The cops will be all over our house. They're going to find all the unregistered guns."

"We knew this would happen," said Julia, placating. "We knew at some point the cops would find out who we are. This way they only know something is up with you and me. With the iPad toast, there's nothing linking us to Inanna and Aarush. This isn't as bad as you make it out to be."

Chen calmed, but still seemed unhappy. "You took a terrible risk. These guys are Special Forces."

"Yeah, well they all hid behind their car like little bitches."

Chen shook his head. "Sometimes you take the rivalry between military branches a little far." He turned to Inanna. "You haven't been home?"

"No."

"Good. How careful are you with your burner phone?"

"I have two, one for you guys, one for the agent selling the estate. That one I pull the battery from when not using. The agent has been instructed to leave messages."

After some discussion. Chen decided everyone was being as careful as possible. Inanna's problems, he pointed out, would arise when sales were made and she had to show up somewhere to sign documentation. If the law knew of her, they would likely be there waiting.

"We'll burn that bridge when we get to it," said Inanna.

With everything packed and ready to go, it only took half an hour to load the motorhome. When Chen and Julia were around, Aarush pretended nothing happened between he and Inanna, laughing and joking as always. But in those rare moments when he and Inanna were alone, he'd reach out to touch her shoulder or the curve of her hip as if to reassure himself she was real.

Is this a subconscious thing to see how I react? Was Aarush trying to figure out if last night was a one-time thing or something more? Was it something more? Did she want it to be?

Maybe for now, it can be what it is. We'll enjoy it while it lasts. If it grows into something else, then…

Then what?

This thing they were doing—the whole plan to change the world—was predicated on the knowledge that they had no future. There was no way this could end well. At best they were looking at jail time.

Julia shot at people.

Why had she done that? Her actions, as well-intentioned as they might have been, really didn't help any future legal case they might face.

"We ready?" asked Chen when the last of the gear was stowed away in the motorhome.

Everyone boarded the vehicle, which smelled like old socks, Chen claiming the driver's seat. He wouldn't even start the engine until he'd confirmed everyone was properly seat-belted. Finally, the motorhome roared to life and he pulled onto the street.

"You drive like my grandmother," joked Aarush.

"How many accidents has she had?"

"This week?"

Chen really did drive like a grandmother taking a carload of kids to church. He sat stubbornly in the slow lane, unwilling to pass the even slower grandmothers in front. After ribbing him for half an hour, everyone gave up and enjoyed the leisurely drive.

"I have a question," announced Aarush. "What is the real problem: drinking while driving, or driving while intoxicated?" He held up a hand to stall arguments. "I can legally drive with a couple of beers in me, right? So why can't I enjoy a beer *while* driving? So long as my blood alcohol is within legal limits —"

"No," said Chen. "I am not okay with you drinking beer back there. It's illegal, and we're on our way to kidnap someone."

Aarush winked at Inanna. "Aw, you're no fun anymore," he told Chen.

The suburbs became less urban and more farm. Long winding roads through fields of corn and clover replaced the maze of city streets.

Loading Google Maps, Inanna set her tablet on the kitchenette table. Zooming in, so the warehouse and gas station became visible, she showed them their target.

"This," she said, pointing, "is a gas station. It's a small privately-owned business with a truck-stop diner attached. There, behind it, this big gray rectangle, is the Children's Dream Foundation. It's a warehouse. They run the business out of an office located inside. I don't know why they rent an entire warehouse. Aside from taking money and advertising, they don't actually do anything. The owners of the business are Glenn and Janet Triantafylloy." She loaded the pictures she'd found online.

Julia took over. "The plan is simple. We're going to pull the motorhome up to the front door and use its bulk to block the view. We'll knock, and grab whoever answers. Everyone will be in masks. We'll blindfold them and drop this bag," she held up a black sack of thick material, "over their heads."

"What if no one answers the door?" asked Aarush.

"Chen kicks in the door," said Julia. "I'll take the driver's seat in case we need to leave at something faster than old-lady pace."

"We're all gonna die," said Chen. "She drives like a lunatic Tasmanian devil on meth."

"He's just angry 'cuz I always win at Gran Tourismo."

"No," he said. "It's because you always drive like you're playing Gran Tourismo."

Julia shrugged. "Then we go in and grab whoever is there. We toss them in the motorhome and fuck off."

"I want everyone wearing the wireless lavalier mics," said Aarush. "I'm going to film and record every aspect of this. The more material I have, the better."

No one complained as he fastened the tiny microphones to each of them and checked recording levels on every channel.

After another hour, Chen spotted the gas station and barked, "Masks on!"

Pulling the motorhome around the front, he passed a black BMW M760 in the warehouse parking lot and drove up to block the main entrance. As he slid from the driver's seat, Julia took his place.

Opening the side door, Chen, wearing the Captain America mask, exited first. Aarush and Inanna followed, Spiderman and Wonder Woman. Glancing about to make sure they weren't being watched, he knocked hard on the door.

Nothing.

He knocked again.

Nothing.

Swearing, he stepped back and booted the door with a practiced front-kick. The flimsy tin construction tore, and the door flew open with a metallic *bang!* Inside, a short woman with big hair and too much lipstick, had just entered the hall, on her way to answer the door. She retreated with a squeak, hand flying to her mouth in shock. When Chen stepped toward her she turned and bolted, screaming, back into the warehouse. All three gave chase, Chen in the lead. Aarush, filming with a handicam and a GoPro mounted on a helmet, came last.

"We're not here to hurt you," Chen shouted, but she didn't seem to believe him.

They caught up with her in an office at the rear. Two cheap collapsible steel tables faced each other, make-shift desks. Each had an old computer and an even older CRT monitor. Binders of accounting and spreadsheets littered both.

Snatching her purse from one of the tables, she fumbled inside, drawing a snub-nosed pistol as they entered.

We're too far away.

The woman turned, gun coming up in a classic gun-range stance. Inanna and Aarush both hurled themselves to the side, scrambling for cover. Chen, however, went straight at her.

She's on the far side of the table. He'll never reach her in time.

He didn't try. Instead, making use of the same kick that opened the door, he sent the table smashing into her hip. The force of the blow doubled her over and dropped her to the bare concrete floor. Sliding across the tabletop like the Dukes of Hazard across the hood of their Dodge Charger, he landed in front of her and took the gun.

Glancing at it, he shook his head. "Safety was still on." Then he popped the magazine and tossed it away. Racking the slide, he ejected the chambered round, catching it left handed.

The woman stared up at him, eyes wide in terror. "Who are you? There's no money here!"

Chen studied her as his hands dismantled the pistol, littering the floor around her with gun parts.

"Janet Triantafylloy," said Aarush, "we'll be playing the part of your kidnappers."

She stared at him for a moment, blinking, before barking a harsh laugh. "Kidnappers? My husband hates me. He won't give you a dime."

"I think he will," said Inanna.

Janet shrugged. "You'll see."

Inanna's prepared speech on the evils of stealing from sick children died on her lips. This woman seemed so normal, so sad. That, and the adrenaline still surging though her, made it difficult to remember.

There'll be time later, in the motorhome. What did Aarush always say? We'll fix it in editing.

Pulling the woman to her feet, Chen spun her around and zip-tied her wrists together. He glanced at Inanna through the Captain America mask and nodded. Stepping forward, Inanna dropped the bag over her head.

Janet Triantafylloy, she reminded herself. *For all her crimes, this is still a person.*

Together they hustled Janet back to the main entrance. Julia met them at the door.

"You're supposed to be in the driver's seat," said Chen. "What happened?"

"Nothing." She flashed a quick grin. "Just taking out a little insurance."

Chen looked ready to argue so Inanna gave him a gentle push from behind to get him once again moving into the motorhome. "Let's go!"

With everyone loaded aboard, Julia threw herself back into the driver's seat and sent the big vehicle screeching out into the street.

The Millennial Manifesto

"A little less noticeable!" shouted Chen as he struggled to maintain balance while zip-tying their captive's feet.

"You'll edit all this to make us look more professional, right?" Inanna asked Aarush.

"And lose the charm? Never!"

She swatted his shoulder.

Once they were on the highway, Julia's driving became less erratic, though she still liked to pass more cars than was strictly necessary. Chen kept darting annoyed glances at her, but was too busy tightening the bag over Janet's head so it couldn't easily be removed to say anything.

"Janet, I want you to listen to me," he said when finished, voice deep and calm.

She nodded.

"If you remove that bag and see our faces, I am going to kill you." He spoke with utter confidence, leaving no room for doubt. "I'll dump your corpse where no one will ever find it. We'll pick our next target and move on. But I will not risk my friends for you. Understood?"

She nodded again.

"The hood only comes off when we say it comes off. If I think you so much as peeked, I'll kill you. You do as we say, you cooperate, and I promise you will not be hurt. No one here has any interest in physically harming you. But if you struggle, if you call out for help at an awkward time, I will put a bullet in your brain." He looked to Inanna. "Ready?"

She glanced at Aarush, and he, camera in one hand, GoPro mounted on a helmet, gave her a thumbs up.

"Janet Triantafylloy," Inanna said.

"Yes?" she answered, voice small and slightly muffled.

"Your charity has pocketed millions of dollars collected for children. For *dying* children."

"That's it?" asked Janet. "You want the money? It'll never happen. Most of it is gone. My husband would rather you buried my corpse than give you a penny."

"We're not interested in your money," said Inanna. "You are, however, going to donate everything you have to charities that will actually help children."

"I told you, it's gone!"

"It's not so much gone," drawled Aarush, "as turned into equity. That expensive home. That BMW M760."

"Exactly," said Inanna. "Your husband is going to sell everything, every property you own, every vehicle, everything in the bank or tied up in investments, and donate all of it."

"He won't—"

"He will, because we aren't doing this secretly. Everything—this included—is being filmed. We will post the videos at regular intervals with our demands. The world will hear his every response. We will shame him into donating his ill-gotten gains."

Janet sat tense for a long while, head slowly shaking. "You don't get it. Glenn set this up, the charity scam. It was all him. He doesn't love me, never did! He married me for money, spent it, and then threatened to kill me if I didn't help him with his scams. *I'm* the fucking victim here!"

"For fuck's sake," muttered Aarush.

"This changes nothing," said Inanna. "We're still exposing him for the shit-stain of a human he is."

"The news articles already did that," said Janet. "There was a dip in income for two months, and then it was back to normal. He'll wait you out, call your bluff. He'll make speeches about not caving to the demands of terrorists like he's the hero." She barked a rueful laugh. "Somehow, he'll come out of this ahead."

"Bluff?" said Julia from the driver's seat. "We don't bluff."

"What will you do when he doesn't pay?" asked Janet.

They'd agreed in advance that they'd let the woman go, that the ignominy of being publicly embarrassed was punishment enough, but now Inanna wasn't so sure. She realized everyone was waiting for her.

When we post our demands, the police will get involved.

Could she use that? She wasn't sure. It would draw attention to Janet's husband, Glenn, he would no doubt prefer to avoid.

The man sounds like a sociopath.

"How do you force a sociopath to do the right thing?" she asked.

"You can't," said Janet.

"She's right," agreed Julia. "You just punish them."

Inanna shook off her doubts. "But he still wants to *appear* to be decent, right? At least in public."

They'd use that, somehow. At worst, everyone would know the truth about the company.

But all this was on national TV and Janet said it only caused a two-month dip in profits.

They had to try.

After making sure everyone's masks were in place, Chen removed the bag from Janet's head. He blindfolded her with a wide band of thick, black cloth, taping it into place, and then replaced the hood. Checking her wrists and ankles were still firmly bound, he carried her to one of the bunks.

"You ready?" Aarush asked Inanna, as she adjusted the mask so she could see more clearly.

"Yeah. I think so." She flashed him a smile. "As ready as I'll ever be."

After checking the lighting, he gave her the thumbs up. "Wonder Woman would be proud."

Would she? Inanna was less than sure. But as long as no one got hurt, and she and her friends effected some real change, she would take that as a victory.

We'll get better at this. Plan more. Hit bigger targets. Every movement had to start somewhere.

"Well, all right, all right, all right," said Aarush in his best Matthew McConaughey drawl, "we're rolling, sweetheart."

Inanna blinked at him. "Sweetheart?"

He stuttered. "I... uh... Action!"

Grinning, Inanna said, "We aren't the super heroes America deserves, but we're the ones she's got. We don't have a name. Who we are doesn't matter. We aren't doing this for fame or recognition. We are going to make the world a better place." She took a deep breath and realized she remembered none of her prepared speech. Should she ask Aarush to pause so she could fetch it?

If you don't know what this is about, if you can't explain to people what and why you're doing this, you shouldn't be here.

"Evil only triumphs," she said, "when good men and women sit idly by and do nothing. We are tired of doing nothing. We are tired of older generations pointing the finger, saying we're lazy, saying we don't work hard enough, saying we're responsible for the decline of America because we don't want to work minimum wage jobs. It has been impossible to support yourself—never mind a family—on minimum wage for decades. Your choices made the world we inherited. Your choices choke the ocean with micro-beads for your expensive body wash, plastic pods because you're too fucking lazy to make a pot of coffee, and grocery store bags because you're too ignorant to recycle or use bags made from reusable products. Michigan towns have gone years without fresh drinking water because you are doing nothing. Scum like Glenn Triantafylloy abuse people's trust and basic good nature and slip through loopholes in the law everyone knows about but no one will close because they're too profitable."

Inanna grinned behind the mask, showing teeth. "You're going to long for the days when Millennials did nothing. The truth is, you fear us. You fear that we're not like you. We don't share your values. We don't share your racism or the outdated class-structure you so desperately cling to. We aren't interested in living in your shadow. We're not going to serve you burgers for minimum wage. We're going to change the world, whether you like it or not. No one is safe. No corporation is too large to be brought low. Government serves at the whim of the people, a fact politicians seem to have forgotten. Yes, we are terrorists. But we are American terrorists. We will terrorize on behalf of the American people. We will use terror to make this world a better place."

Inanna drew a deep breath, let it out slow. "I know how that sounds. Terrorism. But I promise you we shall never hurt an innocent person. We strive for a better world. Our targets are those who believe themselves above the law. You, sitting in your huge office, making decisions that hurt hundreds, thousands, or even millions of people, all so you can meet investor expectations. I know you're laughing at us. I know you think we're a joke, just kids. And maybe you're right. For now. But know this, we aren't attacking your giant impersonal company. We aren't going to sabotage work-sites or equipment. That never works. We're coming for *you*. We'll drag you from behind your comfy desk, and we'll parade your crimes before the people you've hurt. And we shall punish you."

She went on to describe, in detail, the Triantafylloy's crime and berate the government and the law for doing nothing.

"We shall punish them where you could not. We will take not a penny for ourselves. Instead, Glenn will donate their ill-gotten gains to charities with a track record of actually helping people."

And now for the critical part of the plan. Inanna knew, from the moment she conceived the idea, that she could not do this alone. Even backed by her friends, she was not enough.

"I ask you, my fellow Millennials, to join us. Hunt those who would flaunt their power, those who exist beyond the reach of the law. Bring them down. Make it personal. Striking at faceless corporate entities will gain nothing. Attack the people making the decisions. It is the only way to enact change."

Swallowing a knot of emotion, she said, "If you're going to join us, if you're going to help us make the world a better place, there are a few rules: Always use your power for good. Never harm the innocent or profit from your actions; we aren't thieves. Be the hero you, yourself, need."

She stilled, waiting, until Aarush gave her a thumbs up.

"How was that?" she asked.

"A little long," he answered, "but everything you said needed to be said. I'll release a couple of versions. One with everything, and one where it's chopped to a thirty second sound bite."

****

Aarush got to work, editing what they had into a cohesive story. After hours of bolting down M&Ms and energy drinks, he posted the video and sent it to all the same news sources he sent the Gartner video to.

Within minutes, the hacker group, Anonymous, picked up the video, and threw their weight behind sharing it.

Once again, within an hour, they'd gone viral.

Turning on the motorhome's TV, the first station they tuned into was reporting on the gunfight at Chen and Julia's home. The two were reported as missing and wanted for questioning. No charges had yet been filed, and no arrests made. Nothing in the report linked it to the kidnapping of Janet Triantafylloy, though police were on the lookout for a black Chrysler 300.

Taking turns driving, they stayed on the move, stopping only for gas, and to upload new videos at whatever unprotected Wi-Fi hotspots they found.

CHAPTER - HIRAN

After three hours in the local ER, they returned to the Henry VIII hotel. Fana immediately claimed the only sofa in the room, wincing as she lowered herself down to lie prone, head propped up by a pile of pillows Chuck grabbed from the bed.

Why do they always end up in my room?

She watched Hiran and Chuck as she always did, but there was something different in her eyes now. An understanding. Being in her early twenties, and suffering the immortality delusion everyone that age seemed to have, she'd likely never before given death much thought.

God, she looks so young.

She was. Just a damned kid.

"You ever been shot?" she asked Hiran.

"Yeah. Twice. It sucks."

She looked to Chuck, eyes following him as he paced the room's confines. "Tick Tock?"

"Smart people don't get shot." No hint that he was joking. And no anger at being called Tick Tock.

Hiran coughed a laugh. "You haven't actually been shot, Fana. So you can't go around bragging about your war wounds."

"The hell I can't," she muttered.

Chuck continued pacing the hotel room. The big man's fists clenched and relaxed over and over, knuckles popping each time. "I'm going to fucking kill them."

"I'm fine," said Fana. "'Tis just a flesh wound," she added in a rather terrible attempt at an English accent.

"They tried to kill you!"

"Actually," said Hiran, "they were trying to kill the iPad."

The Millennial Manifesto

Fana stretched and groaned, rubbing her belly. It might have been a flesh wound, but the ER doctor still spent an hour digging bits of plastic out of her side. She'd made up some story about the battery exploding due to some crazy charging experiment she was working on. The doc, a middle-aged Ukrainian woman who asked Hiran out for coffee when she caught him alone in the hall, accepted this with a skeptical half shrug.

"Look," said Hiran, trying to calm Chuck. Tick Tock stopped being reasonable if he got excited or angry enough and he was never all that reasonable at the calmest of times. "Whoever shot at us was good enough to hit a damned iPad. If he wanted us dead, I'm pretty damned sure we'd be dead."

"Fucker was showing off," said Chuck. "Fucking snipers."

"Actually, I don't think it was the sniper." Hiran explained the low rate of fire. "Marine snipers are much faster."

Chuck wasn't buying it. "He shot my—He shot Fana. She's one of us, Boss. Part of the team. You don't let shit like that go unanswered."

"You're cute when you're protective," said Fana and Chuck flushed bright red and focused on his fists.

"We aren't in Afghanistan," said Hiran. "Different rules here."

"The rules are *exactly* the same." Chuck stopped, turned to face him, eyes hard, fists clenched. "Eye for an eye, Boss. Eye for a fucking eye."

"That's sweet," drawled Fana, "but calm your tits. I'm fine. It only hurts when I move. Or breathe."

Oddly, that seemed to relax him. For a moment it looked like he was going to sit by her on the sofa, maybe hold her hand. Then he glanced at Hiran and collapsed into a nearby chair.

Hiran's phone rang. It was Gartner.

"You useless clowns watching TV?"

"No, Boss," said Hiran, gritting his teeth. "We're after the folks who grabbed you. We were really close and they shot at us. Fana got hurt. She's okay—"

"Well you clearly aren't all that close. Turn on the fucking TV and then go get these assholes."

And Gartner was gone. Hiran hadn't even got the chance to report that they knew who two of his abductors were, that he had pictures of them.

And the girl. Were you going to tell him he might be responsible for their daughter's death?

Fuck no. It wasn't like Gartner would care anyway.

"Yeah," said Hiran to the dead phone, "she's fine. Thanks for asking. Chuck? Yeah, he's good too. Me? Oh, I miss my wife and daughters. Really just want to go home. Lovely chatting with you… Asshole."

"Did Gartner really ask after me?" asked Chuck.

Fana shook her head, rolling her eyes.

Grabbing the remote, Hiran told Fana to scootch and sat by her legs. The three watched the news. Their eco-terrorists were holding some woman for ransom. They demanded that her husband sell all his properties and valuables and donate all his money to charity.

They listened to Wonder Woman's insane speech.

"Holy shit," said Fana, "they went after those douche-nozzles who run that charity that pockets ninety-five percent of the donations meant for dying kids." She shook her head in awe. "If they hadn't shot at me, I'd wanna shake their hands."

"This doesn't make sense," said Chuck. "What's the angle? What does this have to do with Gartner and Tessier Waste Disposals? How is this helping the environment?"

"Nothing," answered Hiran. "It doesn't."

"The masks say it all," said Fana. "They're goddamned super heroes! I mean, don't get me wrong, they're still dicks for shooting me, but even then, they weren't trying to kill us. If I'd left the iPad inside—"

"They could have killed you," said Chuck. "They're social justice warriors. They're… They're hippies with guns!"

Fana's brow crinkled. "I think I saw that movie."

"Okay," said Hiran, trying to sort his thoughts. "They're on the road, in an RV or something."

Fana sat up, wincing at the sudden movement. "Whoa, whoa, whoa. We can't still go after them."

"Why?" asked Hiran. "What's changed?"

"Everything! Fuck Gartner, these people are heroes! You know what handing them over to him makes us?"

Hiran glared at her. "It makes us paid."

"It makes us the bad guys."

"Bad guys?" said Chuck, forehead wrinkled in confusion.

Oh jeez, he's thinking. That couldn't end well. "Chuck," said Hiran, "how much is Gartner paying us?"

"A lot."

Chuck and Fana made less than Hiran, but they didn't need to know that.

"He pays us a lot to do what?"

"Whatever he wants done and doesn't feel like doing himself."

"Right. There are no good guys or bad guys. There are people who get paid, and people who don't. Which do you want to be?"

Tick Tock hesitated, then said, "The paid kind."

"Right."

"But we do his dirty work," said Chuck, blinking. "Does that mean we're the bad guys?"

How many legs has this idiot broken for Gartner and only now he asks?

"It doesn't fucking matter," said Hiran.

Chuck looked unconvinced, like he'd never considered the moral implications of his actions, never thought of himself as anything less than the hero of his own fucked up story.

"Good guys," said Hiran. "Bad guys. Whatever. We're the paid guys. You know why you can afford all those stupid guns?"

"They aren't stupid."

"You know why you have that huge condo you never spend time in?"

"Too quiet. It's lonely in there."

"You know why you can afford all those expensive escorts and buy drinks for hookers?"

Chuck darted a guilty glance at Fana. "Lonely. Don't do that anymore."

"You can do all that stupid shit because we work for a sociopathic asshole who pays us to be bad guys."

And when the girls asked what daddy did at work? He told them whatever he needed to so they slept well at night and knew the world was a beautiful place. Then, at Christmas, he bought hugely extravagant gifts to assuage his guilt. Hell, maybe he'd take the whole family to Europe for a couple of weeks during the summer. Joan would love that. She'd been talking about touring wineries in Italy since before they were married.

So that's it? That's your price?

Yep. Yes, it fucking was. If these hippies with guns didn't want to end up dead in a ditch, they shouldn't have taken Gartner. This was all their own damned fault.

"Fana," said Hiran. "When you're done lounging about, there's work to do."

She looked ready to argue, but something in his expression stopped her. "I'm in IT," she said instead. "I can lounge *and* work."

"Good. Track the video uploads. I want locations. We're going to figure out where they're going next and be there waiting."

"On it, Boss." She pointed at her laptop on the far side of the room. "Get that for me would you please, Chuck?"

Hiran never saw the big guy move so fast.

The two are getting along, being polite to each other. Was he missing something? *These must be the end times.*

An hour later Fana looked up from her computer. "They posted the first video using the public Wi-Fi at a repair shop in Midland, twenty miles west of where they took Janet Triantafylloy. They aren't moving very fast."

"West? But that's on the far side. I would have thought they'd grab her and bring her back to familiar territory. They certainly didn't venture far to grab their first target."

"They posted another video while I was tracking the first," said Fana. "They were even farther west, not far from Mount Pleasant."

"They know we're on to them," said Chuck, "and they know the gunfight at their house brought in the law. They're running. I bet they aren't coming back."

Damn, he was right. So much for going home tomorrow.

"On the bright side," said Fana, "they do seem to be traveling in a fairly straight line. It looks like they're following the M20."

Hiran once again paced the room. "Okay. Let's think this through. They're on the road. There's the four superheroes and the kidnap victim. The video looked like it was shot inside a motorhome or Winnebago."

"They might have multiple vehicles," offered Chuck.

"No," said Fana. "They're going to want to stay together. If they're running, they want to take turns driving so they can keep moving."

"You're tracking credit cards for Chen McClure and Julia Iliadis?" Hiran asked.

"I do actually know my job," huffed Fana. "Neither has used their cards since Chen ran his to the limit at MEC."

"MEC?"

"Mountain Equipment Co-op. High-end camping gear. Everything from tents to clothes to kayaks and mountaineering equipment."

"They're going off the grid soon," mused Chuck.

Hiran thought it over. "Any big parks along their current route?"

Fana tapped at her keyboard, fingers a machinegun blur. "Several. The biggest, Newaygo, is about ninety miles west."

"Figure out which will give them the most privacy. Chuck, we're going on a road trip. We're going to need another car."

"On it."

"Don't steal another damned black 300."

"Gotcha, Boss."

"I want everything packed and ready to go in one hour. Can you do that?"

"Steal a car and get all of Fana's nerd shit packed in an hour?" Chuck rubbed his chin, head tilted. "Yeah."

"Good. We're going to move fast. We probably can't get ahead of them today, but I want to be waiting at their most likely stop tomorrow."

"They're in a motorhome," pointed out Fana. "They don't have to stop."

"There's chicks aboard," said Chuck. "They'll only tolerate a chemical toilet and no showers for so long. They're going to need to replenish water and eventually someone will want a hot shower with some elbow room."

"Sexist pig."

"Would you take a shit in a chemical toilet where everyone can hear you and smell the utter devastation you leave in your wake?"

"One point for Tick Tock," admitted Fana.

"We drive through the night," said Hiran. Turning to Fana, he added, "I want travel radiuses."

"Radii."

"Whatever. I want to know how far they can go each day assuming they travel at the speed limit and make minimal stops. Give me likely destinations if they do decide to pull off for a night, or even for a dump."

"And if they do drive straight through the night?" asked Chuck.

"Then this is going to be a lot harder. Fana, I want to know where they are the second they upload a new video. That's basically the only way we can track them unless they're dumb enough to use a credit card."

Chuck forgot himself, saluted, and left the room to go in search of a car to steal. Ten minutes later he was back, grinning.

"Whatcha get?" asked Fana.

"A Chrysler 300."

"For fuck's sake," growled Hiran.

"So why the grin?" she asked.

"I got the 363 horsepower five-point seven liter HEMI V8."

"I thought I told you not to steal a—"

"It's red!"

"Oh goody," said Fana. "Want to see the latest video, Boss?"

Hiran stared at Chuck, blinking, before surrendering. "Fine. Fuck it. Sure."

She turned her laptop so he could see the screen.

The video started with a still of Janet Triantafylloy, and a voice-over accompanied by scrolling text for those without sound. A detailed account of the Children's Dream Foundation charity, how much money the business had collected, and how much had actually found its way to dying children. Sources were sited, and exact dollar amounts listed.

"They did their research," Hiran noted.

"Or they tortured it out of the woman," offered Chuck.

Fana nodded agreement. "I checked some of their numbers, and all were accurate."

Why the hell did she do that? Their accuracy had nothing to do with the job.

Next, followed an interview segment where Wonder Woman asked Janet Triantafylloy about the business.

Based on the build, Gartner's description, and the fact she seemed to be in charge, Hiran guessed she was the black girl. Janet looked like an aging Florida trophy wife, still attractive, but showing her years. The interviewer's voice was somehow digitally disguised, while Janet's wasn't. They discussed Janet's husband, Glenn, who Janet claimed was a sociopath but high-functioning and extremely intelligent. She said she'd had no choice but to go along with his plans, and even showed faded bruises on her ribs and wrists. She spoke of multiple visits to the hospital, once with cracked ribs, twice with a broken nose, and all the times she'd hidden behind large sunglasses and a thick layer of makeup.

At the end, they discussed details of the business, which advertising agencies they hired, and how much each agency knew of the charity's practices. They spoke about local politicians who accepted bribes to ignore reports. They named names, flinched from nothing.

They don't care who they bring down.

"Of the over one hundred and ten million dollars we made in the last decade," said Janet, "we only pocketed about seven million." She stared into the camera. "The rest went to advertising, buying silence when people dug too deep, and bribes."

"She's on their side," said Fana, voice soft. "She hates her husband. She's spilling everything."

"Your husband was always able to buy people off?" asked the curvy woman in the Wonder Woman mask.

"No. There was the news special a few months back. But they listed a bunch of charities working the same scam. We mostly slipped under the radar. And then…" She swallowed. "Once, there was a reporter for 60 Minutes. He made a few calls trying to arrange interviews. Then he drowned in his swimming pool. That was six years ago. Glenn said—I don't know if it's true or if he was taking credit for an honest accident—but he said he 'took care of it.' He bragged about killing the man." Janet licked her lips, nervous. "He won't do it, you know. He will never surrender the money. He doesn't give a shit about me. He doesn't care what you do to me. He doesn't care about anyone at all."

"These hippies are idiots," said Chuck. "That Glenn guy will never pay. I'd say he's going to call their bluff, but they haven't actually threatened the wife."

Hiran glanced over his shoulder to find Chuck behind him, watching the video. Much as he hated to agree, Chuck had a point. They really weren't very good at this kidnapping thing.

"Anyone see anything useful?" Hiran asked.

"Not much," said Fana. "They're definitely in a motorhome and were driving while filming. The camera and people swayed a bit—probably when they changed lanes or accelerated—and a couple of times I heard large trucks in the background. They've got noise-gates on the microphones to cut down on background sound."

Hiran thought it over. "Fana, forget about campgrounds for now. Look for unsecured Wi-Fi hotspots. Particularly those at restaurants and diners, and especially those attached to gas stations. They'll stop to upload their next video, fill up the tank, and grab a meal all at the same time. Look for all that near shopping centers too. They'll need supplies at some point."

"And showers," said Fana. "With three women in there, they'll go through water fast."

"Who's the sexist pig now?" asked Chuck.

"Fuck off."

"And toilet paper," added the big man. "Chicks eat toilet paper." He stopped, noticing them staring at him. "What? It's the only way to explain how fast they go through TP!"

Hiran stood. "Chuck, go load the car. We leave now."

CHAPTER – INANNA

Selecting a bag of apples, Inanna tossed it in the cart.

She, Julia, and Chen wandered the aisles in Target, picking up supplies, food, and toilet paper. Aarush, wanting to play with his audio gear—he had some idea about wiring the entire motorhome for audio and video—had volunteered to stay with Janet. As she was handcuffed, hogtied, blindfolded, and gagged, no one argued.

"We've danced around this for too long," said Julia, catching up with Inanna, and tossing a large bag of bison jerky in the cart. "What are we going to do when Glenn ignores our demands?"

"I don't know," said Inanna. "I wasn't planning on dealing with a sociopath."

"Well what kind of asshole did you *think* would steal from children?"

"I don't know! I always imagined that with all the media attention he'd care. At the least I figured he loved his wife."

"We still haven't made any threats," said Julia. "We look weak, and he's totally safe. We need to catch his attention."

"Threats? Like what? We aren't going to hurt her, and we sure as hell aren't going to kill her. We lose the people if we do that. Public support is critical to our long-term plan."

Though she'd often mentioned the long-term plan, truth was it was pretty thin on details. But murder was definitely *not* part of it.

"I get that," said Julia. "We can't hurt her. The problem is that he knows that too. You literally spelled that out in your intro speech."

"So, do we just cut her loose?" asked Chen, adding several packages of bacon to the cart.

Inanna grabbed a huge bag of M&Ms for Aarush. "If we do that, no one will take us seriously."

"Exactly," said Julia. "Luckily, I have a plan. We're going to film a video of a conversation with Glenn. Aarush can set it up so we capture audio for both sides. We won't tell Glenn what we're doing. But…" She paused for dramatic effect. "This time *I* do the talking."

Inanna eyed Julia. *What is she up to?* The woman clearly had a plan, except planning wasn't really Julia's style.

You got a better plan? No. No, she didn't.

"Fine," said Inanna. "Once we're back in the motorhome, we'll give him a call." She peered into the shopping cart, trying to remember if they got everything. "Shit."

"What?" asked Chen.

"We forgot Aarush's energy drinks."

****

Back in the motorhome, Inanna found Aarush tightening the screws on the hinges of the overly thick arms on his glasses.

"You know you can get lighter glasses that don't need so much fussing and look like they were actually designed for this century," she said, tossing him the family-sized bag of M&Ms.

Catching the candy, he winked. "Nope. I like these." He ripped open the bag and tossed a handful of M&Ms into his mouth.

How the hell does he stay skinny?

With five people living in close proximity, the motorhome was beginning to smell a little ripe. To make matters worse, the on-board shower coughed rusty brown water and then refused to work. Chen had looked at it and said he couldn't fix it without a day or two in a full garage. No one had showered since they'd been on the road, and the environment wasn't going to get any better.

Janet seemed to have accepted that she wasn't in any real danger and made no attempts at escape. Not that she had any opportunities. Her wrists and ankles were zip-tied at all times and the mask only came off so she could eat.

Inanna explained to Aarush that Julia had a mysterious plan she wasn't willing to share, and that he needed to record a phone call.

"Easy," he said. "But won't the video be kinda boring?"

Julia smirked, promised it would not be boring. "It's gonna be the fourth of July exciting!"

With a shrug, Aarush had her burner phone wired in seconds.

The Millennial Manifesto

Putting Janet in one of the bed nooks and drawing the curtains, Julia took her place on the sofa. Chen drove, and Aarush joked about how steady the video was compared to when Julia was behind the wheel.

Green Lantern mask in place, Julia sat lady-like and proper, legs crossed and demure, completely out of character. When Inanna finished checking the room, making sure they hadn't missed anything that would give away their location, she gave the thumbs up to Aarush.

"Aaaaand...rolling!" he said.

Julia lifted her phone in a gloved hand. "Earlier today I asked Janet Triantafylloy for her husband's phone number." She winked behind the mask. Blue eyes bright with mischief, she dialed the number. While the phone connected and started ringing, she drew out a second phone, entered a number, but didn't hit send.

"I don't have audio for that phone," complained Aarush.

Julia ignored him, listening to the first phone.

"Hello?" answered a man with a deep smoker's voice.

"Glenn Triantafylloy?"

"Who is this?"

"Hi Glenn, I have your wife. I just wanted to talk to you before we post the next video."

"I already called the cops."

"No doubt. That's fine. We knew you would."

"You people are fucking cowards. I know you won't hurt her."

"Of course not. We're not barbarians."

"I have no reason to bow to your demands. You've got nothing."

"Actually," said Julia, "that's not quite true."

"I'm not donating a fucking penny. I *earned* this."

"I'd like to ask you—"

The harsh sound of a car horn over the phone interrupted Julia.

"Are you driving?" she asked.

"Yeah, why?"

She laughed. "Well, I was going to ask you if you were at the warehouse because there was something I wanted to show you."

"Well I'm not."

"No, no, this is better. I'm guessing the Black BMW M760 is yours?"

"Yeah."

"Nice car."

"Fuck off. You don't scare me."

"That's what you're driving now?"

He didn't answer.

Julia looked at Inanna, bit her bottom lip, and closed her eyes. "Last chance," she said. "Are you sure you won't change your mind? Do the right thing, *please*."

"I like that," Glenn said. "That desperation. Try begging, bitch."

"Please," she whispered.

"Go fuck yourself."

"Goodbye, Mister Triantafylloy." Opening her eyes, she stared straight into Aarush's camera and hit send on the second phone.

There was an instant of deafening noise causing Aarush to tear off his headphones with a curse. Then, silence.

Everyone stared at Julia.

"What did you just do?" asked Inanna, dread twisting her gut.

"I told you I took out some insurance. When you guys went in to grab Janet, I put a bomb in his car. I figured he'd be at home or at the warehouse. I was going to detonate it to scare him, so he'd take us seriously. But then… He was such an asshole. He'd never do it. We'd never win. We'd look weak and no one would take us seriously and all this would have been for nothing."

"You killed him."

"Oh yeah. He's definitely dead."

"You murdered him."

"Murdered?" Julia stood, radiating rage. "Now they will take us seriously."

Inanna opened her mouth to argue and Julia talked over her.

"When you kill during times of war, is it still murder? Are you saying Chen and I are murderers? Because we've both killed. Chen, he's killed a lot. Either we're at war, or we're not. How badly do you want to change the world? Enough to fight for it?"

Inanna glanced toward the front of the vehicle, caught Chen's eyes in the rear-view mirror. They were stone, empty, cold like death.

It's so easy to forget what he was.

And too easy to forget what they'd lost. Glenn stole money meant for sick children just like Jenny had been.

Chen never talked about it. But this was a man capable of taking lives. Julia, she hadn't known about, hadn't known her friend killed in service to her country. She always assumed Julia worked strictly in disposals.

Is it still murder, to kill during war?

It felt like it should be, but she wasn't sure. Soldiers were heroes. They fought and died to protect the American way of life, everything she held dear. They were the reason she was doing all this, fighting to make the country they fought for worth fighting for!

"No," said Inanna. She shook her head. "I don't know. We talked. We said no violence. We said no one would get hurt."

"*You* said no violence," said Julia. "Chen and I always knew this was a possibility. Hell, we knew it was a damned near inevitability."

Inanna looked to Chen in the front and he nodded once, not taking his eyes from the road.

"We're dealing with the worst humanity has to offer," said Julia. "If they were halfway decent people, they wouldn't do this shit. We're dealing with people who knowingly poison rivers and don't care. We're dealing with people who steal from dying children and say 'I *earned* it'! Did you really think they'd suddenly see the error of their ways and become decent humans?"

"No. Of course not. But you *killed* him."

"And when we make demands of our next target," said Julia, "they will remember this. They will know we are serious. They will know we are dangerous."

This was getting out of hand. No one was supposed to get hurt. Inanna felt control of the situation slipping away, like maybe she'd never really had it. Like control was an illusion.

From the very beginning, the intent had been to inspire others to take up their cause. If that happened, she would have no control over what others did.

Suddenly, that frightened her very much. What if she'd started something terrible?

She pushed the thought away. Doubt gained nothing.

What worried her most was that on some level she agreed with Julia. What was going too far when you fought to save the world, to make the country you loved a better place?

Or had she? Aarush was clearly surprised, though he showed none of the horror Inanna felt. Chen was impossible to read. Even if he'd been surprised—

and he really didn't look it—he clearly accepted this as a reasonable course of action.

What should I do?

Julia and Aarush waited, eyes on Inanna. Even Chen kept checking her in the rearview.

If I call this off, Julia will go to jail for sure. Chen would never let that happen. *All this will have been for nothing.* Leaving her life behind, sacrificing her future. It would all be wasted. They'd all go to jail and they'd have made no difference. Prison had always been a likely outcome; she was fine with that. But not like this. Not without changing the world first. Not without achieving *something*.

And that's what decided her.

"I'm sorry," said Inanna. "I wasn't ready. I was naive. We call ourselves terrorists, but I was crippling our effort by ignoring a terrorist's most critical tool: Violence." It hurt to say. She hated the truth of it.

Julia flashed a sad smile. "I'm sorry I did this to you. I wanted to tell you, but you'd never have agreed. You had to be shown."

Inanna breathed long and deep, searching for calm. "This isn't easy. We have to be very careful here. We tread a thin line. This may have cost us any chance at winning public support."

"Only one way to find out," said Aarush. When all eyes were on him, he continued. "We have to post the video now, before Glenn's death hits the news."

"And we have to show a united front," said Julia. "Folks have to see that we are together in this."

"Actually," said Aarush, "I filmed all of it. Even the conversation after."

Inanna saw the red light on the handycam. "You're still recording now."

He smirked. "I'm always recording. Everything. Always." He shrugged a apology. "It's an addiction."

Inanna thought it through, trying to weigh the already surging public outcry against Glenn Triantafylloy and the Children's Dream Foundation, against the fact they'd just blown him up.

"He was a shit-stain," said Julia.

"Now he's just a stain," joked Aarush.

How do they do this? How can they be so calm about killing?

Julia she could at least kind of understand. She'd been in the military, done a tour in Afghanistan, no doubt witnessed horrors. But Aarush? He always seemed so gentle.

The Millennial Manifesto

Maybe because it's distant, because he didn't actually see the man burned alive.

"Do it," said Inanna. "Post the video. Minimal editing. Let people see us discuss it after. Let's be honest, transparent."

With the video of Julia's phone call being so simple, all Aarush had to do was digitally disguise her voice, do a couple of quick edits for flow, and post it when they pulled into the next coffee shop with Wi-Fi.

Half an hour later the internet was in an uproar. YouTube crashed. They were the top trending hashtag, #americansuperheroes, on twitter and virtually every social media outlet. Radio hosts argued with callers about the morality of vigilante justice, even if the victims deserved what happened to them. Chiefs of police were interviewed and claimed they were following leads. Inanna and her friends *were* the news. If anything else was happening anywhere in the world, no one seemed to care. The president's latest insane barrage of self-centered tweets, both condemning and applauding their actions, were background noise, drowned out as people picked sides.

Cable news anchors interviewed terrorism experts who made all manner of inaccurate claims about how many there were in the group and their mental state. While repeating over and over how they didn't want to speculate, they speculated wildly about everything. Could this lead to copycats? Was this the millennial version of hippies and sit-ins? Students and recent graduates, hell, anyone born between 1980 and 2000 was asked how they felt about these young terrorists—and somehow everyone knew they were young. Their hopeless idealism was mocked repeatedly. They'd be caught soon. The police were even now pursuing leads that would end in their arrest. It went on and on, and the more Inanna watched, the more she realized that they knew nothing. The authorities had no idea who they were.

They were superheroes to one generation, criminals to another.

"Hey guys," said Aarush, looking at his phone. "There's a new hashtag trending: #nexttarget. Folks are suggesting who we should go after next. We have politicians from the President all the way down to local mayors. Sporting goods manufacturers using child labor in China. A collusion of oil companies killing solar power." He thumbed the screen, scrolling.

"I like the last one," said Julia. "Is it real?"

"It looks like it. I can trace it to one specific company. Texak Oil has been buying up solar companies and then putting them out of business. They also lobby heavily against solar power."

"Let's do that one."

The Millennial Manifesto

"There's so many suggestions. Priests diddling children. Companies firing staff a day before they retire. School bullies. Ha! Someone wants us to do a mass shooting at the NRA Headquarters in Fairfax, Virginia!"

"The oil companies can wait," said Julia. "I want to headhunt the NRA."

"But you love guns!" said Aarush.

"But I also think they should be controlled, licensed. Hell, we have to take a test and pay for a license to drive a car. Are guns any less dangerous?"

"First things first," said Inanna. "What are we going to do with Janet?"

Aarush flashed that grin. "I have an idea. It might not amount to anything, but the people will love it." He dropped his voice to a whisper so their prisoner couldn't hear. "We tell Janet we're letting her go, and we ask her, on camera, to sell her stuff and donate it to charity. We ask her to *prove* that her husband was the evil one."

Grins all around.

"I like it," said Inanna.

"And," said Julia, "if she agrees to do it and doesn't follow through, we kill her."

All eyes were again on Inanna. "How about we burn that bridge when we get to it," she said, remembering Julia saying something similar.

One of Inanna's burner phones rang. "Shit! I forgot to turn it off!" Pulling it from a pocket, she checked the screen. "It's the estate agent."

She answered, listening, nodding. "Fine. That's acceptable. Do it."

She hung up and grinned at her friends. "I just sold everything. There are offers on both the estate, and all properties. Our funding problems are over! I have to go meet my agent, to sign things."

"Too dangerous," said Chen from the front. "I have a better idea. This agent is making a commission, right?"

"He'll be well-paid," Inanna agreed.

"Then he'll be willing to make a little road trip. We tell him to meet us in Fremont. But we give ourselves time so we arrive first, to scout things, just in case. If the cops know who you are and it's a trap, we'll know."

"Good plan," agreed Inanna. "Okay. Julia, you explain things to Janet and then Aarush can film when you're ready. I'll call my agent and tell him he needs to come out and meet me."

Julia headed to the back to explain things to Janet, the death of her husband and their decision to let her go. She explained that they wanted her to donate everything, except one year's reasonable income—fifty thousand dollars

The Millennial Manifesto

—which she could use to get herself back on her feet. Aarush followed, filming everything.

Janet took it well, no tears, just a stunned disbelief.

Julia told the camera that Janet was under no duress, and that there would be no repercussions—at least not from them—if she lied. However, the video would go live shortly, and the world would know the truth. If, as she claimed, she was innocent, a victim, then she wouldn't have any qualms with selling the ill-gotten gains and donating the proceeds to charity.

The woman seemed to be in a state of shock, but she swore to sell everything and make sure the children got every penny.

When they pulled into an otherwise empty parking area at the side of the road, Chen, Captain America mask in place, sat with Janet. Once he was sure everyone had their masks on, he lifted the bag off Janet's head and removed the blindfold. She sat blinking at them, eyes squinting against the sudden light.

"Here's the deal," he said, unzipping a rifle case to expose the M40 sniper rifle within. "We're going to put the bag back on your head and let you out in a moment." He stared straight at her, hands going about their business opening the breach and slotting in a round as he talked. "You're not going to be handcuffed, or restrained in any way. We're also going to leave you enough cash to buy a meal and bus fare home."

Inanna noticed Aarush still filming but said nothing. Everyone had agreed right from the beginning that he'd capture everything. Noticing her attention, he winked.

"We're going to face you away from the highway," continued Chen. "so it isn't immediately obvious to motorists that you're blindfolded. You're going to count slowly to one thousand before removing the bag." He worked the bolt, pushing the round home. "I'll be watching out the rear window," said Chen, patting the rifle. "If you remove the bag early, I'll blow your brains all over the highway. In a moving vehicle, with this baby, I can kill you at half a kilometer. Maybe more if the road isn't too bumpy." He leaned forward, staring her in the eye. "Understood?"

Face pale, she said, "Understood."

Leaving the woman at the side of the highway, they headed for the motel where Inanna had arranged to meet the estate agent.

****

"Should we park in the mall lot?" asked Inanna. It was her turn to drive, but now all she could think of was how good a hot shower and clean sheets would feel. She'd already called dibs on the first shower and Chen promised to get a load of laundry started in the motel's coin-op laundromat.

Pulling the motorhome into the shade created by a couple of towering oak trees, she dropped it into park and shut it down. Chen rose from the passenger seat, stretching long muscular arms and rolling his shoulders.

"You go ahead, babe," said Julia from the back. "I want to get changed and then go for a run. If I have to sit around waiting for Inanna to finish showering, I'll kill her."

Scooping up their combined dirty laundry into a big green garbage bag, Chen bent to give Julia a quick kiss and exited the vehicle.

He stood, breathing the clean air with a big grin. "I never knew how bad four people living off McDonald's could smell."

"I farted this morning," said Aarush, following him out. "It smelled *exactly* like a Big Mac. Not even kidding."

"Yeah," said Inanna. "I caught that. I would have applauded, but I lost consciousness."

"You could try eating better," said Chen.

"Crazy talk," said Aarush. "And very un-American."

Chen spotted the laundromat and set off with his bag of laundry. "I'm going to hang out there until it's all done," he said to Inanna. "I'll be a while," he added, winking.

Ah. They do know.

She and Aarush hadn't exactly been secretive. They touched each other often, a small caress on the shoulder, a hand on the knee. She'd known they knew, but having them admit it felt different. Made it more real somehow.

Inanna and Aarush went into the motel office and booked a single room. The estate agent would be here in a couple of hours with the papers for her to sign. They'd move the motorhome out of sight before then, as everyone agreed the fewer people who knew about it, the better.

After paying cash for the room, they waved through the window of the laundromat to Chen, who gave them a straight-faced military salute, and went in search of their room. Aarush kissed her the second the door closed and they stood, groping and caressing, tongues dancing.

Aarush broke away first.

"You taste like a Big Mac," Inanna said

"And you taste like Chicken McNuggets."

"We gotta brush our teeth."

"Maybe," he said, leaning close to sniff her neck. "We should shower together to make more time for other stuff after."

"If we shower together, is there going to be other stuff after?"

"Do naps count?"

"Hardly."

"Insatiable wench. I'll get the shower started," he said, disappearing into the bathroom.

Sitting on the edge of the bed, Inanna kicked off her shoes and peeled off her socks.

"You should take your socks off," she called to Aarush. "It feels amazing!" She wriggled her toes.

"I was hoping you were going to 'rock my socks off," he hollered back. "And I guess that explains the sudden stench. I thought someone brought a wet dog into our room."

"You really know how to charm a girl."

"It's a gift." He exited the bathroom wearing only a pair of black boxers so threadbare she could see through them.

"How old are those?"

Glancing down he said, "I think my mom bought them before I left for college."

Outside, something went *bang!*, rattling the motel window.

"That was loud," said Aarush, "and close."

"Car backfire?" asked Inanna.

"I don't think so." Hurrying to the door, he opened it a crack and peered outside. "Oh fuck."

CHAPTER – HIRAN

Hiran drove west in the recently acquired red Chrysler 300, always staying within the speed limit, but never going slower. He felt most comfortable when behind the wheel. It was peaceful, calming. The roads were a mess, a non-stop *thump thump thump*, but even that was somehow hypnotizing.

Sitting in the back, Chuck snored, his smoker's lungs bubbling. It was peaceful when the big guy slept. Hiran didn't have to worry about him shooting at fellow motorists. Tick Tock hadn't had a cigarette in over twenty-four hours, and had been turning into even more of a ticking time-bomb before Fana told him to take a nap.

I'll give him one more day to shake the mood and then order him to smoke a few.

Chuck's longevity was not Hiran's concern. Anyway, if he had to listen to him shout racist epithets at everyone on the road, and the sincere apologies each time Fana berated the big thug, he'd kill him. Smoking would only extend Chuck's life. Fana, in the passenger seat, talked in her sleep. A steady mumble sometimes broken by an odd laugh. Thankfully, he couldn't understand what she said.

When awake, Fana tracked the video upload locations. After the most recent one, they sat watching, stunned, as the Green Lantern—who Hiran assumed was Julia Iliadis, due to the blue eyes—killed Glenn Triantafylloy. Sure enough, confirmation soon came that his car exploded on the freeway. There were a few other minor injuries to folks in nearby cars, but no other fatalities.

"That's it," said Chuck. "Now they're fucked. They're murderers."

That's rich coming from you.

But Tick Tock wasn't wrong either. This group of corporate terrorists—or eco-terrorists, or whatever they were—just put themselves at the top of the manhunt list for law-enforcement agencies across the country.

"Why is it called a manhunt?" demanded Fana. "Half of them are women."

The Millennial Manifesto

The publicity of their stunts guaranteed this would end in a spectacle of some kind. Would they go out in a blaze of glory, a classic gun battle against the forces of evil, only to be reborn as mythological martyrs to the American public? God, he could already see the Netflix mini-series.

Based on what Hiran heard on the radio, that certainly seemed to be what Joe America wanted.

Or, would they come peacefully, using the ensuing trials to preach whatever it was they thought they were doing?

Probably the latter. At least if Hiran didn't find them for Gartner first.

The curvy black chick—as Hiran had begun to think of her—liked to talk. Every video started with her spewing on about how they were going to make the world a better place and how evil only thrived where good people did nothing.

The car bomb, however, had been a surprise. One of the terrorists had shot a tablet out of Fana's hand, careful not to kill her. Whoever that shooter was, they'd chosen not to kill one or more of Hirans' team. and he had no doubt they were more than capable of it. Did that mean Hiran, Fana, and Chuck weren't considered evil enough to be worth the superheroes' justice?

If they had any idea of the shit we've done, we'd all be dead.

How many bones had he broken in service to Gartner's greed? How many basic rights and laws had he trampled for this man he loathed?

What did Fana call Glenn Triantafylloy? Oh yeah, a douche-nozzle.

And Chuck? Though he had no proof, Hiran was pretty damned sure the big guy moonlighted as a hit man. He wouldn't be at all surprised to learn Chuck helped Gartner bury a few bodies behind Hiran's back. He certainly had enough guns, and no compunction against using them. His so-called Travel Bag —which he joked was just for day-trips—included an assortment of automatic pistols, a Steyr Aug submachine-gun, and a heavily modded Armalite with a sniper scope.

It'll be over soon.

Either the cops would get these kids first, which he figured was pretty fucking unlikely as they seemed to have none of the information Hiran and his team possessed, or Hiran would deliver them to Gartner to be punished or humiliated, or whatever his twisted little perv mind dreamed up. Hiran prayed he could drop them off, bound and gagged, and be on his way home.

The Millennial Manifesto

I don't need to see that shit. Hopefully Gartner would be smart enough not to want witnesses. Or, if he was dumb enough to want an audience, hopefully he chose Chuck.

By Hiran's best guess, they were ahead of their target. According to Fana, they'd passed Wonder Woman and The League of Justice while the superheroes were parked outside a diner uploading the last video of Janet Triantafylloy promising to sell everything and donate it to charity. The video ended with a shot from the rear window as the woman stood, blindfolded, at the side of the freeway. They'd been careful, and shown nothing that might give away their location. Street signs were digitally blurred as were the license plates of every passing car.

They let her go unharmed.

It made them instant darlings, celebrities of the media world, who cursed them with one breath while lauding their goals, with the next. Everyone agreed someone had to do something about the state of the nation, but no one agreed what.

America, folksy rurals said, was going to hell, and the greedy corporations were leading the way. Even in the cities, almost everyone one agreed that rule by corporation had gone on long enough. Corporations had raped the planet and showed no signs of stopping, denying climate change and lobbying for a repeal in the Environmental Protection Act. Due to loopholes designed to benefit the wealthy, they'd paid almost no taxes for decades.

It was time to pay up.

"This is ridiculous," said Hiran. "There's too much media attention on these people. Gartner shouldn't want anything to do with this shit-show. The law is all over this and we're going to get stuck in the middle. They're going to get caught anyway. We should blow this Op and go home."

"Boss," said Chuck, shaking his head. "It ain't gonna happen. Have you ever seen Gartner back down from anything? Ever?"

This was bullshit. Doing this clown's dirty work because he turned bitch and embarrassed himself on camera was a crap job.

"What if we suggest Gartner as their next target," joked Fana. "There's a trending hashtag set up for that."

Damned kids and their Twitter. Hiran stared at her, mind churning. Of course the terrorists knew about the hashtag; they were all over this social media thing.

"Can we manipulate that?" he asked.

"Really? You want them to kill Gartner?"

"I do, but that's not what I meant. If we manipulated the hashtag, could we maybe define their next target? Pick someone close by so it's appealing to them and then be there waiting."

"Look who's using his prehistoric man-brain!" said Fana. "You are a sneaky motherfucker."

Chuck snorted laughter.

"I like it better when you two were bickering," said Hiran and Fana blinked at him, mouth working in silence as Chuck busied himself staring out the window.

"Anyway," she finally managed, "It is possible, maybe, given some time and enough computing power. I could set up a click-farm to storm the hashtag we wanted to the top. But that's probably the difficult way. It'd be easier to keep an eye on what makes it to the top naturally and then get the jump on them." Sitting in the passenger seat, she tapped at her laptop, fingers a blur. "Right now, the millennials are all up in arms about the fossil fuel industry killing solar power. Apparently, they got the laws changed so folks couldn't sell power back to the electric companies. They basically murdered a cheap and renewable energy source to protect their own profits."

"Can you pin this on one man?" asked Hiran.

"Hmm. Let me do some digging."

"Okay. We'll put that on the back burner for now, but keep it in our pocket. Tell me you know where they're going to stop next."

"I have it narrowed down to three possibilities, depending on what they need. I'm putting my money on the Target shopping center in Fremont. It's just off the freeway, and there's a cheap motel right across the street if they need showers. There's also an Irish pub near the motel if they're in the mood to celebrate."

"Good stuff."

Fana preened a little, reminding Hiran just how young she was. She made fun of millennials all the time, but she was one.

Christ, I have pants older than her.

"How fast can we get there, and how long a wait before they arrive?" he asked.

Glancing at the laptop, she said, "We'll be there in fifteen. By my best guess we have about an hour on them. Could be more or less depending on how fast they're driving."

"Fana, can you show me a satellite image of the area?"

"Of course."

After calling up Google Maps, she spun the laptop so he could glance at the screen while driving.

"Right." Hiran thought it through. No matter how he looked at it, there were too many angles to cover, too many possibilities. They knew Julia and Chen by sight, had memorized the picture of the two back at their house. Hiran had seen the skinny brown kid at the cafe, but the others hadn't. Gartner's description of 'curvy black chick' was not a lot to go on. If the terrorists split up, they'd be easy to miss. And what if they went to the hotel but didn't stop at Target, or went to one of the bars for a beer but didn't stop to shop or shower?

"We're going to have to split up," he said, not liking it. "We'll stay in constant contact. Regular check-ins. Chuck, if you forgot to charge your phone again, it's gonna be used as a suppository."

"Isn't that where they keep books?"

Fana muttered something under her breath and shook her head in disgust. "Not unless you have a library up your ass."

Chuck shot her a confused, hurt look.

The Target seemed like their most likely stop, so Hiran decided that would be Chuck's watch. The pub seemed like a stretch, but from the parking lot one could see both the bar and the entrance to the motel. Fana would take that position. Unlike Chuck, she could be counted on to watch two things at the same time and not wander into the pub for a quick beer. Hiran would stay on the move, wander the Target parking lot, particularly the far end where the motorhomes and RVs usually parked. After two days in the car, he needed to move, even if it meant popping a fistful of ibuprofen for his knees.

First, they swung by the Irish pub, dropping Fana off. She blew them kisses and said that if anyone needed her she'd be in the pub getting shit-faced. Next, Hiran parked the 300 and pointed out where he wanted Chuck.

"Keep an eye out for them both together and individually. You've got the picture of Julia and Chen?"

Chuck nodded, holding up his phone.

"Call if you see anything, even if you're not sure. They may have changed their hair or appearance."

"Yeah, Boss. I know the drill."

"Good. Stay sharp."

"Frosty as fuck."

Finally, Hiran took the 300 out to the far end of the lot. All the Recreational Vehicles too large to fit into regular spots were out here. Families gathered around, hosting impromptu barbecues, sharing a beer with a new neighbor, or comparing notes on the makes and models of their vehicles. Hiran watched as a motorhome slowed near the entrance to the parking lot and then pulled past to park in the much smaller lot in front of the pub where Fana stood, pretending to play with her phone. At least he hoped she was pretending.

He called, and she answered instantly with, "Yes, I see the motorhome that just cruised past the big spacious parking lot to park near the pub. Maybe they're just fat lazy Americans who want a beer and don't feel like walking a few hundred yards."

"Maybe."

He killed the call.

Climbing from the 300, groaning from the grinding noises his knees made, Hiran straightened, rubbing his lower back.

God, I miss being young and immortal.

When had he lost it? Was it the first time he watched a friend die, blood leaking from a bullet wound as Hiran fought to stanch the flow? Was it that time his squad got jumped by insurgents and it degenerated into a mad brawl in the street and one of them pinned him, face down in a two-inch puddle of murky piss water, drowning him? He remembered barely hearing the pistol shot that blew the insurgent's brains all over Hiran's back even though it had been fired from maybe three strides away. He recalled sitting up, soaking wet and confused, stinking of gas and urine, the damp feel of bone and brain sliding down the collar of his shirt. Or was it the first time he got shot? He spent two weeks in the hospital as doctors removed fragments of steel from his perforated gut.

When that sniper round snapped past at Chen McClure's house, he thought for sure he was dead. He remembered scrambling to get behind the car, not even sure where the shot came from. He hadn't given a thought to the others until he saw Fana sprawled, bleeding, in the dirt. For an instant he'd just been happy it wasn't him. All that mattered was that he might still get to go home and see the girls.

You work for a dangerous asshole. What do you expect?

Later, at the hospital, he'd suggested to Fana that she take a week or two off. She wouldn't listen. Where all he wanted to do was go home, that was the *last* thing she wanted. 'Hell begins at home,' she told him once. He never asked what she meant by that.

Hiran's phone rang, startling him. *Slipping old man, you haven't been paying attention.*

He answered. "Yeah?"

"Three people just left the motorhome," said Fana. "They rented a room in the motel. Care to guess?"

"No."

"Big Asian dude. Skinny brown kid. Curvy black chick."

"Was it Chen?"

"Can't be certain. Wasn't at a good angle to see his face."

"We're on our way. Stay on the line. Going to add Chuck in for a conference call."

"I'm amazed and impressed you know how to do that."

He hung up on her twice before getting it right.

"Boss?" Chuck finally answered.

"Fana may have found them."

"There's someone still in the motorhome," said Fana. "I just saw the curtain move a bit."

"They see you?" Hiran asked.

"Dunno. Don't think so."

"On my way," said Chuck, hanging up.

"Fucking idiot," Hiran swore.

"Someone doing something inside," said Fana. "Window just slid open a crack. Maybe getting some air."

Window. Hiran remembered the *crack!* of the sniper rifle. "Fana, get—"

A rifle shot echoed off the concrete parking lot and cinderblock stores. Years in the military. Years of shooting and being shot at. There was no mistaking that sound. Too loud to be a pistol, but without the weight of a fifty-cal.

Across the parking lot he saw Chuck suddenly burst into a sprint, SIG-Sauer P226, coming from its shoulder holster as he ran. People screamed, scattering from Tick Tock's path. He ignored them. Hiran prayed some underpaid mall-cop didn't see Chuck and decide to be a hero. Then he realized he too had drawn his firearm. People fled before him, ducking behind vehicles.

Great. Brown guy with a gun in a parking lot full of white people.

Fucking serve him right if someone shot him.

The Millennial Manifesto

A car window blew apart as Hiran passed it, showering him with beads of safety glass. The bullet traveling faster than the speed of sound, an instant later he heard the shot split the air, echoes slamming around like a drunk in a mosh pit. Throwing himself down, he rolled into the nearest car. At least this time he knew which direction the shots were coming from. Several people stood around blinking stupidly at the broken glass, frowning in dumb monkey confusion.

"Get the fuck down!" Hiran screamed at them. "There's a sniper!"

Seeing him cowering behind a car, gun in hand, convinced them that at least someone, somewhere was dangerous.

Across the parking lot, Chuck's SIG barked like an angry dog. After the rifle, the sound was small and flat.

Oh fuck. They pissed off Tick Tock.

Another shooter, probably in the hotel, returned fire with what sounded like a nine.

CHAPTER – INANNA

Inanna followed Aarush to the door, looking over his shoulder. "I don't —"

Another shot shattered the air, louder now that the door was open, and a puff of smoke wafted from the rear window of the motorhome.

"The hell is she shooting at?" said Aarush.

Inanna, needing to see, pushed the door wider. There, sprawled on the sidewalk behind the motorhome, lay a young black woman. Blood pooled around her. Inanna stared as the woman fumbled at the light jacket she wore.

Julia shot her. She'd stayed in the vehicle. It was the only thing that made sense. But why?

"It's the girl from TV," said Aarush. "The one with Gartner's goons."

She heard more gunshots from farther away, somewhere in the parking lot of the Target shopping center across the street. One of the motorhome windows blew apart and something smacked into the motel wall less than two feet from Inanna.

Julia shot back.

More bullets punched holes in the motorhome. It was too fast. She didn't know what to do. Run? Where?

As Chen exited the laundromat, gun in fist, the woman on the sidewalk rolled over and drew a pistol from her jacket. Inanna watched in horror as she fired, over and over, into the back of the motorhome.

Chen screamed something incomprehensible, raw anguish, and the girl turned, lifting the gun to aim at him.

He shot her dead.

Two in the chest, and then one in the skull, blowing her head back and spraying the sidewalk behind her with brain, bone, and blood. Without hesitating, with no pause for thought or doubt, Chen raised the gun and shot at someone in the parking lot. He moved sideways, gun up, firing each time his hands reset to the ready position.

"Get in the camper!" he shouted without looking. "Get in the fucking camper!"

Inanna, wearing no socks or shoes, and Aarush in his aging boxers, dashed for the motorhome. Aarush dove for the driver's seat only to discover the keys missing.

Crack!

Crack!

Two new holes appeared in the tin wall.

He turned to stare at Inanna, eyes wide.

Julia! Julia had the keys.

Inanna turned and dashed for the rear of the vehicle. Bullets had smashed through the cupboards, shattering plates and mugs and glasses. Her last two steps left bloody footprints on the faded linoleum floor.

She found Julia in the back. The sniper rifle still sat propped against the window frame, just the tip of the muzzle poking out. Her friend sat on the floor, face fixed with a perplexed grimace. Blood stained her chest.

"Julia."

She didn't move, didn't blink.

"Julia?"

Bloody feet forgotten, Inanna moved closer. Leaning down, she touched her friend's hair.

"Julia?"

This couldn't be happening. This couldn't be real. Outside, beyond the tin walls, a cacophony of gun-play.

Aarush yelled something from the front and more plates exploded into sharp little fragments and Inanna blinked tears.

"No. No."

Chen screamed out his rage and loss.

Grinding her teeth, Inanna forced herself to search through her friend's pockets until she found the keys.

Numb, barely aware of the glass in her feet, or the snap-hiss of bullets passing through the home, she returned to the front. Aarush, seeing her face, nodded and said nothing as she handed him the keys.

The moment the engine roared to life Chen burst through the door screaming "Go! Go! Go!"

Aarush stomped the gas pedal, and the vehicle lurched clumsily into motion.

Bracing himself against the small table in the kitchenette area, Chen fired shots out the side window as they pulled away. Someone returned fire, bullets punching holes in the walls, and sometimes *spanging* off something solid.

Then, they were away.

Inanna's ears rang in the silence. She stood, swaying with the movement of the RV, tears falling.

Chen moved to stand beside Aarush, placed a hand on his shoulder. "Slow down." He spoke in a soft and calming voice. "Drive like nothing happened." Glancing over his shoulder he said to Inanna, "We have to ditch this vehicle."

"Chen," said Inanna.

"I know," he said, looking away.

"Julia…"

"I know." He breathed deep, jaw set. "Right now, we have to focus." He pointed to a side street, and Aarush made the turn. "We have to get off the main streets. We have to find somewhere without street cameras."

"Were those cops?" asked Inanna. "Did we just flee a gun battle with the law? Did you kill—" She couldn't say it.

"I don't think so. I think Julia—" His voice cracked. Closing his eyes, he brought his emotions under control.

He's locked down tight. She imagined him bursting from the pressure, exploding into violence.

"Julia must have recognized them. She shot the woman on the sidewalk, but didn't kill her. She knew what she was doing. She could have killed her if she wanted." His jaw muscles clenched and relaxed, his eyes unfocused as he replayed the gun battle. "She should have killed her. Julia was distracted shooting at the others—and she was only shooting to keep them running for cover, not to kill—the woman shot her. I knew…" He swallowed. "I knew when Julia didn't shoot any more. I knew." He pointed to a narrow alley. "There."

Aarush turned into the alley.

"Here," said Chen, pointing into a narrow lane between rows of aging townhomes.

Aarush stopped the RV, turned the engine off.

"Chen," said Inanna. "I'm sorry. I…" She what? She'd been helpless. She'd left her father's Glock in its case because she didn't think they were in danger. Even when the bullets started flying, not once had she thought to get it. Maybe if she'd kept it on her, taken this more seriously, she could have saved Julia. The memory of the woman on the sidewalk firing into the RV while Inanna stood watching, helpless, frozen in fear, played over and over in her mind.

I could have saved her.

"You're bleeding," said Chen.

"I am?" She looked at her feet, blood pooling on the floor around her. A shard of glass jutted from the heel of her right foot.

"I'll clean the wound," said Chen. "Then we'll go."

He disappeared into the back, returning a moment later with a first aid kit she hadn't known they possessed, and a bottle of vodka they kept in the freezer.

"This will hurt," he said.

Without waiting for a response, he pulled the shard from her foot and opened the wound wide, peering in looking for more. "Looks clean."

Inanna whimpered but made no other sound as he examined the other foot.

"A few minor cuts. Nothing serious."

Then he dumped ice-cold vodka all over her feet and she loosed a long hissing screech. He worked fast, expertly wrapping her right foot and applying a few bandages to her left. Eyes clenched, she waited until he finished and the pain subsided to a throbbing roar.

"You did good," he said gently.

Opening her eyes, she stared at the wrapped foot and its pristine white bandages. Pain pulsed up her leg with each heartbeat.

Aarush stood nearby, watching. He offered her the second pair of shoes she'd packed, a pair of white sneakers. Grimacing, Inanna donned them. She only laced them up tight enough they wouldn't fall off if she had to run, and prayed she wouldn't need to.

"Aarush," said Chen. "Help her outside. I'll join you guys in a second." When Aarush nodded, he frowned at the two of them and added, "Hold on." Climbing into the back of the RV, he returned a moment later with two baseball caps. "Keep these on. Heads down. It'll help protect you from any streetlight-mounted cameras."

The Millennial Manifesto

"One moment," Inanna told Aarush. Limping, she found her backpack, her father's gun tucked in the bottom. After putting the concealed carry holster on her belt and moving it to the small of her back, she put the gun in place. It was stupid. When the bullets started flying, she hadn't once thought about the gun. She doubted that, even had she had it on her, she would have thought to draw it. But she couldn't leave it here, couldn't chance some kid finding it.

Aarush helped her from the motorhome and the two stood waiting. Chen joined them a minute later, eyes red but dry. Over one shoulder hung the sniper rifle in its soft-case. Unlabeled, it could have been anything.

"Let's go," he said.

"Wait!"

Chen and Aarush turned to Inanna.

"I just remembered that I set up a meeting with the estate agent at that motel."

Chen checked his watch. "They're due in half an hour. Call and cancel."

Inanna phoned the agent and got his voicemail.

Damnit! Who the hell doesn't have Bluetooth these days?

She wanted to cry with frustration. She wanted to run away and hide. This was all too much. Julia dead in the back of a shitty camper. She still couldn't believe it was real. What the hell happened? How had Gartner's goons found them?

They were waiting. We must have been predictable somehow.

Had the estate agent tipped them off? Where were the police? Had she made a mistake somewhere and got her best friend killed?

She called again, and got voicemail again. This time she left a message saying she had to cancel the meeting due to a last-minute emergency. Her voice shook and cracked. When she finished the call, Chen stood staring at her.

"It's not enough," he said.

"Why?"

"They might not get the message before they arrive. The place will be crawling with cops. They'll be questioned, and that will lead to you."

He was right. "So what do we do?"

Chen said nothing, adjusting the rifle bag on his shoulder. He looked back the way they came.

"No," said Inanna. "You can't kill him."

He shrugged.

"You *can't*," she repeated. "It won't solve anything. The police will look into why he was there, who he was meeting with. That will still lead them to me."

"It would buy time."

"But it will solve nothing. And killing innocent people doesn't make the world a better place. That is our goal. That is what this is all about."

"Julia is gone," said Chen. "The world will never be a better place."

His voice flat, devoid of emotion, dead. Haunted. Inanna's heart broke. The two had been together forever. Polar opposites, Julia's adrenaline-junkie recklessness and Chen's locked down military perfection, they were each other's world.

Does he blame me? Could she blame him if he did?

"We have to go back," said Aarush. "We have to try to intercept the agent."

He was right. "I can't ask you to risk yourselves," said Inanna. "This is my mess."

"You don't have to ask," said Chen. "And this is *our* mess."

Aarush nodded agreement. "Let's go."

CHAPTER – HIRAN

The bullet-riddled RV roared out of the motel parking lot, jumped the curb, and careened away down the street just as Hiran reached Chuck. Another magazine already loaded, Chuck raised his SIG to keep shooting.

Hiran grabbed Chuck's arm. "It's gone! Too many people!"

The big man turned on him, eyes ablaze with rage.

Chuck was gone.

This was all Tick Tock.

For a heartbeat Hiran wondered if he was about to get shot again.

"The cops are coming," said Hiran. "We have to get out of here."

"Fana." Chuck turned away, ignoring Hiran's grip on his arm, and stared at her crumpled form, the halo of blood and brain surrounding her shattered skull.

"She's dead. Cops are coming. We can't be here."

Hiran pulled Chuck's arm, tensing in case he lashed out. Surprisingly, Chuck didn't resist. Leading him away, Hiran glanced over his shoulder one last time. Fana lay still, motionless in that way he'd seen too many times. Motionless like she'd never move again.

I did that. I put her there.

Could he have done it differently? Should he have known? He replayed the scene over and over, trying to figure out where it all went wrong. The *crack* of the rifle, Fana falling on the sidewalk. He thought she was dead. At that range, a blind idiot could kill someone with an M40 and this was likely the same person who shot the iPad out Fana's hand. Then the sniper started shooting at them. At first, Hiran was sure he, too, was dead. Then he realized the shooter was intentionally missing. Each bullet went somewhere it wouldn't hurt anyone. Engine blocks and concrete bore the brunt of the attacks. It was, however, enough to keep he and Chuck ducking for cover. Chuck, in full-on Tick Tock mode, shot back, blasting away with that SIG like a madman. He peppered the

RV with bullets, uncaring who or what might be beyond those flimsy walls. Hiran had shouted at him, screamed himself hoarse trying to get him to stop, but Tick Tock was beyond reason.

When Fana rolled over and Hiran realized she still lived, he damned near found god. He knew then, beyond any shred of doubt, that the sniper intentionally avoided killing the girl.

We're going to be fine, he remembered thinking. *As long as no one does anything stupid.*

He watched, helpless, as Fana drew a pistol he didn't know she had, and fired it into the RV until the slide locked open. He'd known elation and fear. At that range there was a damned good chance whoever was hiding in the back of the RV would be out of commission. But he'd been in enough shootouts to know how easy it was to miss a concealed target at any range.

And then that big Asian came striding out of the laundromat, calm as death. He put Fana down like she was nothing. Two in the chest and one in the head to be sure. He'd yelled something at someone out of sight behind the camper, and laid down a barrage of cover fire. Unlike the whoever was in the RV—Julia Iliadis, Hiran guessed—he wasn't trying to miss. Bullets punched holes in the car Hiran hid behind, narrowly missing him. But two hundred yards was a long shot with a pistol and Chuck sprinted, ducking and dodging and returning fire.

Hiran watched as Chen McClure turned away and disappeared behind the motorhome. Even though Chuck sent round after round into it, the vehicle fled the scene tires screeching.

What a shit show.

Hiran realized he was still numb. The adrenaline dumped into his system when the bullets started flying soured, gutted him, left him stupid and empty of emotion. It would come later, he knew. It always did. You didn't watch a co-worker—a *friend*—get gunned down without feeling something. He'd cry. He'd lie in bed hating himself for living, for failing her. For getting her killed. But for now, he was shielded from the brunt of the pain to come.

Fana deserves better.

Hiran dragged the unresisting Chuck back to the 300.

Chuck hesitated after opening the passenger door. "Shotgun," he whispered, before entering.

Dropping the car into gear, Hiran eased the vehicle out of the parking lot. It was a scene of chaos. People ran or cowered, according to their personalities. Several had drawn guns and were scuttling about like they thought they thought they were Special Forces on a seek and destroy mission.

Idiots.

Most had no idea the excitement was over. A group gathered around someone sprawled on the pavement who'd either taken a stray round or fainted. Hiran didn't want to know which.

What a fucking mess.

"Gartner is going to be furious," said Chuck, looking back at the scene they left behind.

"Does he seem to be the type to be upset by a little collateral damage?"

Chuck tilted his, thinking. "No. He's an asshole."

And you, Chuck, the man who likely caused most of that collateral damage, what are you?

"This is a mess," said Hiran. "Too much attention. We should call Gartner for new orders."

"The orders haven't changed," Chuck said. "And you know it."

"Fuck."

Pulling into traffic, they left the violence behind. The car felt oddly quiet, empty without Fana, without her barbed nerd humor.

She was too smart for this filth. And yet there she was, dead in the street.

The more he thought about it, the more Hiran saw that there was no way this wasn't his fault. He hired her when she was in her third year of her Computer Science degree, lured her away with quick cash and the promise of shoddy deals and getting paid to hack, instead of living the life of an assembly line code-monkey. She'd leaped at the chance, walked away from school like it was nothing, like a future in crime was so clearly preferable to a job at Microsoft or Google.

It was her choice.

It felt like a lie. She was smart, far smarter than he and Chuck, but she'd been naive.

Damned kids always think they're immortal until the world proves them wrong.

"I gave her the gun." said Chuck. "I got her killed. If she hadn't shot at them, she'd still be alive." He sagged, looking down into huge hands. "She said something about 'going all John Woo on the bitches.' I got her killed."

"*We* got her killed," said Hiran. "My fault she was there at all."

The Millennial Manifesto

"We." Chuck glanced out the window at the passing traffic, people going about their lives like Fana's brains hadn't just been blown all over the sidewalk. "It doesn't feel any better."

They drove in silence for several minutes.

"The question now," said Chuck, "is what are *we* going to do about it?"

Hiran knew that tone. Chuck sounded sane, sounded reasonable and in control, but Tick Tock waited below the surface. Nothing Hiran said would change Tick Tock's mind. Tick Tock did whatever Tick Tock wanted. Maybe, if Hiran stayed with Chuck, he could limit the damage, make sure no more innocents were hurt. And of course Chuck was right: Gartner wouldn't give a shit about any of this. The job wasn't finished and Gartner didn't pay for unfinished business.

And maybe you want a little bit of payback too.

It wouldn't change anything. It wouldn't bring Fana back and it wouldn't bring meaning to her death.

And closure? What the hell was that anyway? People went on and on about needing closure, how it would make them feel better, make it possible move on with their lives. There was no closure. Closure was bullshit, a sap tossed to bitches too weak to face the truth.

Okay, decided Hiran, *maybe there was one closure.*

Death.

Death was the final closure, that last door, the final step in getting over all life's hurts, all the terrible things you saw. All the terrible things you did.

Chuck punched the leather glovebox door, leaving a line of knuckle-shaped indentations. "Why?" he asked, voice tight.

Why? Hiran waited.

"Why me? Why did she… I'm…"

"A racist shit-stain of a human?"

Chuck shot him a dangerous look, but it folded, caved in on itself. "I'm not racist."

"She's smart *for a black*," said Hiran, throwing Chuck's words back at him.

"I was joking."

"Not funny. Most of you are meek lazy little bastards. You remember saying that?"

"You're the exception. Most of you—"

"Chuck."

"Sorry."

"I have no fucking idea why Fana chose you. Maybe she saw something worthwhile in there. Maybe she just wanted to fuck a stupid cracker and laugh about it after." Anger fueled Hiran's words. "I don't know what she saw. Whatever it was, I don't see it."

They drove, not going anywhere, just putting distance between themselves and their crimes.

"You think she saw something in me worth something?" Chuck asked. He sounded impossibly small for such a monster.

"I don't know." Hiran drew a calming breath. How this big idiot still managed to piss him off after all these years was a mystery. "Sorry about what I said."

"You weren't wrong. Fana… She was an uppity black—"

"For fuck sakes, Chuck!"

"Let me finish. She was an uppity black, but sometimes, when she wasn't making fun of me, she'd talk to me. Nothing big. Nothing serious. She'd talk about politics or science or those nerd books. She'd talk about ideas, what she had planned for some computer program or hack or whatever. I realized pretty early on she was a fuck-ton smarter than me."

"No shit."

"Smarter than you too, Boss, and you're the smartest guy I know."

"If that's true, we're both in trouble."

"I could barely follow half of what she said. Anyway. We were talking about race one day, and she said it was a grammatical fallacy, a cultural myth. She said we were all one species. She dared me to get a DNA test that would trace my ancestry. Never one to back down, I did. I'm not white. I mean, I am, but I'm not *just* white. I'm Russian or Slavic or something with some African and Middle Eastern mixed in." He laughed, shaking his head in disbelief. "Hiran, I'm a Brownie just like you."

I should shoot him. Hiran said nothing.

"She was small," said Chuck. "I could crush her so easy." He held up a meaty fist, knuckles crunching. "But she wasn't afraid of me. She got in my face and pushed me and the angrier I got the harder she pushed." He laughed again, a rueful bark. "Tick Tock. She knew who I was. She knew *what* I was. Still, no fear. Fuck, she was brave. Brave and smart. So much better than me." He turned away, stared out the passenger window. "Hiran?"

"Yeah?"

"We're going to kill them."

"I don't—"

"That was always the job. Gartner wants them to die. He called me, told me. Told me not to tell you 'cuz he says you're too soft. He wants us to find them and bring them to him and then he's going to kill them. Wants to do it himself. He's a sick fucker. Fana said he's a psychopath. But he said if shit went wrong and we couldn't bring them in, then I should pop all four myself. He offered me a bonus if I brought pictures."

"A bonus you would have, of course, shared with your colleagues."

Chuck shrugged, not bothering with a response.

"How we going to do this?" Hiran asked, changing the subject. "Without Fana, we can't hack cop files or access traffic cameras. Aside from Chen and Julia, we have no idea who the other two are. They'll ditch the RV first thing."

"I put a lot of bullets into that thing," said Chuck. "What if I clipped one? Stupid hippies will run straight to the hospital."

Still clinging to the hippy idea? God*damn* the man was stubborn.

"Yeah," Hiran admitted, "You may have wounded or killed one."

Chuck blinked. "Problem."

"Christ, what now?"

"Why the hotel? Why did they go there?"

"Showers, like Fana said." Hiran winced. It hurt to speak her name.

"Never bought that," said Chuck. "Those damned campers have showers. What if they were there to meet someone. More hippie terrorists, maybe. Another cell. Their handler. I don't know. They went right past the Target and straight to the motel."

That did make some sense. "The hospital is still a better bet. Like you said, you put a few pounds of lead into that RV."

"We can't chance it," said Chuck. "We have to cover both contingencies."

Every now and then he's smarter than me.

"You're right. I'm going to drop you off so you can catch a cab to the nearest hospital. I'll head back to the motel."

"Either one of us sees them, we call the other."

"Chuck, how much was the bonus?"

Chuck stared at him, no doubt deciding whether or not to lie. "Ten grand."

"Chuck."

"Twenty."

"Even split."

"Yeah, of course."

Of course. Asshole.

Hiran pulled the car over. "Call if they show, and I'll haul ass."

Chuck nodded, climbed out, and immediately hailed a cab with a sharp whistle.

Knowing it was a dead end, knowing it was a waste of time, knowing that finding these people would just mean he'd have to wait even longer before he saw his girls again, Hiran drove back to the Target.

Slowing as he got close, he pulled over at a good distance and parked the 300. After fishing his tactical binoculars from his bag in the trunk, he returned to sit in the driver's seat to relax and watch. His knees and back ached.

Hiran spent several minutes scanning the scene. The local police arrived and set up cordons, taping off things of interest with that yellow tape they loved so much, and dropping those little plastic triangles by every shell casing.

A *lot* of little plastic triangles littered the ground.

I hope Tick Tock was smart enough to wear gloves while loading his magazines.

Hiran watched a cop pull an emergency blanket from the trunk of a cruiser and lay it over Fana's body, hiding it from the gawkers already gathering. The spray of brain showed past the edge of the blanket.

Tarping the body, that's what they called it.

The body.

Fana.

A TV crew had already made the scene and filmed everything.

Humans are vultures.

He'd never see her again. Not unless his mom was right and there was a heaven, though in that case it seemed unlikely he'd wind up there. But would Fana? Whatever bad decisions she made, she was still a good kid.

This is a stupid idea.

Hiran scanned the crowd.

They'd never be so dumb as to—

There, watching the police through a pair of tactical binoculars, was the big Asian, Chen. The black curvy chick, as Gartner called her, stood beside him, petite and sexy. The skinny brown kid from the cafe was there too. Using the camera function in the binoculars, Hiran snapped several pictures.

Fana can find out who they—

"Fuck," he swore, more for the sheer unwillingness of his brain to accept reality than from the inconvenience of no longer having access to someone with computer skills beyond opening email.

What was he going to do, go find another student, get another innocent kid killed? He couldn't do it. He and Chuck would just have to make do on their own.

Maybe it's time to walk away. One last job and then retire on whatever he had. He and Joan would figure it out. Somehow, they'd survive. Maybe they could down-size. Joan was always complaining about how much a pain in the ass the house was to clean. And the girls would be going away to school soon.

What would he do with himself if not this? A life in the military hadn't left him with much in the way of valuable skills beyond hurting and killing, and he was too damned old for that shit anyway. Maybe he could find a soft part-time corporate security gig. Mall cop? He laughed at the thought.

His laughter died, choked to silence.

Focus on now.

His phone rang. "No luck at the hospital," said Chuck. "Already on my way back to you."

Hiran hesitated. Walk away. Forget all this shit. "They're here."

"Don't fucking let them out of your sight," Chuck said, voice all Tick Tock. "I'm on my way."

CHAPTER – INANNA

Helpless, Inanna watched the estate agent's car approached the motel parking lot and get flagged down by the police.

If only we'd been here five minutes earlier!

She watched him talk with the officer at the cordon, no doubt explaining he'd been asked to meet someone here, and yes, that was a little odd, and no, of course he wouldn't mind discussing the details. Her heart sank as the agent climbed from his gray Mercedes and went off to be questioned by two officers.

"We're fucked," she said. *I'm fucked.*

Chen already lost everything. Jenny. His home. Julia. How did he deal with it so well? How did he lock it down so tight? Inanna was sure she'd be curled up on the ground screaming. She wanted to anyway.

"We don't know that," said Chen, still looking through the binoculars.

Inanna's burner phone rang, the one only the agent had the number for.

"Should I answer?"

"What happens if you do?" asked Aarush.

"They probably ask me to come to the station and answer some questions."

"Bad idea," said Chen.

"If I don't answer, I'll still become a person of interest."

"Don't answer," said Chen. "That's the choice that leaves us the most options in the future. Maybe we can fake your kidnapping, make it look like the terrorists took you for some reason." He glanced at her, eyes gentle. "A least you'll get your life back."

My life back. She wanted that more than anything. She wanted all this to be done. She wanted to go home and hide in those massive closets.

"I don't want my life back," she said. "I'm in this until the end. We change the world."

"You can call him back in a couple of days," said Chen, "say there was an emergency. Tell him you already spoke to the police."

Inanna let the call go to voicemail. "How are we doing for cash?" she asked.

"I have a few thousand left from selling my pickup," said Chen.

Aarush shrugged. "I was busted-ass poor *before* we started."

"Okay," said Inanna. "If we live on the cheap, cockroach motels and ramen noodles, we can last a few weeks. Certainly enough time to figure out what's up with the estate agent and whether the police are onto me."

Chen lowered the binoculars. "We have to get out of here, put some distance between us and…and all this." He waved a hand at the swarming police officers.

And Julia. Every time Inanna thought of Julia, she saw her sitting motionless, eyes open, in the back of that shitty RV. Tears welled up and again she cried. She couldn't help it, couldn't stop. Glancing at Aarush she saw tears in his eyes too. Only Chen remained hard-eyed, dry.

I know he loved her. God, it must hurt him so much.

Chen took a long breath and let it out. "We have to keep moving. We need to find somewhere that'll sell us a cheap car for cash. Wrecking yards are good for that."

And that was it. Chen hailed a cab and they left Julia behind. Forever.

The cab driver who picked them up caught the mood and didn't speak. He dropped them at a junkyard with a big spray-painted sign advertising 'Cars for $200 on up!' Chen paid cash and the driver left without a word.

Aarush looked lost, blinking at the lot, shaking his head like he couldn't believe he was really there. Gone was his boyish grin, the constant jokes. He looked like he aged a decade in the last hour.

Will he ever laugh again? Will the Aarush I know return?

She knew, intellectually, that time healed all wounds. Or at least it wore the sharp edges to blunt corners still capable of hurting. For months after each of her parents' deaths she'd thought she could never be herself again, never go out into the world as a whole human. But slowly, day by day, bits of her leaked back into the gaping wounds left behind. Years later, she still cried sometimes, but it was rare now. And she could remember them with fondness. But right now, she couldn't imagine going on. Julia had been there from the beginning, the first one to jump on Inanna's suggestion that they change the world, the first to truly embrace the idea.

The first to die for it.

Chen looked at cars for an hour, test drove a gray 1988 BMW 325IS, and said, "We'll take it."

He paid $450.

Moments later, the three were in the car and heading east. Chen, behind the wheel, drove at the speed limit.

"Where we going?" asked Aarush.

Chen shrugged. "Anywhere."

Aarush nodded. "So, why this car?"

"These cars are tanks. I checked underneath, and the chassis is solid, not too much rust. This engine—a straight six—will go forever."

"A little small," said Inanna. After the RV, it felt positively cramped.

"The front seats go way back," continued Chen, "until you're practically lying down. The passenger can sleep. It's got 170 horsepower—or did when new—and it handles like a dream. And even if all the computerized stuff dies, the car will keep running."

"And, as an added bonus," said Aarush, sitting in the passenger seat, digging through the glovebox, "the previous owner left us a pile of punk music. All MP3s burned to CD, so I hope you're not too picky about audio quality." He turned to flash a fractured smile at Inanna in the back seat, but it wasn't the old smile. A crack of pain ran through it.

It's the eyes.

"What are you in the mood for first?" he asked. "The Forgotten Rebels, or the Circle Jerks?"

"Neither," said Chen.

That broken smile died and Aarush shoved the CDs back into the box. He sat facing forward, shoulders hunched.

They left Fremont behind, winding country roads replacing the streets of the small city.

"Damn," said Chen.

Inanna sat up. "What?"

"No one look back, but we're being followed. They're good, but there's not enough traffic out here. And a cherry-red 300 stands out."

"What do we do?" asked Aarush. "Can we outrun them?"

Chen glanced up at the rear-view mirror. "We probably have the handling advantage, but they have twice the horsepower." He allowed the car to slow a little without braking. "Everyone has their seat-belt on, right?"

Inanna and Aarush answered affirmative.

"Hold on."

Chen slammed the brakes, yanking the parking brake at the same time. Opening the door, he drew a pistol and stepped out before the car had come to a complete stop. Striding back down the street, he shot at a steady pace.

Perfectly calm.

Inanna peered over the backseat, frozen and unable to look away.

The red 300 didn't brake or turn away. Instead, the driver gunned the engine and ducked from sight. Beside him, whoever sat in the passenger seat, ducked too, but shot blindly at Chen out the open passenger window.

Chen stumbled, straightened, and fired into the engine of the approaching car. He acted like he had all the time in the world, each shot aimed and squeezed off. He stepped around the car as it passed, ejecting the spent magazine and replacing it with another.

The 300 turned abruptly, smoke pouring from under the bullet-riddled hood, leaped the ditch, and crashed into the embankment on the far side. It sat there, front end crushed.

Inanna watched Chen examine the car, make a decision, and walk back to the BMW. When he turned, she saw his torso was a mess of blood, the sodden shirt clinging to him. Climbing back into the car, he put it in gear and calmly drove away as if nothing had happened.

Aarush, sitting beside him in the passenger seat, stared, eyes wide. "Are you—We have to get you to a hospital."

"No." He drove, jaw clenched.

"You've been shot!"

"Yeah."

"We're taking you to a hospital," said Inanna, reaching forward to put a hand on his shoulder. "We'll face whatever consequences—"

"No," said Chen. Glancing up, he flashed a pained smile in the rear-view. He coughed blood, staining his chin, and the smile died. "I took one in the chest and one in the gut. I'm done. I can feel it."

"You'll be fine," soothed Aarush. "The doctors—"

"I don't want doctors."

"A trauma unit—"

"Julia's gone," he said. "After Jenny, I had one reason to keep breathing and she's dead. After the war—the things I did over there—I couldn't be here. I didn't think I'd ever fit in. And then you," he met Inanna's eyes in the mirror, "you and Julia had this crazy idea and I thought it might be my redemption."

"Chen." She didn't know what to say.

"They killed Julia. That woman on the sidewalk. I blew her brains everywhere." A sob tore from him and he coughed more blood. It fell from his chin, disappeared into the gore of his shirt. "I don't know who she was. Was she an undercover cop? Did I kill someone sworn to protect the people, someone who was just doing her job?"

Remembering Aarush's words as they exited the hotel, Inanna said, "I think it was the woman with Gartner's goons. The one we saw on TV."

"Julia was a damned good shot. She could have killed her, easy. But she didn't. Why not?"

Inanna had no answers.

Chen drove in silence, bloody teeth bared in a snarl of pain. Once he had them back in a more populated area, he turned the old BMW into a narrow alley and turned it off.

"I'm sorry," he said. "I thought I could protect you." He coughed, groaning and spitting blood. "Whoever that was saw the car. You have to leave it." Chen laughed, a weak grunt of humor. "Anyway, I bled all over the front seat."

"Chen," said Aarush.

"Don't argue." He waved them both to silence. "You'll find cash and a Glock in my bag. There are three loaded mags in there."

Inanna suddenly remembered the gun in the holster pressed against the small of her back. When Chen stopped the car and got out and started shooting, she could have helped. Maybe she'd have made the difference. Maybe he wouldn't be bleeding out in a damned alley. She hadn't. She'd watched like a goddamned spectator.

"I'm sorry," she said.

"Don't apologize," he said. "I believe in you. Julia does too. Did. You're going to make this shitty world a better place. Your next target should be the NRA. That school shooting. Eighteen children dead because of lobby groups and cowardly politicians. After them, hit the oil companies. Most of what we did in the Middle East was to protect their interests." He coughed more blood, closing his eyes. "Fuck them." He grinned, red, mean, and feral. "I wanted to hit those alt-right Nazi motherfuckers too. Always wanted to fight Nazis."

Chen whispered, "I wish I hadn't killed that woman," and was still.

"Chen?" asked Inanna. She gently shook his shoulder. His head lolled, loose. "Aarush, is he breathing?"

"I don't think so." Unbuckling himself, Aarush reached over to check Chen's pulse. Then he sat back, expressive eyes wide.

"Aarush?"

He shook his head.

"What do we do?"

Aarush swallowed. "We do what he said. We go."

She watched as Aarush collected Chen's bag and took the car keys to open the trunk. Slinging Chen's bag over his shoulder, he opened the rear door for her and she exited the car. They stood, blinking tears, each saying goodbye to their friend in their own way.

She remembered wondering where she'd lost control and wanted to scream at the futility of the notion.

I never had control.

Had they gone too far?

If she'd left Gartner alone, her friends would still be alive.

Julia. Chen. Glenn Triantafylloy. That woman on the sidewalk. Four dead. Had others died in the gunfight back at the motel? She hadn't seen the news, had no idea how bad the carnage might have been. And what about those two men in the car that Chen shot at? Were they dead? Wounded? Had they survived the crash?

"How many people?" she whispered.

Aarush took her hand. "Let's go."

Inanna let him lead her away. They left Chen in the car, sitting there, staring at the dashboard as if waiting for something. Aarush guided her to ever busier streets, going nowhere, just looking for wherever had the most people.

Lost in a crowd. God, she wanted that to be true. Was there any way back to that? What if she went home, never returned the estate agent's call? Could she sink away to nothing, disappear into her old life?

"Inanna?"

"Hmm?"

"I filmed it all." Aarush squeezed her hand, pulling her into another street.

How does he have the presence of mind to do that?

Should she give him the gun? She couldn't imagine him using it. Aarush could never hurt someone.

"I can't help it," he said. "Shit starts happening and I have capture it."

"I didn't notice."

He winced. "Whenever I don't have a handycam running I use the wireless microcam mounted in the frame of my glasses."

Stopping, he removed the glasses, held them up for her inspection. There, in the corner by the hinge, he pointed out the tiny lens.

I thought that was just a design detail.

"That's why the arms are so thick," he said. "Data storage is built in."

She remembered how he put his glasses away in the hotel when they kissed, how careful he always was to remove them any time they were intimate, tucking them away in a case.

He could have recorded any and all of that, and didn't.

People passed them by on the sidewalk, lost in their own lives, blissfully unaware. The air smelled of car exhaust, the promise of rain, and the sweet scent of coffee and donuts from a nearby bakery.

"Sorry," said Aarush, once again pulling her into motion. "I should have told you. Should have said something."

She tried to remember all the moments he must have captured. Conversations with Julia and Chen. The group planning or arguing.

He said he was always filming. She hadn't realized what he'd meant.

"You filmed the two men in the car?" she asked, as they dodged around knots of pedestrians.

He nodded.

Think this through. You always knew your old life was over. Just because this didn't go as planned, just because you're scared, is no reason to roll over and quit.

Hell no. It was a reason to fight harder.

"That was Gartner's goons Julia was shooting at, right?" asked Inanna, her mind racing.

"I think so," said Aarush.

"Julia saw them at her house, shot at them. At the iPad," she corrected. "She must have seen them again, at the motel. They've been tracking us somehow."

"Uploads," said Aarush. "Fuck. We drove in basically a straight line uploading videos. They predicted our next stop and were there waiting."

"I bet that was them in the car Chen shot off the road."

"Easy enough to check," said Aarush.

Ten minutes later, sitting in a dingy cafe sipping burnt coffee, Inanna won that bet. They huddled together, watching video on his phone, each taking one earbud so they could hear. They saw Chen carefully place his shots into the car's engine, disabling it. Shaky as it was, they were still able to grab several screen-shots. They recognized the two Special Forces men they saw on TV out front of Gartner's.

Inanna felt an odd wave of relief. *Chen didn't kill them.*

Though they killed him. Mixed emotions, grief, anger, relief, and a desire for revenge, tore through her.

"It's them," Aarush repeated. "It was them. Gartner sent them to kill us. Gartner killed Julia and Chen." Delicate artist's fingers clenched into angry fists.

"We have him," said Inanna, struggling to rein in her emotions. "We have the clip of them from the TV, and we have them shooting Chen."

I caught the entire gunfight at the hotel, too," admitted Aarush.

Neither felt ready to watch it.

"We post this video," said Aarush. "Once I've got it edited." He darted a look at Inanna. "No one needs to see that Chen started shooting first."

Inanna agreed. "What's our play once the video is up? Do we go to the police, turn ourselves in?"

Aarush considered the options, eyes narrowed in thought. "What's our goal here?"

"Well, when the authorities see the video, they're probably going to pick up Gartner for questioning at the least."

"That's not very satisfying."

"And he's a rich bastard," said Inanna. "Best lawyers. What are the odds he gets away with this somehow?"

"Everything we have on Gartner is circumstantial," agreed Aarush. "Gartner isn't actually doing any of this. His goons will take the fall."

An idea took root. "Unless…" She grinned at Aarush. "Unless we film a confession."

"He'll never confess."

"We have to trick him."

"How?"

"What does a man like Gartner understand?" she asked. "Greed and money. If we offer to sell him the video, he'll assume we're after the payday. He'll know he can buy us off."

"He'll think we're idiots."

"And he'll betray us."

"Those goons will be there," pointed out Aarush. "We'll have to be ready for them."

Inanna grabbed his hand. "I have a plan, but it's going to be dangerous."

He squeezed back, grinning just a little of that boyish charm. "And I have a backup plan for when everything goes to shit."

"I love your confidence."

"I love you."

The Millennial Manifesto

CHAPTER – HIRAN

"Fuck," said Chuck, sneezing white airbag dust.

Hiran, ears ringing, groaned and looked around, trying to figure out what happened. His nose throbbed and hot, salty blood trickled down the back of his throat.

Chuck sneezed again, spraying more white powder. Pushing the deflated bag off himself, he climbed from the car. "You hit?"

Hiran checked himself for bullet wounds. "Only by the airbag." He clambered from the car with a groan, his knees popping as he straightened. "He saw us."

"No shit. I told you not to follow so close."

"How about next time you steal something other than a cherry red car."

"Beggars can't be choosers."

"You're stealing, not begging. And you do know you're allowed to steal cars other than Chrysler 300s, right?"

"I like 'em." Chuck eyed the car, the front end crumpled in. "Ain't going anywhere in that."

Even if it could still be driven—which Hiran doubted—the chassis straddled the ditch, leaving the front tires spinning in the air. He considered climbing in and seeing if the rear-wheel drive would drag it out of the ditch, but the car was riddled with bullet holes, and not the kind of vehicle a couple of criminals on a manhunt needed to be seen in. They'd be pulled over by the first cop that saw them. Add in the fact that the car was stolen, he and Chuck armed, and Tick Tock's bag of toys in the trunk, and it was an ugly picture all around.

"We walk," said Hiran, limping out of the ditch. His knees made wet crunchy noises like fresh celery being snapped. The left one felt bruised and tender. He must have hit it during the crash. Once out of the ditch, he fished out his depleted bottle of ibuprofen and finished the last four, swallowing them dry.

A car approached, heading into town, the direction the old BMW had gone. Hiran stepped out and waved, trying not to look scary. The woman driving pulled into the far lane and accelerated past.

Good call. He couldn't blame her; seeing two people looking like him and Chuck, he'd have done the same.

Going around to the driver's side, Chuck popped the trunk and then retrieved his bag of guns and ammunition.

"Why the hell do you carry that shit everywhere?" Hiran asked, irritably. "Every damned job, and I've never seen you need anything more than your pistol. And even that's been rare."

"Boy Scouts," said Chuck. "Be prepared."

Hiran couldn't imagine Chuck as a Boy Scout. Hell, he couldn't even imagine him as a boy. He'd been Tick Tock since they met in Afghanistan.

That's not true, Fana named him that.

But Chuck had been deserving of the name even back then. War had done nothing to calm him. If anything, where Hiran came away intimately aware of his mortality, Chuck left the army convinced he was invincible.

He never got shot.

No matter how many people shot at the big bastard, he always walked away unscathed. And the fact he got medals and commendations for killing people further skewed any moral compass he may have once had from true north. Not that Hiran's compass was doing much better. But unlike Chuck, he always turned down the killing jobs. He had enough ghosts already without adding to their numbers. Sure, he'd collect people so someone else could kill them, but he never did the killing himself.

That was worth something, right?

Gun bag thrown over his shoulder, Chuck joined him at the side of the road. "You ready?"

"Yeah."

"I grabbed the plates off the car, tossed them way off into the trees."

"Good."

Hiran turned and began the long walk back into town. Spotting something in the road, he went to it, groaning as he crouched. His knees did that wet crunchy thing again. Dipping his finger into the fluid, he lifted it to his nose, already knowing what he'd smell.

"Blood," he said. "We hit him." Scanning the road ahead, he saw more. A lot more. Ejected shell casings littered the asphalt. "Maybe more than once."

"Good," said Chuck. "Fucker killed Fana."

They walked for half an hour before a craggy old man in a rusted Ford pickup truck offered them a lift and drove them the rest of the way into Fremont, dropping them at what looked to be a major intersection.

Hiran's nose dulled to a slow pulsating throb—due more to the ibuprofen than anything else—and he was pretty sure it was broken. Touching it sent waves of nauseating pain through his skull and his gut grumbled unhappily at the blood he'd swallowed.

He spat red, staining the sidewalk. Some passing man in an expensive suit scowled in disgust. For an instant Hiran considered siccing Tick Tock on him, but they were already in enough trouble.

"What's next, Boss?" asked Chuck, turning a circle. He hadn't even been scratched, his wrinkled suit looking the same as always.

What's next?

Without Fana to hack local police networks and access street cameras, what chance did they have of finding their targets? His head hurt too much to think. He wanted a couple of whiskeys, a bucket of pain-killers, and twelve hours of uninterrupted sleep. He wanted to hug his girls, tell them he loved them, and then pass out on the sofa while Joan ran her fingers through what remained of his hair.

"We shot him" said Chuck. "They're going to a hospital for sure this time."

Right. Hospital. He couldn't summon excitement at catching their prey.

Hiran wondered who hit Chen. Both he and Chuck had ducked beneath the dash, firing blindly. Thank god they were out in the middle of nowhere.

Fucking miracle we hit anything.

It was also a miracle they hadn't been shot dead. Then again, with the number of bullet holes in the hood of the car, the sniper had clearly been more interested in killing the engine rather than them. What stayed the man's hand? He and Chuck had been stunned by the crash and resulting airbag face-punch. Chen had plenty of time to wander over and blow their brains all over the interior of the 300.

There was the blood, though. Had they critically injured him?

Have I killed another man?

Did not knowing absolve him? That seemed unlikely.

"Boss?"

"Sorry. Thinking. Hospital. Yeah, I guess so."

"Right. I'll go steal another car and we'll be on our way."

Chuck wandered off, hands in pockets.

There was no hesitation in the man. See need. Fulfill need. A couple of days ago, Hiran would have said that's all Fana was to the big man, a need fulfilled. But Chuck had changed. Or at least the way he was with Fana changed. It was like she found something buried deep inside Tick Tock, and pulled it out into the light.

Or maybe I never really knew him.

It was fucking weird, that's what it was. *You think you know someone.* They'd both surprised him. He felt like he'd just begun to learn who she was, and then she was gone. Dead.

Checking his phone, Hiran glanced at the local news. He saw the firefight from a few different perspectives, shaky video shot on the phones of shoppers. He watched as the bullet-riddled RV jumped the curb and roared away. Amazingly, neither he nor Chuck appeared on any of the clips shown. Hopefully that meant no one had filmed them rather than those clips having been grabbed by the police in an effort to apprehend suspects. He listened as the reporter somberly detailed the deaths. One young woman, identity unknown, gunned down outside of a motel. One middle-aged man, father of three, pronounced dead on arrival at Spectrum Health Gerber Memorial Hospital after being shot in the Target parking lot. Another young woman had been found dead in the back of the RV which fled the scene and was discovered, abandoned.

Julia. He wondered who killed her. Fana emptied a magazine into the back of the camper at damned near point-blank range. Chuck fired god-knew how many rounds into the vehicle. Hiran, too, had shot back several times, though somewhat more carefully than Chuck.

How would Fana feel, knowing she may have killed someone?

Doesn't matter.

The dead are freed of guilt.

Hiran's phone rang as he was putting it away.

Gartner.

Fuck. "Yeah, Boss?"

"Guess who just fucking called me?"

I have no idea who fucking called you.

"The police?"

"Why would the fucking police—Never mind. Those four assholes that kidnapped me."

Three," said Hiran, needing something positive to report. "Maybe two."

"Explain."

"Julia Iliadis, the blond woman, is dead. Fana killed her." That seemed the most likely.

"Didn't think she had it in her. Well, tell her she earned herself a sweet bonus."

"Fana's dead."

"No bonus then."

"Chuck and I shot Chen McClure. Pretty sure he's hurt bad."

"So a bonus is back on the table."

One of your team is dead but don't worry you might make some extra money. Motherfucker. "You said the terrorists called."

"Yeah. It was the black bitch. I recognized her voice. They say they have incriminating evidence that will put me in jail and are willing to sell it."

They can't be that dumb. "They want to meet to arrange a swap?"

"Yep. Only we're going to grab the idiots."

Of course we are. "What are we going to do with them?"

Gartner hesitated. "Nothing, Hiran. We'll see that they have nothing incriminating and then we'll send the stupid fuckers on their merry way."

The CEO was too paranoid to ever say anything incriminating over a cell phone.

"Of course, Boss."

"Haul ass back here. If you run into them on the freeway, you know what to do."

"Yep."

"You get this done right," said Gartner, "and there's sweet bonuses for you and Chuck." He killed the call.

"Goodbye to you, too, asshole." Hiran pocketed his phone. Sweet bonus. Like that would remove the pain of Fana's death. Like a few thousand more dollars would make any of this worthwhile.

And now, a couple more hours in a car.

His back hurt and his knees never ceased their constant complaint. The thought of breathing Chuck's farts and contributing to the overall miasma with his own, left him wanting to call Gartner and quit.

Except Chuck wouldn't. Chuck would drive back there by himself, if he had to, and kill those hippies or terrorists or kids, or whatever they hell they were. He'd do it because he was raw about Fana.

Tick Tock could do no less.

Gartner was a bastard, but he was a smart bastard. Gartner would set it up so Chuck took the fall for all this shit if anything went wrong. He might even do it so he wouldn't have to pay him.

Or he might do it for fun.

So Hiran was going with Chuck. He was going because he needed the money, but also because Chuck, for all his many faults, was about as close to a friend as he had. And yeah, maybe he, too, was a little raw about Fana.

Chuck pulled up in a blue Chrysler 300 and called, "Got one," through the open window.

Sliding into the passenger seat, Hiran asked, "What the hell is it with you and 300s?"

"I just like them. And I think it's really cool that they named a car after the movie."

"What movie?"

"300. Remember, the one with all the Greek guys killing Persians. That's my favorite movie of all time."

"Oh." *Should I tell him?* "That's cool."

Chuck nodded happily.

"Didn't you make fun of Fana for liking movies like that?" Hiran asked before his brain caught up with his mouth. He winced.

"Yeah," said Chuck. "It's different though. She's a girl. Chicks aren't supposed to like that stuff."

Supposed? It was like talking with his eldest daughter, back when she was six. He was continually explaining that there weren't boys toys and girls toys, and that anyone could play with anything. She'd listen. She'd nod. And then she'd explain that toy cars were boys toys, and sometimes she played with them, but that didn't stop them from being boys toys. Hiran was pretty damned sure both his kids and his wife were a hell of a lot smarter than he.

"I didn't want her to know I liked that nerd stuff," added Chuck.

"But you liked her. That was something you could have shared."

Chuck sighed and looked out the window.

Hiran blinked and shut his mouth.

Could have shared.

The Millennial Manifesto

How about you shut your fucking pie-hole.

She was dead and here was Hiran giving Chuck relationship advice. The big guy probably would have laughed at him anyway. Chuck and relationships weren't exactly the kinds of topics one typically associated. He was always bragging about women he'd picked up in bars or strippers he'd taken home. He once explained at great length how 'pulling a stripper' was the greatest test of a man.

But he never said anything about Fana. He never bragged or even mentioned it. It was like he'd been afraid to jinx in by admitting it out loud.

"Boss?"

"Yeah, Chuck?"

"Where we going?"

"Back to Gartner's."

"Fana deserves a proper burial," he said, suddenly changing the topic.

"Yeah. I guarantee Gartner won't pay for it."

"Cheap fucker."

"The rich always are, in my experience."

"You know many rich people?" asked Chuck.

"Every person who has ever hired us to hurt someone has been rich."

Chuck thought about it, lips pursed. "I think maybe you're getting a skewed perception of the wealthy because of what we do."

"Could be," said Hiran. "Could be." *And you continue to surprise me.*

It was like Chuck's brief time with Fana shook something loose.

"Anyway," said Chuck, "if the people who hire us are so cheap, then why do they pay us?"

"Because we're the kind of people who hurt people who don't pay us."

"True." Chuck scowled. "I know you don't like killing."

"You don't like it much, either."

"But I'll do it if the money is right." He glanced at Hiran. "You going to be okay with killing these hippies? You *know* that's the job right. That was always the job."

"Am I okay with it? No. Am I going to do it? Yes. I guess. Maybe." *I fucking hope not.*

"Shit we do for money, eh?"

They drove in silence until Chuck cleared his throat. "Do you think Fana would be okay with us killing?"

"Mostly we don't kill people. Mostly we just scare or hurt them."

"But sometimes we do. *This* time."

"Fana knew what we do. Maybe not all the details, but she knew. She helped us. She helped us find people so we could hurt them. She was no angel, Chuck. She broke the law too."

"I know. But, I mean, do you think she would have been okay with us killing *these* people?"

"They killed her."

"Yeah, but I kinda got the impression she admired them, that she thought they were doing the right thing. She told me they were modern Robin Hoods. Not perfect, flawless heroes, she said, but they're the heroes we need. The heroes we deserve."

I never heard him talk so much in all these years.

"What I'm saying," continued Chuck, "is would she be okay with us killing these heroes?"

"Are they really heroes? They forced Gartner to drink poisoned water."

"Water *he* poisoned. Anyway, doesn't seem to have bothered him none."

"They killed Glenn Triantafylloy, blew him to shit."

"He stole money from sick kids' charities. Fucker deserved to burn in hell."

Hiran couldn't argue with that. "No," he said finally. "I don't think Fana would be okay with us killing people she thought were heroes."

"But we're going to do it anyway, aren't we?"

"Yeah. We are."

The Millennial Manifesto

CHAPTER – INANNA

Unsure what the authorities knew, and whether anyone had connected Chen and Julia—both of whom had now been found dead—to them, Inanna and Aarush purchased a rusted-out Chevy Nova which sounded a little like the burbling thunder of a Harley Davidson. The man at the junkyard assured them it would keep running as long as they topped up the oil every hundred miles.

As they drove home, Aarush insisted they stop at an electronics store so he could purchase supplies for what he called his Awesome Backup Plan For When Everything Goes to Shit. They uploaded content to a multitude of email accounts at a variety of free Wi-Fi locations along the way. Inanna did all the driving, as Aarush needed to edit and prepare the videos, and he had an unimaginable amount of material to go through.

Too tired, too emotionally wrung out, to make the drive in a single evening, they found a motel willing to take cash. That night they curled up together, taking comfort in each other's warmth, and slept, exhausted. In the morning, they made love, slow and gentle, exploring and kissing in a way very different from their earlier, more frenzied, efforts.

After, Inanna lay entangled with Aarush, the dark chocolate of her skin a warm contrast to the milk-chocolate of his.

It's like it might be our last time and we want to breathe each other in, miss nothing, lock each moment in stone.

"Do you think Chen had Post Traumatic Stress Disorder?" asked Aarush.

"I don't know." Inanna thought about it, remembering how he was with people, the cold distance until he decided he liked you. He avoided crowds more than mere introversion could explain, and he never discussed his time in Afghanistan. Somehow, Julia came back unscathed. Or at least less so. Was that adrenaline junkie search for danger and excitement her way of dealing with whatever she brought back?

"Sometimes someone would say something," Inanna said, "a casual joke, and Chen would change."

"Julia called it 'the Jimmy eyes'," said Aarush. "He got them if there were too many people around, or if a situation got tense. I was at a bar with him and Julia once, and some dude hit on her. He asked her out right in front of Chen like he wasn't even there. I remember thinking the poor bastard had no idea what he was getting into, that I'd need to mop him up off the floor. Julia saw Chen's eyes, made some crack about Jimmy making an appearance, and hustled him out of there. Chen was going to kill him."

Inanna had seen the look a few times too. It was hard to know what caused it. Sometimes a news report would set it off. Sometimes, she had no idea. He never acted on it though. Whatever was going on inside, he never let it out.

The sun edged over the horizon, lighting the room through stained curtains.

"I heard that people who came back from war mentally scarred did so because of things they'd done," she said, "not because of things they saw."

Aarush shrugged. "I don't know. He was a sniper, a decorated one. He definitely killed people over there."

"Julia killed that Glenn asshole, blew him up. It didn't seem to touch her. I don't think she missed a wink of sleep."

"Yeah," said Aarush, "but that was at a distance. I don't think it's the same as looking at someone through a sniper's scope when you blow their brains all over a wall."

"Nice visual."

"Sorry. Movies. Can't help it."

"Could you have done that?" Inanna asked. "Could you intentionally blow someone up?"

Aarush pursed his lips, thinking. "No. Not unless they were threatening someone really important to me." He darted a glance at her, half shy, half mischievous.

"My hero." Though, in truth, she couldn't imagine him getting angry, never mind actually being violent.

Aarush studied her in the half light. "I think that's why Chen and Julia were willing to do all this. The war. And then losing Jenny. I think they both suffered—each in their own way—from the things they did and saw. I think the chance to do something really right, to make a genuine change, was…I don't know. A chance at redemption? Atonement for their sins?"

Was that true? She'd never know.

"What about you?" Inanna asked. "Why are you here?"

"Oh, you know me. I need to film things. I need something interesting to point the lens at. You guys were the craziest thing going."

Were. That hurt.

"And that's it, eh?"

Aarush shook his head, midnight hair falling before his eyes. "No. Not at all. None of that was true."

"So then?"

"You. I'm here because of you."

Inanna's heart soared. "You believe in me, in what I'm doing?"

"I do, but that's not what I meant. I'm here because I want to be with you."

"You are?"

"I had to see those fantastic—"

She smacked him playfully.

"I'd tear down society if it meant I got to spend time with you," he said, face serious.

She kissed him, and they held each other, reminiscing about Chen and Julia. Favorite moments and treasured memories. They cried for the pain of friends lost. They agreed that they had to go on, that they had to see this through. They'd bring down Gartner, but they'd do it on their terms; even though they knew that Julia and Chen would probably rather have shot the bastard from a safe distance.

When she awoke the second time, Inanna found Aarush working on his project. She watched for a while before giving up.

"Okay. What's your secret project?"

He grinned that boyish grin. Each hour he became more himself, but there was always an edge to him, something in the eyes she'd never before seen. "Defense in depth. Wheels within wheels."

"Explain."

"I've set up all the edited video to auto-post to a pile of sites and upload to news outlets. Once I arm it, I'll have to check in every thirty minutes to tell it not to. I'll trigger it just before the meeting. If shit goes wrong, the media, YouTube, Anonymous, everyone will get everything."

"Not bad," said Inanna. "What happens when they point a gun at you?"

"I tell them to go ahead. They kill me, and nothing can stop this."

"And when they point a gun at me?"

"I've been thinking about that. They have to believe we're both willing to die for this."

"Are we?"

"I'd rather not."

"Same. And the 'wheels within' part?"

Bright eyes glinted mischief. "I've got the micro-camera in my glasses, and I'll be wired for sound. I'm going to hide a tiny Wi-Fi hotspot."

"Going prison-style? Going to hoop a hotspot?"

"Uh… I think not. I'll be streaming live the entire time. We're double-crossing them before we even meet. This is no time to play fair. We can't let Gartner win."

"The authorities will shut down the account," pointed out Inanna.

"It takes anywhere from five minutes to an hour to find and kill sites. I've notified my contacts that there'll be interesting posts and they're ready. It'll be spread far and wide before anyone can do anything. On top of that, I've set it up to broadcast to a new account every ten minutes. It's a cascading system with overlap."

Not having the technical savvy, she decided to take his word for it. "They still might kill us."

"If they do, everyone will know. Everyone will see it."

"And if they search you?"

"Unless they strip me naked, they'll find nothing. Modern microcams are tiny."

Inanna had a backup plan of her own, her father's Glock tucked against the small of her back in its concealed carry holster. Meeting in a public space like a restaurant, she figured they probably wouldn't search her. As a last resort, she also had a second burner phone, a tiny little thing, the smallest she could buy, a Zanco T1, tucked into one sock. She'd pre-dialed 911. All she had to do was wake it up and hit send.

More likely, Gartner will meet with us to buy our silence and send his goons to kill us after. We'll be ready and waiting.

Or so she hoped. This was so far beyond her experience, beyond what she'd imagined when she first set things in motion, she felt lost. She worried she and Aarush were making a million mistakes Chen and Julia would never tolerate. But no matter how hard she thought it through, she couldn't find a better plan. Except maybe the one plan she knew the two would like: Stay at a safe distance, and put a bullet in Anthony Gartner's head.

I'd probably miss.

She doubted Aarush would do any better.

"Do you feel like they've been ahead of us every step of the way?" Inanna asked. "They showed up at Chen and Julia's. They were waiting for us at the hotel."

"They even had people covering the mall."

She remembered Chen talking about how different people handled fear and adrenaline. Some froze. Some ran away. Some cried or puked. Some went cold and calm and saw each action and reaction with crystal clarity. She knew which kind Chen was.

She worried she knew which kind she was too.

"We stay together," Inanna said. "No matter what."

"Agreed."

She hugged him tight. He wasn't huge. He wasn't a big, burly man. He couldn't fight, knew nothing about guns or martial arts. But all of that made him the bravest man she knew. He'd fight injustice, make the world a better place with his camera.

His use of technology is his super power.

Inanna grinned at the thought. The masks had been his idea. 'It's not subtle,' he'd said, 'it's product positioning. We're the heroes, and Americans love heroes.'

They'd left the masks behind in the RV. With Julia. Inanna cried then, great tearing sobs as she remembered her best friend, body riddled with bullets, dead, in the back of the camper. Aarush held her tight, stroked her hair until she stopped.

****

After showers and a quick breakfast at a nearby diner, they drove the last leg of the journey. Inanna took the wheel while Aarush fiddled with his gear. When he felt confident that everything was working, she called Gartner. They recorded the call on the off-chance he said something incriminating they could use.

"We meet today," she said. "You bring the money, we'll bring the files."

"I know you're recording this," said Gartner. "I've only agreed to meet with you to put this ugly situation to rest."

The Millennial Manifesto

Damn. Catching him saying something incriminating had been a long shot at best. She realized she'd been half hoping they'd get something useful from this call and not have to go through with the meeting.

"We're doing this somewhere public, because we don't trust you," she said.

"Whatever. I want it somewhere public too. Pick a place."

He sounded too confident, like he'd thought of everything and they were walking into a trap.

But he doesn't even know where we're meeting.

Was he planning on killing them before they made it there? Or maybe he'd have a sniper waiting to kill them as they left.

"You know that if anything happens to us—"

"Whatever," he drawled. "Just tell me where and let me get back to my life."

"Like Chen and Julia are getting back to theirs?" Angry, it came out before she could stop it.

"Never heard of them."

"You know the Olive Garden restaurant in Bay City? Be there at 5pm. The reservations are under your name."

"Thought of everything, have you?"

He sounded so fucking smug she wanted to hit him. *It doesn't matter, we've covered all the angles.* If anything happened to them, the blame would fall on Gartner.

"We meet once," said Gartner, "and then we're done. I don't ever want to hear from you again."

Was that him admitting he planned on buying them off without ever actually admitting it? With the very real possibility she'd lost her house and everything she owned and was now destitute, that suddenly became enticing.

You don't really know who you are until you're tested. How many times had Dad said that? *I won't fail.*

"We have taken precautions," she told Gartner. "If you—"

"Whatever." And he was gone.

Aarush, who'd been listening in, asked, "So, what do you think?"

She shrugged. "Don't know. He seems too confident. Shouldn't he be at least a little worried?"

"He assumes we're driven by greed, just like him. He figures that once we accept a bribe, we're done as heroes. I bet he's planning on recording the meeting too, to use against us if we try a double-cross. If we try asking for more money, he threatens to show us accepting a bribe. He doesn't understand that we don't care, that our double-cross will be donating his money to charity and airing the meeting anyway."

That makes sense. But she couldn't shake the feeling she missed something.

"Try to see this from his angle," said Aarush. "It's easier and less dangerous for him to buy us off. If he tries to harm us, he has to rely on his goons not to talk. And they're goons, it's only a matter of time before they run into trouble with the law and need something to trade, right?"

"He won't be able to trust us, though. People like that can't trust anyone."

"True," said Aarush, "but he's going to assume that what he has on us keeps him safe."

"I don't know. I think he's the kind of guy who needs to win," said Inanna. "He won't be happy with anything less than total victory."

Back in Bay City, they arrived at the Olive Garden an hour early and claimed a table for five, assuming his goons would be in attendance. Aarush ordered a huge plate of cheese fries and a nonstop stream of Cokes that mysteriously disappeared into him. The only outward sign he gave of being nervous, was the double-kick blast-beats he maintained with his feet under the table.

Inanna ordered a coffee and sipped at it as it slowly went cold.

At 5:05pm Anthony Gartner strolled in carrying a bulky black briefcase at odds with his usual sleek style. Two muscular men followed, one at each shoulder. They both wore their hair cropped short, the Indian man letting his grow out to the edge of what was acceptable by military-standards. He was big, six foot three at least, and round with muscle. The white guy was bigger, bullet-headed with a neck like a tree trunk. Inanna recognized them from the TV.

Grinning perfect teeth whitened to a bright shine, Gartner collapsed into a chair and placed the box on the table before him. The goons sat, one either side of him.

"Good to see you without the masks," Gartner said. "You're quite the looker. Not just a great set of tits."

Inanna resisted the urge to retort or retreat by crossing her arms.

The brown man studied Inanna and Aarush with a critical eye. "The other two, Julia and Chen…"

He paused, and Inanna's heart dropped at the mention of her friends. *They know us.*

"They were the muscle," he continued. "You two don't look military."

"We're not."

She expected him to gloat, to try and scare them. Instead, he looked glum, like he'd rather be anywhere else in the world.

Gartner snorted. "How rude of me not to introduce everyone!" He nodded at the man who'd spoken. "This is Hiran. He works for me as a security consultant of sorts. The big racist motherfucker—"

"I'm not—"

"Shut the fuck up. The big racist motherfucker is Chuck." He smiled sweetly at Inanna. "And you two are?"

"I'm Spider Man," said Aarush. "And she is Wonder Woman."

Gartner laughed. "Fine, fine."

"I assume you have someone recording this?" asked Aarush. "Maybe a telephoto lens? Outside in the bushes?"

"Pardon?" said Gartner, looking genuinely confused.

"You're recording this so we can't double-cross you and try and blackmail you again."

"Why would I do that? My friend here," he nodded at Chuck, "has a gun on Wonder Woman. Either of you do something stupid, he'll put one in her gut. She'll die. Long and slow. Terribly painful, I'm told."

"We're surrounded by people," said Inanna. "Witnesses. You kill us and everyone will know it was you."

"Yep. And thanks for that phone call," said Gartner. "You see, everyone knows you murdered Glenn Triantafylloy. And after that gunfight in Fremont, no one will be surprised you tried to kill me. My security personnel will be forced to defend me."

He won't even get his hands dirty.

"We have files set to go public," said Aarush. "If you don't let us go—"

"No," said Gartner, "you're coming with us. Both of you. You'll undo whatever failsafe or backups you've created, or we'll kill her."

"Fuck them," said Inanna. "He's bluffing."

"My dear," said Gartner, "I never bluff. I have, however, made a career of reading people." He nodded at Aarush. "He loves you. He won't let you die. Not if there's a chance he can save you."

"And after the files are gone?" said Aarush. "What assurances do we have?"

"None." Gartner showed teeth. "I win. I always win. You crossed the wrong man. Once I've got what I want from you, you're nothing to me. You can walk away."

They haven't searched us. They think those files were our only plan.

These two burly military men discounted them as a physical threat. She saw it in the way they lounged comfortably in their chairs. If she drew a gun now, neither could stop her.

"Or maybe," leered Gartner, "I'll let you *earn* your forgiveness." His eyes roved over her, drinking her in, measuring her like she was a choice piece of meat.

Aarush's hands clenched under the table, and Inanna put hers on top of his fist. *Calm. Stay calm.*

Hiran, she noted, looked away with an uncomfortable grimace. Even Chuck, the big dumb one, darted a glance at Gartner.

"So what's the play?" she asked Gartner

"The four of us are going for a little drive. I have some property ten minutes north of here on Saginaw Bay. Very nice. Very quiet."

Inanna squeezed Aarush's hand. He might not be broadcasting yet, but he was still recording. And Gartner hadn't said anything incriminating enough.

I want to hear the words. I want a confession.

She'd only get that when he was sure he was safe, when he was positive he'd won. He had to think he had them at his mercy.

"We'll go with you," she said. "If you promise to let us go after, once all the files have been deleted." She poured desperate hope into her eyes. Of course he'd lie. She knew it. She planned on it. She needed him thinking they were cowed. "Otherwise," she said, "I stand up right now and start screaming and we'll see if these two goons really will shoot an unarmed girl in a crowded restaurant."

Chuck looked hurt by her assessment whereas Hiran seemed to accept it.

Gartner licked his lips. "Fine. I was just fooling with you, trying to scare you. Once the files are deleted, you can go. I promise."

CHAPTER – HIRAN

Gartner's grin gave Hiran a severe case of the heebie-jeebies. The man was a fish. A worm. A soulless parasite.

Don't fucking believe him. He half prayed the girl would stand up and scream. It was her only chance of escape. No way Hiran would shoot her, and even Chuck couldn't be that stupid. He glanced at his partner, saw tight-wound rage.

Unless Tick Tock blames these two for Fana's death.

"Okay," said Wonder Woman. "We'll come with you."

Fucking hell. Idiot.

She just signed her death warrant, and Hiran had a pretty damned good idea who would have to execute it. Gartner talked big, but he doubted the man had the balls to kill someone.

I'm an idiot too.

He saw it, clear as day. Gartner would be sure that Hiran and Chuck were both implicated, that there was blood on their hands. He'd make sure they both killed someone. He'd hold that over them forever. They'd be trapped. Trapped, but paid. And with two girls that would someday go to college, Hiran *needed* that money.

They all stood, Gartner tossing a fistful of bills on the table, Chuck with a hand inside his jacket like he'd draw a gun and start blasting if they decided to rabbit.

"Hiran," said Gartner, "grab the case."

Hiran did as instructed.

Together, Hiran leading the way, they trooped out to the van waiting outside. Neither Wonder Woman nor Spider Man made an attempt to escape. They walked like cows to the slaughter, too ignorant of what they'd embroiled themselves in, too stupid to see Gartner for the psychopath he was.

The Millennial Manifesto

Does Chuck understand? Hiran doubted it. If it came down to it, where exactly did Chuck's loyalties lie, with the wallet, or with his partner? *Like you've ever treated him like a partner.* Hiran realized he really didn't know. Before Fana, he would have sworn that Chuck would stab in him the back the moment it was profitable. Now, he was less sure.

"You drive," Gartner ordered Hiran. "You're in the back with them," he told Chuck.

He knows. He reads people. He knows he can't trust me to kill these two. Did that mean he knew Chuck would?

Hiran climbed into the driver's seat, Gartner taking the passenger seat beside him. Chuck and the two terrorists sat in the back.

Terrorists. He remembered thinking they were hippies or corporate, or muscle hired by one of Gartner's many enemies. Men like Gartner always had enemies. Shit, he probably takes pride in his enemies, thinks it says something important about himself.

How else could he feel superior unless he won and had victims to gloat over.

But that picture: Chen and Julia with their daughter. There'd been no child's room in the house, no toys. It still haunted Hiran. So maybe he understood their motives.

But these two are just kids. They barely looked twenty.

Would Gartner let them live so he could gloat?

Not a fucking chance. He'd gloat, but he was too smart to leave them alive.

Hiran followed the GPS to Gartner's property. It was, of course, a palatial cottage a thousand times more impressive than Hiran's home. A long dock jutted into the pristine blue of Saginaw Bay, so unlike the rivers Gartner's company poisoned. Two sailboats, masts laid down, bobbed at the pier. A third boat, a forty-foot powered yacht, sat at the end. The cottage was new, but made to look old and rustic. Fieldstone walls and log cabin chic, married to what had to be six thousand square feet of living space. The nearest neighbor was a mile away.

Chuck, Wonder Woman, and Spider Man were quiet in the back. It was weird. A month ago, Chuck, sitting in the back with a pretty black girl and a scrawny brown kid, would have been spewing racist shit, terrorizing the two and generally enjoying himself. But every time Hiran glanced in the rearview, the big man looked to be lost in thought. A contemplative Chuck was something he never thought he'd see.

Ah, Fana, if only you could see him now.

His chest tightened at the thought of her.

Eyes on the prize. Focus on the job. He couldn't. He hated the job, hated what he was going to do.

He hated what he was.

"Bring the case," instructed Gartner.

Briefcase in hand, Hiran exited the van first and went to the back to cover the two as Chuck exited in case they tried to run or suddenly put up a fight. He knew they wouldn't; they were scared kids, beaten. In a real op, or back in Afghanistan, he'd have drawn a weapon, been ready for anything. He didn't bother. Swinging the door open, he stepped back. Wonder Woman and Spider Man followed Chuck out of the van, meek as sheep, and stood waiting.

Only the girl seemed unimpressed by Gartner's show of wealth. She glanced at the dock and the cottage, but was more interested in watching Gartner. There was something in her eyes, buried deep. Maybe a seething anger. Rage, he assumed, at her helplessness.

You should have run. No way this ended well for her. Hiran watched her watch Gartner. She was beautiful. She moved as if unconscious of how attractive she was. If anything, that somehow made her even sexier.

Hiran glanced at Gartner. The asshole leered at the girl, waggling his eyebrows. He made no attempt to hide how he undressed her with his eyes, gaze lingering and caressing.

And when he wants to rape her, when he wants to lord every aspect of his victory over her, what then?

Killing her for Gartner was acceptable but rape was crossing the line?

A coward like Gartner wouldn't do it on his own. He'd want help. He'd want to drown Chuck and Hiran in his filth, make sure they were all on the same level.

If I didn't need the money so bad, I'd walk away right now.

Would walking away from what he knew was going to happen absolve him?

No, it fucking wouldn't.

Jesus Christ, what would the girls think?

What would his wife think?

Wonder Woman turned her back on Gartner and stared out into the trees. Not like she contemplated running, but as if simply appreciating the beauty.

Gartner, realizing he was being ignored, ground his teeth, fists clenched.

She did that on purpose, knew how much it would piss him off.

She possessed, Hiran saw, something of Fana's strength, her utter lack of fear. He remembered the way Fana faced off against Chuck, daring him.

And look where that got her. Brains spattered all over the sidewalk.

Glancing at Chuck, he saw the big man scowling at the girl. There was no anger there, just a maelstrom of emotion and conflict.

"Let's head inside, shall we," said Gartner.

Anger suddenly gone, he sounded pleased, excited. Hiran had never seen the man so jovial.

The skinny brown kid, Spider Man, fished a pair of thick-rimmed glasses from a breast pocket, and put them on. He glanced at Hiran and turned away, studying Gartner from behind.

Trying to see a way out of this? Good luck.

They trooped toward the palatial cottage, Hiran taking the lead. Chuck followed at the back, behind everyone. Gartner walked beside the young woman, chatting like they were chums, eyes locked on the way her breasts swayed under her t-shirt. Chuck, who Hiran would have sworn was the crudest and rudest man he ever met, looked everywhere but at the girl.

He doesn't want to be here any more than I do.

Chuck had asked if Hiran thought Fana would be okay with killing these people.

Since when does Chuck give a fuck what anyone else thinks?

They entered the cottage via a huge marble foyer, a massive brass chandelier hanging overhead. A rack of expensive coats, hunting jackets, and rows of sturdy hiking boots sat near the door. The coats and boots were in different sizes, ranging from small children to adults.

Christ, he brings his family here.

Everything was spotlessly clean.

The foyer opened into a kitchen containing miles of white marble counters and white cabinets all offset by a black granite floor and matching back-splash. High-end pots and pans and cooking utensils hung over a huge breakfast island like hunting trophies. None looked like they'd ever been used. The two monstrous double ovens finished in stainless steel also looked pristine.

Gartner gestured at the breakfast bar. "Put it up there."

Hiran placed the briefcase on the granite.

The Millennial Manifesto

Gartner, suddenly playing the host, pulled out stools for everyone. They looked hand-carved, each one custom-made. No doubt an attempt to add character to the soulless display of wealth.

"Who wants a drink?" he asked. "Wine? Red or white?" Turning to Hiran, he said, "Scotch, right? I have some Lagavulin that's fantastic."

I like whiskey, asshole. It's different. "No thanks."

"Beer?" Gartner asked Chuck, Hiran already forgotten.

Amazingly, Chuck didn't look to Hiran for permission. He just shook his head, eyes hooded.

Gartner ignored the skinny brown kid like he didn't exist, wasn't worth noting. "Wine?" he asked Wonder Woman.

"White," she said.

"Of course, of course," he answered as if she'd somehow turned that single word into innuendo.

Everyone watched him putter about, selecting a wine glass. "Spiegelau," he said, holding the glass up to the light and inspecting it for smudges. "Very expensive." He opened the wine fridge, exposing rows of labeled bottles. "This is an excellent Pinot Grigio," he said, choosing a bottle. "Very dry. Hints of oak and lemongrass."

"I hate lemongrass," she said. "And that is a seven-dollar bottle of plonk."

Gartner's mood faltered and then he shrugged, once again jovial, and picked out another bottle. "Chardonnay, then." Pouring a very large glassful, he set it on the counter before her.

She raised an eyebrow. "That's a red wine glass," she said. Lifting the glass, she turned it in her fingers. "Meant for Barolo, if I'm not mistaken."

Gartner plucked the glass from her hand and hurled it against the wall. She twitched when it shattered, showering the counter with shards of glass and splashing the cupboard doors with white wine, but otherwise didn't react.

"It'll be better if you're sober for this," he said. "Best if you can't hide behind the excuse of alcohol. You'll know you loved it no matter how much you fought."

The skinny kid stiffened, but said nothing. He looked everywhere but at the girl, like he couldn't bring himself to meet her eyes, couldn't admit that he was out of his depth here, helpless.

The Millennial Manifesto

Hiran knew that look, that pent up helpless rage. He'd seen it on the faces of every man he'd beaten in a fight, every man who knew they couldn't win and who caved before the fight even started. It was the look of defeat.

"Oh," said Gartner, voice casual, "I almost forgot. See, I noticed you millennials are kinda tech-savvy. But us old dogs can be too. Well, I didn't want you recording this little meeting and broadcasting it. Yeah, I'm sure you've got a little microphone somewhere on you. Didn't you wonder when no one bothered to search you? Well, see, this," he nodded at the case, "is a cellular and Wi-Fi scrambler. I'll be honest, I haven't a fucking clue how it works. But it does. So your stupid little plan to catch me saying something incriminating and broadcast it to some safe cloud-site or whatever…is just that. Stupid."

The two would-be terrorists sagged, fear written clear across their features. Spider Man still refused to look at Wonder Woman.

"Is it just me," said Gartner, "or are kids getting stupider every year? Like I wouldn't see this coming a million miles away and take precautions." He took a mocking bow. "I win, as always."

He glanced from person to person, as if expecting some response.

"Okay," continued Gartner, when no one said anything. "I guess the fun is over. Strip them both naked. I need to know they aren't hiding a wire or anything." He nodded at the girl. "Her first, so her boyfriend can watch."

No one moved. The skinny kid couldn't take his eyes off Gartner.

"Chuck," said Gartner. "An extra five large if you rip the bitch's clothes off her."

Chuck pushed himself up from his stool, jaw set, fists clenching.

"No," said the brown kid, drawing a snub-nosed .38 revolver.

Maybe he expected everyone to freeze, seeing as he had the drop on them. Maybe he thought he'd have a chance to tell everyone to drop their guns, and that he and the woman would waltz out of the kitchen.

Whatever he expected, he got something else.

Chuck and Hiran reacted with a speed and sureness screaming years of experience. Guns cleared holsters even as Gartner squealed and dove for cover.

Younger and faster, Chuck drew first.

The kid, however, shot first. Driven by anger, he fired at Gartner. The CEO's mad dive saved him, the bullet shattering the counter top. In that granite and marble kitchen, the *crack* of the gun was deafening. When Chuck's much larger pistol went off a fraction of a second later, the .38 was dwarfed by the bone-shaking boom.

The Millennial Manifesto

The bullet punched the kid in the chest. Staggering, he gritted his teeth in a snarl and fired again at Gartner scrabbling on the floor. Black granite blew apart, peppering the CEO with sharp stone shrapnel. He screamed and curled up tight, arms over his head, legs tucked against his belly like that might save him.

Chuck's second shot, point-blank into the youth's chest, straight into his heart, put the kid's lights out. Knees buckling, the boy crumpled, boneless, to the floor.

Hiran spun, leveling his gun at the woman. She sat unmoving, frozen, as surprised as everyone.

We got sloppy, underestimated them.

She blinked and tears ran. She didn't seem to notice Hiran had a gun pointed at her. She didn't move, didn't twitch.

She's in shock.

Hiran holstered his pistol with a sigh of relief. He hadn't had to kill anyone. Yet. Adrenaline crashed about in his chest, stuttering his heart and left him breathing like he just sprinted the four-hundred-yard dash.

That kid could have killed me.

Had the boy been smarter—or maybe just less scared and angry—he'd have shot Chuck first and then Hiran.

Chuck stared at the girl, his jaw working, eyes glinting hard with rage. Glancing at the kid on the floor, he kicked the .38 away. Not that the boy was ever going to reach for it.

"Fucking Christ!" screamed Gartner, climbing to his feet. "The little bastard had a fucking gun!"

"Sorry," said Hiran, wincing.

"Fucking *sorry*? He almost killed me!"

Hiran watched Gartner check himself for wounds and find many nicks and scratches left by shattered granite. "I'm bleeding!"

"It's not bad," said Hiran. "Nothing serious."

"Nothing serious, he says. You two boobs are fucking incompetent," said Gartner, ignoring the fact that a moment ago he'd bragged about why they hadn't searched the two.

But he wasn't wrong. Or not completely wrong. *We don't want to be here. We don't want to do this.* And their apathy for the job made them sloppy.

Or it's an excuse and you're getting old.

Gartner spotted the kid's .38 and bent to retrieve it. "It's a goddamned toy."

"Will still kill," said Chuck.

"Yeah?" Gartner turned and pointed the revolver at the big man. "Will it."

One-handed, Chuck fished a crumpled pack of filterless Lucky Strike cigarettes from a pocket. Holding the pack to his lips, he withdrew a cigarette before returning the pack to its pocket. Taking his time, he pulled out his zippo lighter, flicked it open. Lighting the cigarette, he inhaled deeply. His eyes never left Gartner. He rushed nothing, looking like he had all the time in the world to enjoy a smoke. The SIG hung carelessly in his other hand, all the more threatening for how he ignored it.

Chuck held the smoke in for a moment, examining Gartner, before letting it out. "Better make it a killing shot," he drawled, "or I'm going to take that gun and fire the last three rounds up your ass."

Gartner blinked at him and burst out laughing. Lowering the gun, he backed away. "That's what I like about you, Chucky. Big brass balls."

Hiran watched. *Coward.*

Gartner turned and pointed the gun at the girl, who still hadn't moved. "I'm going to fuck this bitch right on top of her boyfriend's brownie corpse."

At the word 'brownie' Chuck darted a look at Hiran, his fists clenching, knuckles popping.

Oh, so now that bothers you.

Gartner pulled back the hammer on the .38 special.

It's a double-action, asshole. You didn't need to do that. People were always mimicking the crap they saw in movies, holding their Glocks sideways, and blasting off rounds as fast as they could. More than once the stupidity of his opponents had saved Hiran's life.

The girl ignored Gartner, stared at the growing pool of blood around the dead boy.

"Let's start with the pants," said Gartner. "I want to save those tits for last."

She blinked, finally noticing Gartner and the gun. Meeting the CEO's eyes, she didn't move. Hiran couldn't tell if she was frozen in fear, deep in shock, or in denial that any of this was real.

Looking from man to man, her attention finally landed on Gartner again. "No," she said.

The Millennial Manifesto

Maybe there's a little iron in her after all.

Gartner smirked over the barrel of the gun. "You'll do it," he purred, "because every minute you're stripping for us is a minute you're still breathing."

Us. Like Hiran and Chuck were in it with him, accomplices.

We are. He pays, and we do as we're told.

Never before had Hiran truly understood the idea that if you're not part of the solution, you're part of the problem.

Chuck stared at the girl, cigarette hanging forgotten in his mouth. There was no lust there, no excitement. If anything, he seemed to look through her like she wasn't there or he saw something behind her. His free hand clenched and unclenched.

Tick Tock.

Gartner had no idea who he shared the room with. He assumed money bought all men and bought them absolutely.

Didn't it? Was Hiran's soul not bought and paid for?

"Pants," said Gartner. "Take them off to buy another minute of life. And then do whatever I tell you next to buy another minute. You will. You'll keep buying minutes no matter what they cost." Licking his lips, he sighted along the barrel, "What's the call, sweetheart? Want to buy one more minute, or are we done here?"

He isn't bluffing. Gartner was about to blow this girl's brains all over the kitchen. *Take your fucking pants off!*

Chuck inhaled another lungful of smoke.

Tick.

And released it.

Tock.

"No?" said Gartner. "Fine."

"Okay," she said, closing her eyes. "You win."

"No shit I win." Again, he licked his lips, tongue wet and pink, as she undid her belt.

Eyes still clenched, she hesitated.

"C'mon, baby, off with the pants. I want to see that ass. I'll be gentle, promise."

Slim fingers fluttered over the buckle, unwilling to go further.

"Fuck this," said Gartner. "Chuck, take the bitch's pants off. She thinks she's a fucking superhero? Well, I'm going to fuck her hero ass on the breakfast bar while you hold her down."

He's doing it. He's dragging us into his shit.

"Hero," said Chuck.

Tick.

"And rip that fucking shirt off. Those tits definitely look heroic."

"Heroic," said Chuck.

Tock.

"Are you fucking retarded?" demanded Gartner, turning on Chuck, but keeping the gun on the girl. "I said get her fucking pants off. Now."

Chuck shot him in the face.

Gartner went over backward, what remained of his skull making a sodden *thwack* as it met marble.

"Christ, Chuck—"

The girl shot Chuck twice in the chest with a Glock nine she pulled from a conceal-carry holster attached to her belt.

Chuck stood, blinked at the blood leaking from the wounds. He stepped back, bumping into the wall behind him, and then slid down to a sitting position.

"Fuck," he said, bubbling blood.

That's why she hesitated, Hiran thought numbly. *Concealed-carry holster in the small of her back.* Even after the kid drew a gun, they still hadn't thought to check the girl. She'd sat there, frozen in shock, and Hiran ignored her as harmless.

Chuck touched fingers to his bloody chest. He sighed, and then stared into nothing, unmoving.

Finally pulling his attention away from his friend, Hiran found himself staring down the barrel of the Glock. It didn't shake, didn't waver.

Getting slow, old man. Didn't even go for your gun.

"We didn't want to be here," he said. "Needed the money." The excuse felt lame. He shrugged. *Duck and go for your gun. She has no training. She'll panic and miss.*

Hell, she was close enough that if his knees were even halfway decent he might have been able to tackle her.

"When you have a gun on someone," he said, "don't stand so close to your target."

She didn't move, didn't blink.

She's got some iron in her, alright.

"It doesn't have to end like—"

CHAPTER – INANNA

Inanna shot him.

He lay sprawled on the floor. Her ears rang like she'd never hear again.

She pointed the gun at Hiran, at Chuck, and then, for a long time, at Gartner.

What the hell just happened?

She struggled to piece together the last few seconds.

Gartner was going to shoot her if she didn't take her pants off and she'd been scared that when she undid the belt they'd see the concealed carry holster. She froze, trying to decide if she should go for the gun.

The big white guy, Chuck, looked like he was ready to kill again. He looked like he *wanted* to kill. Gun already in hand, no way she could get to her Glock fast enough. Gartner was going to kill her. She knew that beyond any doubt. The only real question: was he going to rape her first?

Take your pants off, buy a minute. But if she did, everyone would see the gun.

Gartner said something—Inanna couldn't even remember what—and Chuck shot him. And there everyone was, staring in surprise at Gartner's body. Even Chuck looked startled by what he'd done. She knew it was her only chance. She'd seen too much. No way they'd let her live.

Sound and blood.

Lowering the gun, Inanna looked from corpse to corpse. No one moved. Not one breath. Still.

Gartner was an asshole, but what about the other two? Chuck. Hiran. They were just names. Chuck killed Gartner instead of stripping her. What kind of man ended up in that situation? She saw no way it could be a good man.

You're here too.

And what about Hiran? He never reached for his gun. When he said she was too close, she almost shot him right then out of fear. He was warning her, she saw now.

He was going to say, "It doesn't have to end this way."

He was wrong. It did. She knew who he was. How could there be trust?

It had to end this way.

Kneeling beside Aarush, Inanna kissed him on the forehead. "I'm sorry," she said. "We failed. We didn't make the world a better place." Not until she rose did she realize she'd knelt in his blood.

Her pants were soaked. She laughed at the irony, a cracked cackle tinged with horror. She'd had have to take them off, find something else to wear, before leaving.

Gartner got what he wanted after all.

She caught sight of the Wi-Fi jammer. Reaching over, she opened the case and shut it off. Everything Aarush recorded would broadcast now. She felt too numb to even consider what that meant. All that video he edited earlier would soon be released too. Maybe it was already out there.

Inanna went to the stupidly large fridge and helped herself to a beer. She needed something normal. Sipping the beer, she surveyed the room as tremors ran through her. Pulling up a stool, she sat at the breakfast bar and drank.

She shook.

She cried.

What am I going to do now?

Did she have a home to return to? Would the police be waiting with questions she couldn't answer? Even if she did still have a home, what then? Should she live out her days in vacuous comfort, surviving off the money her parents left?

Or should she go on, continue what she started.

Could she do it alone?

"There are too many men like Gartner," she said to a room of dead men. "Too many people focused on themselves, on profits no matter what the cost to the future." She sighed, finishing the beer. "I can't do this alone."

Julia, Chen, and Aarush, all dead. Gartner and his goons, Hiran and Chuck, dead too.

"When is the cost too high? When do you give up and let the bastards win? When is the fight to make things better just not worth it?"

Grabbing another beer from the fridge, Inanna went upstairs in search of clean clothes. Finding the master bedroom, she hunted through the closets until she found a long skirt and loose t-shirt that fit. She tried not to think about the fact these clothes must belong to Gartner's wife. She couldn't imagine him married. Was he different with her, less of a sociopathic asshole?

Could someone be two radically different people like that?

Or did his wife live in fear of him, like Janet Triantafylloy had feared her husband, Glenn. Would she feel relief when she learned of his death, or would the loss crush her?

Good job not thinking about it.

After dressing and finishing the second beer, Inanna found the keys to the van. Grabbing a towel from the kitchen, she wiped down everything she thought she might have touched, careful to avoid the blood on her way out.

Not knowing what else to do, where else to go, she drove home. Parking several blocks away, she walked.

Life went on around her. People rushing about their business. Birds in the trees. Buses and taxis. All the smells of the city. Car exhaust and pizza. The echoing shouts of school-yard children out for recess.

No one was waiting for her. There were no police cars, no media. Nothing. Her home, her normal life, seemed to await her return.

I can disappear in here.

God that was tempting, the thought of abandoning everything she thought she had to do and spending the rest of her life in quiet obscurity. No one would die, and the world would remain the same shitty place it had always been.

Entering the house, she shed Gartner's wife's clothes, tossing them in the trash, and climbed into bed. She lay curled in a tight ball for a long time before sleep finally took her.

She dreamed of Aarush. She dreamed of his playful eyes and boyish grin. She dreamed of his fingers and of his lips.

She dreamed of his death, and woke crying.

The sun shone through around the edges of the blinds. Somehow, she'd slept through the evening, the night, and well into the morning.

Climbing from bed, Inanna donned a comfortable pair of track pants and one of her father's old shirts. She padded into the kitchen, took a beer from the fridge, and retired to the living room. Collapsing onto the sofa, she turned on the TV.

"Oh my god."

There, in front of her, was Gartner as he'd been just a few hours ago. She watched the entire event from Aarush's perspective, as he turned from Gartner to Hiran to Chuck, and refused to look at her.

He did it on purpose. The entire time, once he put on those glasses and began recording, he'd been careful to keep her off camera.

The video cut to the anchor woman just before the guns came out and she described what followed in such detail they might as well have shown it. Next, they broadcast live video shot from outside Gartner's cottage. Police had the driveway blocked and a dozen emergency vehicles, cop cars and ambulances, littered the manicured lawn.

"Early reports," said the anchor woman, "suggest at least three dead and one woman missing."

Inanna's heart kicked in fear. She struggled to remember her last minutes in the cottage. In the horror of the aftermath, she totally forgot about Aarush's recording gear.

Did I put myself on camera after all Aarush did to protect my identity?

The TV cut back to Gartner threatening to rape her on her dead boyfriend's corpse, and then jumped to after the shooting had ended. She heard herself sobbing. Listened as she moved to kneel at Aarush's side. Watched as her hair fell across the camera lens as she leaned in to kiss his forehead. She saw herself move away, padding about Gartner's kitchen, talking to herself.

"There are too many men like Gartner," she heard herself say. "Too many people focused on themselves, on profits no matter what the cost to the future. I can't do this alone."

Cut back to the woman in the news room, and Inanna listened in shock as the anchor described how Aarush's videos—edited and uploaded while Inanna drove or slept—had gone massively viral overnight.

An underground movement had been born.

The anchor called them copycats, but across the country young people were rising up against the corporations they perceived to have wronged them. Bankers were kidnapped, stripped of their belongings, left penniless and naked in the poor end of town. CEO's of companies guilty of pollution were forced to eat, drink, and breathe the poisons they produced. Officers of companies utilizing child and slave labor were taken, forced to work in terrible conditions, videos of their experiences posted hourly. The owner of a company owning several brands of bottled water was found dead, his bloated corpse filled with ocean water and shards of plastic. Companies gouging the public with artificially-inflated prices for life-preserving drugs were attacked, their HVAC systems infected with doses of deadly poisons requiring costly vaccinations.

Inanna watched in horror as she learned of the assassinations of bankers, lawyers, NRA spokesmen, and politicians guilty of colluding in scams and scandals. Senate lobby groups were bombed and shot at. In a single day the death toll had climbed to double digits. This was a country, crushed for too long beneath the corporate boot, lashing out in anger. Superhero masks were everywhere. People wore them on the streets in protest, or to show support.

This isn't what I wanted.

No one was supposed to die. Violence was terrible, a crime. Taking a human life should be a last resort, only when all other choices had been removed.

Again, she saw the lack of surprise on Hiran's face when she shot him. Chuck sitting on the kitchen floor, back against the wall, looking at the blood on his fingers.

What have I done?

According to the news, no one knew who she was. Authorities were looking for a young black woman, likely in her early twenties, with long hair. Chen and Julia were in the news, their deaths connected to the acts of terrorism, though authorities remained unsure in what capacity.

Did I get away with murder?

A thrill of fear and excitement ran through Inanna and she couldn't decide how she felt. People died. All her closest friends were dead. She, herself, shot two men in cold blood.

But this…this movement that seemed to be going through some rather brutal birthing pains…what of it? Did the way things ended make everything she and her friends accomplished wrong or evil? If companies were forced, literally, to clean up their acts, to pollute less, to sell lifesaving medicines at reasonable prices, was that not a good thing?

What cost is too high to make the world a better place? What price am I unwilling to pay?

The phone in the kitchen rang. It was the land-line her parents, slow to let go of old technology, had insisted the house have. Rising, Inanna walked to the phone as if sneaking up on it.

There's no hiding.

She answered. "Yes?"

"Inanna Williams?"

Her heart lurched. "Yes?"

"It's Steven So, you're estate agent."

Silence. She didn't know what to say. How did he get this number? *Phone book. Duh.* She smothered the desire the laugh.

"Hello?" said Steven.

"Yes, I'm here."

"I got your message, heard it while the police were waiting to question me. I figure the chances of it being a coincidence were pretty slim. Look, I don't care what you're up to. I don't care why you want to liquidate all of your holdings so fast. I told the police nothing. I still have buyers lined up."

"You do?" Did she still want to sell? She could hide here forever, disappear.

"I do. Here's the deal. I want an additional two percent for my discretion in looking after your affairs."

Roughly one hundred and forty thousand dollars for saying nothing. Peering round the door, she watched TV for a moment as the station replayed the juiciest moments sure to boost ratings. Again and again, Gartner talked about her tits, threatened to fuck her on the breakfast table, though of course all crude words were censored. Seeing it from this angle, knowing how it all ended, she saw Chuck's anger differently. He wasn't some cold killing machine like she'd thought. He had no intention of holding her down while his boss raped her. He was conflicted, scared. She saw his eyes change, decision made, when Gartner mocked her for trying to be a hero. When he shot the man, *he* was the hero. He was saving her. But at the time, she hadn't seen his face. She saw her opening and acted instead of freezing. She killed him.

"Miss Williams?" said the agent.

"Your discretion is appreciated," she said. "Your terms are acceptable. Sell it all."

"I'll have the new agreement drawn up and couriered to you ASAP."

"Excellent."

Cold purpose filled her. Chuck killed Gartner when the CEO mocked her attempts at heroism. *He believed in me. He* wanted *me to be a hero*. How or why, she couldn't imagine. But she wouldn't let him down. She wouldn't let Julia or Chen or Aarush down either.

"I'll have it signed and returned as soon as my lawyer has looked at it," she said, and hung up.

The Millennial Manifesto

And then?

There was no rest, no respite from her calling. She swore, at the very beginning, to make the world a better place, and that was what she was going to do.

Inanna returned to the living room. On TV she saw student marches proclaiming Wonder Woman the hero of the millennial generation. Minimum wage was a joke. In a nation where housing prices had gone insane, what prospects did they have? Health-care was in the process of being murdered by greedy old men. The lakes and rivers ran thick with pollution.

Millennials were tired of being shit on by a system they hadn't asked for, had no say in. Here was a generation looking at a future worse than that enjoyed by their parents. Even the most menial jobs were being replaced by robots or sent overseas where human rights didn't raise the cost of production. She'd seen reports of fast food chains mechanizing burger flipping stations so they didn't have to pay some college student the whopping $7.25 an hour. It wouldn't be long before the only remaining jobs were in the service industry.

How many waiters will we really need when only a tiny percentage of the population will be able to afford restaurants?

Her peers, her fellow students, they would be her recruits. It was time to stop thinking small. With some intelligent investing, she could fund dozens of terrorist cells across the country.

Turning off the TV, Inanna sat back and closed her eyes. She'd need to distance herself, protect her identity.

Recruiters.

She'd pretend to work for someone else, and start by hiring recruiters to travel the country, hitting all the universities, setting up cells. The cells would need to be autonomous, yet open to communication from a central authority. There would, she knew, be violence. People would get hurt. She had to be sure it was the *right* people. Public support was everything. No one liked the massive corporations and banks. They'd see what she was doing. They'd understand.

Inanna laughed when she realized the irony of her plans. The corporate model was an effective one. Fighting fire with fire, she'd run the revolution like a business, start franchises across the country. Eventually, however, her funds would run out. Could she run this as a profitable organization, pay members, fund future actions?

Why not steal from the corporations who have been stealing our futures, selling our natural resources for short-term gain?

The Millennial Manifesto

Was this the path of the modern Robin Hood?

Paid terrorists.

No one asked to sacrifice themselves for a cause.

She'd need to look into healthcare plans and legal services. If she could offer every member legal council should they run afoul of the law—which was exactly the plan—it might go a long way toward aiding recruitment.

First, she needed to lay out a mission statement detailing the organization's purpose and goals. She wanted it to be clear from the very first day what conduct was acceptable, to spell out the movement's philosophies and values.

A moment's thought, and she knew exactly what to call it: *The Millennial Manifesto*.

"Getting tired of waiting tables?" she asked her generation. "Come help me change the world."

ABOUT THE AUTHOR

Michael R. Fletcher was born in one of those rural towns with more dogs than people. He grew up milking goats, thinking sticks were amazing toys, and pretending that used nine-volt batteries were spaceships. He thought the rabbits in the barn were pets until one day Blackie appeared on the dinner table.

Things got a tad dark after that.

After dropping out of university in his second year of a Philosophy degree, he decided it was time to grow up and get a real job. He promptly moved to Toronto to become a rock star, which strangely involved less drugs and alcohol than his attempt at Philosophy.

After working for twenty years in the music industry as an Audio-Engineer, he decided it was time for a change and set his sights on becoming a famous author.

Once again, things got a tad dark.

Sometimes he thinks he should have become a ninja like his mum wanted.

Made in the USA
Monee, IL
18 August 2024

64057552R00118